Take This Man

TAKE

BY

THIS

FREDERICK BUSCH

MAN

Farrar · Straus · Giroux / New York

This book is for

Benjamin Busch,

my father

Take This Man

❧❦❧

He rose with the fog. It always came dripping from the sea to announce itself in sunlight which it captured on the rise and magnified. When he was at home, as he had been for some days now, he felt it lying on his window and, he would have sworn, against the clapboard and plaster and lath of the walls themselves, and on his pillow and on his face.

He woke under the weight of that light, and he put on the clothes he had packed in fright and haste, and he walked down, past the room in which his mother maybe slept, and past the room in which, he hoped, his father slept, and out into the chill and wetness of a summer morning in Maine, where his family had *slunk*—he always used the word, when he was alone and thinking of that trip—starting in darkness and arriving in darkness, fleeing cross-country, pioneers in reverse.

But that was long ago enough for him to have aged a quarter of a century, he thought, rubbing a young man's gut that soon would want to be a paunch. The tall hand-some lawyer from New York, he thought, walking in the dark morning, which was lighted from the sea by sun hanging in fog. The dodgy bachelor from New York, prac-ticing the law and every emotional evasion he could dream —even walking away, even while he heard himself thinking this, from the house in which the trouble lay.

Down the steep track, which leveled off near a tall wet spruce, then down onto the rocks and boulders of the beach, black and purple with moisture, slippery and shining in the light suspended over the sea; he bent into his sweater and himself because of cold wind and hanging damp and the slow ticking thunder of the Atlantic before him. In the early morning, alone, a fugitive from the house in which his father lay, he thought of a night five or six years before when he'd been wakened, earlier than this, by the fearful sudden telephone. It was Tony, his father, a little slurry with the whiskey he rarely drank too much of, nervously pausing after he'd announced himself to Gus, his son, the distant lawyer in distant New York.

"Is it about Mom?" Gus had asked.

"No. It's only me. Did anybody tell you Duke Ellington died? You know that?"

"Yes," he'd said. "I'm sorry. He was an elegant man."

"He was a blues musician. Do they play him up there? They used to."

"New York's a black city, some parts of it, Dad."

"I used to love to listen to him."

"I didn't know that."

"He had this song—do you know who Johnny Hodges was?"

"Uh—no, sir."

His father had sighed. "His saxophone. He came up with

Sidney Bechet, who you don't know who he is, for certain. Well, listen, Gus, they had a song they did together called 'Just Squeeze Me,' and when it started out, before I was born, some black man someplace wrote it to go with the dirty words of 'The Boy in the Boat.' I used to listen to that. I was young. You sleepy, Gus?"

"Right here on the line."

"Mom's asleep. Listen, I don't know what the boat was supposed to be, except the slave boat somebody's great-great-grandfather was imported on. Except there was talk about it sometimes, and some kids I knew at home, the black musician ones, it was kind of a puzzle with them. One night, they let me sit with them, it was summer after college, and my father had moved on, but I came home to my old high-school neighborhood. I worked there that summer at a public swimming pool which was surely, let me tell you, for whites only. They had black kids doing maintenance at night, though, and we drank some beer. One of those boys was a bass man. He played for cash in low saloons, every now and again. He played the way Slam Stewart played, you know what I mean? Singing the note when you bow the string? Well, Harry Howard Fanning Carson was his name, and he told me things. He trusted me because I was so plainly ignorant, I suppose." His father had laughed, and Gus had laughed with him, charmed by the ramble of the call. "He said he'd learned the boat was the Moses boat— the bullrushes business? A kid drifting. I liked that. Another one, Wesley Fish, very squat and coffee-with-cream, and not a musician, but the authoritative sort, *he* knew that the song was about putting your tongue into a woman's crotch. Well. And whenever Duke Ellington and Johnny Hodges—George Hannah sang it, I believe. The Delta Rhythm Boys, did it too. But when *Ellington* did it, I always thought about the sweaty walls of that tiled room under the city swimming pool. And the blues, Harry Howard Fanning Carson said—I don't know if he ever came up to be a good player, you know. He said, when the black man played the blues, he made up the happiness part. Now this is what I wanted to tell you, Gus. He said when the *white* man played the blues, it was the misery he faked. You understand that?"

"Are you black?" Gus had said. "I once thought you were Indian, you'll recall."

His father's laughter had been low and slow and genuine. "I got a little drunk, Gus. You want me black, I'll be black. It's a color good as any other I know."

The silence got longer, and all Gus could think of saying was "Dad."

"Good boy. I got a little bit drunk, and I wanted to tell you something. All right?"

" 'The Boy in the Boat.' "

"That's right. Let's go to sleep, and I'm sorry to wake you. But you call me up sometime, will you?"

Now, an August nearly a couple of thousand early mornings later, was as good a time to cry as that night had seemed—better, for obvious reasons, really. He was working himself into a quiet hysteria, his shoulders jumping all over the back of his neck, when his mother hailed her way into his day with a thermos of coffee and her dimming hair, still carried as if it were a flag to men, and her handsome small face, which at night could look as worn as one of the stones she stepped on, strong, this early, with whatever power or pride or even arrogance had carried her this far, this long.

She ignored his tears and she poured them coffee, telling him his father had wakened, been tended, and had returned to the comfort of his drugged sleep. Gus couldn't imagine that she wanted to talk about anything but the man who slept in the house above them, but they talked—about the cost of fuel oil, about the pollution of the coast, about what was large in the lives of others and merely secular, civilian, in theirs.

And then his mother, small and taut, wincing at the heat of coffee on her lips and tongue, called in a voice too strong for the distance between them, as they sat on a slab of volcanic stone in the center of the rock beach, "So I never married your father."

"I never thought it made much difference. I even actively like the idea, most of the time. When I was a kid, I was proud, really. There I was, a bastard in the name of breaking dumb rules. There you were, a couple of rebels. You know. I was a kid. And of course I still don't care."

"No."

"You never said why you didn't get married."

"Well, as you know well, I *was* married. Before."

The word *slunk* nibbled, like a rat behind the woodwork, in his mind. "They had divorce even then," Gus said, laughing his lawyer's laugh—the kind that makes clients certain that you're thinking of their lives when you're actually bound inside your own. "Somebody would have been glad to take your money and set you free."

"I *was* free," his mother said. "I only was married. But I was free. I think I showed that by what I did. It started out with me thinking that if I didn't ask for a divorce, nobody would know where we'd gone. Then, once we *were* gone, and once nobody did know, I liked the idea of being married to someone who couldn't find me, and of not being married to someone who could. I think you might have to be a woman to understand that."

"No," Gus said. "I do. But Dad didn't?"

"No."

"He takes it as some kind of lack of faith in him?"

"He'd never say that."

"No, he wouldn't. But he feels it?"

"Yes," his mother said, "you probably would, too. But you probably also would do something just like it. Note, for example, how many times you haven't been married."

"Yes. Yes. But I always thought it was because of the *rules*. Church. Justice of the peace. Any of that. I thought it was because you didn't want to swear those oaths and say those prayers."

"You think I'm in my adolescent-rebellion phase at my advanced age?" She finished her coffee and threw the dregs at the rocks. "Well, maybe that too. I have to go up."

She stood. She was a shape in the light, now harsh, which broke around them like the water below breaking on the beach. Her stiffness as she stood, and then the way she strode, told him that the journey up was hers, and that he had come here to be useless—comforting to him who nearly was absent, and stinking of the fear of death to her who was stranded in life. He had come there to be no more than what he couldn't help being. His mother moved past the spruce above them with a sudden haste. He gathered the thermos and cups which she had left behind, and he went too. When he looked back at the sea, it was bright and smooth beneath a sky undirtied by fog: smooth sailing for boys in their boats.

1944

He was on the air of another black dawn. The wind knocked one of the corporals over. Guy lines holding the Wright Cyclones on their concrete stanchions sang. The other corporal laughed, and Prioleau heard him, then didn't, as wind from the west blew the corporal's mouth empty. Prioleau was certain that he heard the steady *hump-drump* of the generator that ran the camp and powered the project, but he always heard it, in his sleep and fifteen miles away in Patoka Plains, and in Washington, where he was flown to report the details of failure. He dreamed to the generator's song, and in his nightmares of running or of crouching in sealed-away places, everything was regulated by that sound of the sea speeded up, crashing too quickly. The wind exploded on them and everyone leaned into it; the morning flickered, then held.

Corporal Prince, who had fallen, was up to help a private check the thick black cables that ran to the four B–17 engines mounted on concrete. The wires came from a wheeled charging unit and were connected to the 1,200-horsepower Cyclones laid out as if on the wings of a Flying Fortress E. But there was no plane. There were the engines and the wailing wires that held them to the frozen ground of Illinois. Where the tail might be, sixty-eight feet away, where a short man might crouch behind .50-caliber machine guns, and where on a bombing mission he might be surprised by rising interceptors, a giant oblong camera aimed at the purple-black morning. Corporal Rita, in his fur-collared flight jacket, spread his arms and flew at the camera, snarling like a child imitating an engine, spitting like a child pretending to fire aerial guns.

Prioleau stood with First Lieutenant Moffit, who spoke on his field transceiver to Master Sergeant Amboise, who was in charge of security. He patrolled the perimeter of the field in a jeep containing a .30-caliber machine gun; Amboise wore a Webley purchased from a Commando in Liverpool two years before. Lieutenant Moffit said, "There are no tanks or German sappers in Illinois, according to the patrol."

"Our luck's holding," Prioleau said.

They watched the big kinescope on which static raced as if blown by the wind that had begun in Missouri. The security jeep slowly circled the field, as one by one the engines of the imaginary bomber fired and roared and added to the wind. Corporal Rita flew at the nonexistent rear turret and fired his make-believe cannon. Corporal Prince and the private pulled the charging unit back toward Moffit and Prioleau. Moffit looked at the civilian, who nodded, and the lieutenant waved his hand in a gesture of disgust. Rita flew closer to the tail of the imagined Fortress and Prioleau reluctantly bent toward the kinescope to see whether an American imitating the Luftwaffe would appear on the dark screen.

And in spite of the shared unfunny joke that this day's work was, and yesterday's, and that of every day for a month and a half, and in spite of what Prioleau was—a prisoner until recently, a conscientious objector; to them a coward, their betrayer; to the National Defense Research Committee, an expert, a resource to turn television into eyes for bombers; to these men, the cause of their being stationed in the flattest and bleakest and emptiest land they had seen —Moffit smiled a little at Prioleau and bent with him toward the pulsing blue-gray screen.

"Nothing," Moffit shouted over the wind and the engines.

"The *usual* nothing," Prioleau answered.

Moffit picked up a .30-caliber carbine with a folding metal stock and aimed it at Rita, then fired high. Rita, seeing the muzzle flashes, dropped to the ground. Prince, seeing Rita fall, shut the engines down, far port and starboard, inboard port and starboard, and soon there was only the sound of the wind, and possibly the detachment's generator, and wind on the guy lines that held the engines in place. Prioleau shut the kinescope off. The security jeep's lights continued to circle the field. The sun rose.

Rita came up screaming, "You coulda killed me, Lieutenant! You coulda killed me!"

Moffit, short and bald and fat and sour, his career ending in the ruins of an Indian camp among wooden shacks and the wiring diagrams of a wartime criminal, said, "I don't *think* I'd of hit you, Rita."

"You do that again, Lieutenant—"

"If you threaten me, Corporal Rita, I can execute you."

"You can?" Rita, skinny, unshaven, wet-lipped and al-

ways in motion, said, "But I wouldn't talk like that if you
didn't fire off at me, see? And then *you* wouldn't talk like
that. Then it wouldn't happen. You see?"

"Ask Mr. Prioleau," Lieutenant Moffit said. "He'll verify
we don't see for shit around here."

Prioleau said, "I'm going back to bed."

"Write your report," Moffit said. "Corporal Prince will do
the typing."

The jeep slowly circled the field. A truck backed up for
the two corporals, the three privates, the lieutenant, and the
civilian who was their misery's source. But after he had
seen to the loading of his circuitry manuals and the kinescope and the camera that Prince removed from the make-
believe tail turret, Prioleau waved the truck away and
walked in its wake. The truck's lights disappeared beyond
a low hedgerow, and then the security jeep came up behind
him, honking, weapon pointing up at invisible danger. He
waved at Sergeant Amboise, who reluctantly saluted, and
soon he walked by himself, curled in winds that blew down
the middle of America's back in 1944.

The sky brightened as he walked, and Prioleau tried to
smell it. He raised his long nose into the paling violet air
and remembered how in the exercise yard in New York
City, each morning at eleven-fifteen, he had been certain
that he smelled hot chestnuts. He remembered the smell of
a shed he and his schoolteacher father had built, and then
the smell of a kitchen when he was little, but old enough
to be working on their houses with his father as they wandered from school to school; he had come up from under
the damp heavy quilts and into the kitchen lit by kerosene
lamps, and a woman had been frying johnnycakes and
singing random lines from the "Dallas Blues." She had
whispered, "Baby, bring a cold towel for my head—and

good morning to *you*. If you aren't Tony, I'm not cooking your breakfast this morning." She had stayed with them all that year and much of the next. He had watched her when she left, walking down a path that would take her to the small road running between their house and the railroad tracks. He had watched his father walk behind her and then stop. He had smelled his father's bay rum, and the starch in his fresh shirt, as his father wooed until the last, when he stopped a dozen yards down the path and waved to her small back. Now Prioleau sniffed at the sky, at the fields opening around him and not ending, and all he smelled was grain. "I could breathe my breakfast," he said.

Then he saw the Kaiser over frozen furrows, coming out of the sun like an interceptor, bucking as if it fought headwinds, honking until he stopped to wait. In the prison yard he had dreaded this: someone walking from the sun, a silhouette tall and faceless coming, perhaps, to punish the coward and traitor with a righteousness reserved for men who, when out of jail, earned money by injuring the very frightened. Prioleau had a scar near his navel to remember such patriots by, and as he waited for the cheese-box car to slow, he rubbed his stomach and planted his feet.

But when the window was rolled down, a round clean-shaven face over a necktie smiled at him with boundless affection. "Mr. Purloo?" the driver called. "Mr. Anthony Purloo?"

"Prioleau, yes. Civilians aren't supposed to be driving out here. This is a military reserve." He waved his hand, but there was nothing to point at except flat ocher fields and the invisible chugging generator.

"Robert D. Dander, Mr. Purloo. Bob Dander, I hope you'll call me. I'm in radio broadcasting. By Jesus, I *am* radio broadcasting south of Vandalia. You can hear me out-

side of Chicago on a good night with a low ceiling and the
clouds banked right, real late. *The Soldiers' Request* we call
it. Sad music until you fall asleep. I understand you folks
are doing a little something with television, and I *do* understand what television's about. I met with Mr. Sarnoff himself
in New York City less than a year ago and he told us plain
—he's aiming for a fifty-million television receiver industry
after demobilization, and that's coming: we are whipping
their asses all over the Pacific and Europe and every place
else. I'm thinking big just a little in advance. You're looking
at the David Sarnoff of the American Midwest, and I think
there just might be room for you in the deal. I'm talking
about the *future*, here."

Prioleau found himself walking closer, into the music of
the national chamber of commerce, bending closer to the
open window, smelling coffee and cigarettes from Bob
Dander's breath. "This is restricted territory," he said, having nothing else to say.

"Catfish," Dander said. "I hired out to plow this land with
horses when I was the youngest boy you ever saw. You
can't restrict it from *me*. Mr. Purloo, I'm talking the first
private television network west of—what is it? the Hudson
River. I'm talking about the future, Mr. Purloo. Come on in
and hear about it." Dander reached to the other side of his
seat and thrust the passenger door open.

"You ever sell herbal medicine in Louisiana?" Prioleau
said. "No, thank you, Mr. Dander."

"Bob. I could use your expertise, son."

"I work for the government, Mr. Dander."

"Bob. Call me Bob, won't you?" He pulled at the lapels
of his heavy gray suit striped with faintest maroon. "I'm
going to try you again. That's my plan. I can't see an
American man with your expertise walking away from the

future. I'll be trying you again. You won't let me give you a ride and talk you into changing your life?"

"I don't think I'll change my life today, Bob."

"Maybe next time you will, then. Think about Henry Ford, why don't you? Think about Mr. Sarnoff starting up his radio stations. Think about Norden and his bombsight."

"That's a military secret, Bob. Just like television is supposed to be out here. Can I ask you how you heard?"

"Carl Melchior. Best-informed man in Patoka Plains. We do some business in a small way. Carl advertises his pharmacy on my *Ask for the Answer* show at noon. If Carl Melchior doesn't know it, you don't need to. Ask him about me. He'll tell you: Bob Dander knows what the future tastes like, and Bob Dander is going to *dine*. I'll be talking to you, Mr. Purloo. I will."

Prioleau stepped back as Dander rolled his window and shifted into first and drove back into the sun. He squinted and then closed his eyes. The image of the car remained beneath his lids and then broke up.

Then it was back to the installation, six small wooden one-story buildings in a semicircle, a small wooden flagpole from which no flag flew, stacks of large crates, wastepaper blowing in the wind, which had grown erratic now, less forceful, and some jeeps and a couple of one-ton trucks, all old and painted for jungle camouflage, and Sergeant Amboise carrying a new M–3 grease gun with its long cartridge clip, staring at Prioleau until he felt that he was walking in the yard again, waiting for the punishment of thugs. Around the camp, which had no name but which Lieutenant Moffit called the Morgue, Illinois spun out its fields, which were level enough to assure no transmission interference—perfect for the purposes assigned by the National Defense Research Committee, and for the work conducted by the prisoner they had seized from a cell and planted, like foreign grain, on ground that ran to the horizon without break. Amboise stared and Prioleau nodded and Amboise stared.

At the far side of the Morgue, behind the semicircle of shacks and their flagpole, fifty yards from the huddled trucks, with Amboise, he felt, still looking into the back of his neck, Prioleau entered the building he'd appropriated. As civilian-in-charge, although Moffit was commander of all but fuses and cathode tubes, Prioleau had the authority to be alone, and he exercised it hard. He stayed as long as he could each day, extending his New York prison to his Army Air Corps bivouac, in this old single room with three windows. Corporal Prince had put glass in the frames, and Corporal Rita had whitewashed the walls, and Private Bagley had found two lawn chairs of heavy white iron and a wide four-poster bed for him. The weak-legged table under a military lamp with metal shade was his dining table and desk; two trunks and a duffel bag were his bureau and closet; an old knee-high barroom refrigerator was his kitchen; shirts and a long khaki coat on hangers swung from the clothesline that ran catty-corner across the room. This was Prioleau's home, and he had allowed few military personnel to enter since he'd begun to work on using television to win the war he wouldn't fight.

When he closed the door, made of tongue-in-groove boards, he saw that he was standing on mail slipped under it. He shuffled the letters with the toe of one shoepac, and leaned down, as if his knees couldn't bend, to read the return addresses. He chose to open none; he kicked at the letters and one flew up. He walked across them to put water from a bucket on the coal stove that heated his room. It all smelled, suddenly, like a room he had lived in with his father and, later, his brothers, but he couldn't remember when or in which state. The fled memory drove him back to his mail, but there was nothing from the South, no one knew where he was except the government, and he dropped the letters again and made coffee, which he drank, still in his flight jacket, standing in a shack that Indians had used between the wars.

The redheaded woman had gone sleepless except for three hours' snoring—she had heard herself, louder than the rain, while she lay curled in the front seat half a day's drive west of Philadelphia. She was Ellen LaRue Spencer— Ellen after her dead father's dead sister, LaRue after her grandfather, Uncle Spaulding LaRue, who once sold cars and who now, in an attic room at their house on the White Horse Pike, counted cars as they passed, by moving matches from a cardboard box to an old Lucky Strike tin and who, before retiring each night, wrote his tally in a blue notebook, then moved the matches back to their carton, looked hard at the dark road, and slept on a cot lined with newspapers. She was in Illinois now, and that was all she knew about this leg of the journey, except that soon, she thought, she would be almost halfway there.

Though he was crazy and almost always holding a conference with the Pike and its fast cars, Uncle LaRue had taken time out, especially when Ellen was younger, to awe her with the secrets of rotors and condensers and carburetors, and she knew that the 1937 Dodge, squat and humped and filthy gray, was either burning oil or leaking enough through the seams of age and wear to blow back at the manifold and stink at her through the firewall. Mike's Boston bag was on the seat beside her, and in it she had gas coupons, food coupons, road maps, a .32-caliber revolver loaded with blanks—souvenir of Uncle LaRue's service as starter for the Chestnut Hill Field Days—and Mike's letter from the Seabee base at San Diego:

Dear Ellen,
As you know, I am safe and well. For now. The sun
rises and the sun sets, but not so pretty without you to
share it. Where the sun rises is where I go whether I like
it or not without you to share it, so I guess you get the
slant of things and you know how much I love you
whether the sun sets with you here or not or whether the
sun rises on me and the guys without you. We have a new
buck sergeant from Lancaster who never got to Phila. in
his life! Imagine that. He's an interpreter, did I spell that
right, teacher? All these guys from the East are the same,
is what Nipper Lewis says. I told you he was from
Frisco, right? I wish I had more time today to tell you
more, but the time is short, so this note will have to get
across all I need to say to you. Whatever happens, I hope
you know I love you. I am signing off because of time.
                                                    Your,
                                                    Mike

And somehow the censor had permitted the letter to pass. So that Ellen, discussing current events with her tenth-grade class, had ordered the children to write a composition on Sacrifice, while she lightly drew lines through extraneous passages about love and sergeants, to isolate the key words of the obvious code: "slant," "East," "sun rises" (for "rising sun"), "interpreter," and "time is short." Mike was going to invade Japan. Everyone knew that Japan would have to be invaded, and Mike had suspected that he might be in the first wave, and now he was telling her goodbye. She nodded at "Nipper Lewis," whom he'd never mentioned before, because what he wanted to say was "Nip." Mike was going to Japan to get killed. Everyone said that: the Japanese would never surrender, the invaders would have to root them out horribly. They never surrendered, and everyone knew that the soldiers who went there would more than likely die.

Which was why Boopi Postelli and Leon Levine and Doris the Slut were writing about Sacrifice. Which was why Ellen took her pocketbook from the desk, her coat from behind the door, walked out of the classroom without a word, and drove home to pack the Boston bag with ration coupons and the suitcase she had used at Kutztown State Teachers College with extra clothes, had walked upstairs in the old cold house to kiss Uncle LaRue goodbye, had come down to telephone, and had started driving west.

And now she was possibly halfway to San Diego, or halfway-to-halfway, she really didn't know, had never traveled except to Kutztown and once to Baltimore and once to New York State, and now she had to sleep because she couldn't steer the Dodge around the curves anymore. When she left, telling Uncle LaRue that she was going after Mike to be with him before he left to die, Uncle LaRue had nodded, still staring from his polished attic window at the Pike, and he had said, "A slip of the lip can sink a ship, Ellen." She had thanked him, kissed him again, gone downstairs to phone her great-aunt's private nurse, who agreed to visit with Uncle LaRue and cook for him, and then she had driven away, taking two hours to find the way west out of suburban Philadelphia.

Now, she pulled the Dodge over to the side of the road and stopped. She closed her eyes, discussed with herself very briefly the purpose of a journey across the whole strange country, alone, unprepared, with little money, in a bad car, to reach a man whose insistence upon their eventual marriage she had always accepted because there was as much reason to accept as reject it, and then she gave the discussion up and slept hard.

She woke harder. She had been dreaming about the time her mother, in the cellar, had screamed that Ellen had been playing with her mother's childhood dolls. Ellen, at six, had replied that her mother was too old to play with dolls and her mother had shouted that she wasn't to be fresh, that she was *saving* the dolls, they were for Ellen's children.

"I don't have children," Ellen had answered. "I'm a kid. And how come if I become a mother I can't play with the stupid dolls but my babies can and I can't now? Answer me *that*."

Ellen's mother had risen from the cellar in thumps of feet and seethes of breath, and had smacked her, once on the cheekbone, once on the buttocks, then had descended again. Ellen had refused to cry. And when her mother, in a different voice, had summoned her, she had set her face— it looked like her mother's, she knew now, and knew whenever she dreamed the memory—and she had joined her mother among the golf clubs and crates and old furniture, under the bright bulb, to find her mother weeping softly, saying, "I'm sorry, sweetheart, I'm sorry." Because dragged out from under a dark-green bureau with only two legs was an old cloth doll. Its fleecy layers of skirt had been gnawed, and lying on one of its limp legs, the head near the stomach of the doll, were the desiccated remains, nearly skeletal, of a rat.

Ellen had said, "*I'm* never being a mother."

It was some of that, something like that, something *from*

that dream or memory—she didn't know now how much was recalled or imagined—and Ellen woke in low red sunlight, her neck sweaty, the car's interior cold, her feet swollen, her right knee sore as if she'd been bitten or kicked. She thought of men in American uniforms stabbed before odd temples by shrieking small brown soldiers, and she pushed the starter while she pulled out the choke and drove off in almost a single motion, looking for a turnoff to a side road with a service station and directions for the best way west.

Prioleau rode into Patoka Plains with Corporal Rita, who never sat still, even when he drove the jeep with wooden bumpers and ruined gearbox. His foot jiggled between clutching and accelerating, he bounced his fingers on the shift stick, pulled at the loose skin of his throat. Rita was the tallest man at the encampment, and the happiest. He had precisely eleven weeks left before he was to be returned east to Utica, New York, for processing out. The country they drove over was not as flat as a table or the first green of an easy golf course; it rippled slightly, varying by feet in height, and its colors changed from burnt sienna to faded brown-green to occasional loam-black. White farmhouses, each surrounded by huge oaks, were islands, miles apart and each a quarter mile or more from the road. The low sun burned orange in the farms' clean windows. Cattle stood still. As the wind picked up, Corporal Rita crouched over the wheel to be shielded by the cloudy window, and Prioleau, his hands in his pockets, sat straight up to watch the land remain the same.

Rita left him at Melchior's Pharmacy, then drove on past the bar and the hardware store toward the small depot where crated tubes from Chicago should be waiting. Prioleau stood before the window, staring at the enormous white china mortar and pestle and the two apothecary jars filled with colored water, red in one, blue in the other. Next to Melchior's door was a six-foot-tall wooden Indian, painted barn-red, from feathers to bare feet. His mouth was a gash, partly open; his feet were arrested in mid-stride; his left hand was over his heart; his right, loose vertical fist was extended toward Prioleau.

A tall and sturdy man in a starched white laboratory coat opened the door and said to Prioleau, "Will you come in, soldier?"

"Melchior?"

"Carl Melchior, pharmacist. Will you enter?"

Melchior's hair was Vaselined straight back from his high hairline, his bony chin was raised, and his eyes behind tortoise-shell glasses were dark and shiny. The hand he used for invitation was big and furred to the knuckles. Inside, he closed the door as if it had opened into his living room instead of a large dark square room of shelves and counters on which the merchandise seemed to glow. Where sections of shelf were empty, the spaces were announced with bright-red shiny paper, as if to say that soon, of course, the stock would arrive and the emptiness be filled. There was no soda fountain, there were no children's toys, no can openers: there were elastic bandages, tubes of unguent, bottles of tablets, pamphlets on sciatica, neuralgia, athlete's foot.

Melchior came close to Prioleau, looked down as if he were eighteen inches taller instead of one or two, breathed a breath of sharp mint at him, and said, in a tone suggesting that Prioleau had entered to report, "So. How goes your work?"

"What work?"

"The work, of course, which you do at your secret encampment at the old-time Indian sheds."

"Could I ask you, Mr. Melchior, how come a German—"

"German-American, sir."

"—doesn't have any trouble about hanging around near a military installation and asking questions—according to a guy named Dander, *knowing* a lot—in a place in a country that's fighting with Germany?"

The huge left hand came up, the right one pried fingers from it, long and stiff: "*First*, I was first here, before the soldiers. *Second*, I had troubles plenty, only recently am I at peace with this town in this war. *Third*, Germany will have soon to surrender. *Fourth*, I ask you this with all respect: Why is a man of the Negro people, is it, do I see the faintest brush of tar, as you say, treating other people like *they* are the foreigners here? May I ask? With all respect?"

Prioleau laughed. "I'm almost as native as you are, Mr. Melchior. My mother claimed to be Choctaw. I had a white man for a father, and I helped to raise two younger brothers, who, you'll be relieved to hear, had an all-white woman for a mother. I surely apologize for making you think I considered you some kind of alien spy."

"Spy?" Melchior said, the fingers still hanging before him.

"No harm done, I hope."

"Spy?" Melchior opened his wide mouth and showed his blue-white teeth and said, "Ha ha."

"Absolutely," Prioleau said. "But you surely know a good deal about the activities out at the Morgue—the base."

"I know that expression for it, Morgue. A morbid sensibility prevails with your officer."

"He's a disappointed man."

"He should be," Melchior said, nodding Prioleau's agreement in advance. "As to what I know—you have seen, I watched you, I confess, you have seen the great mortar and pestle in my window. It is an emblem of pharmacists, no? Ha. It is the sign of the earliest medicine man, your shaman. Just so, as in your tribes. The sign of the man of magic. It tells me my responsibilities. So: I make it certain that little is unknown to me that affects my people."

"Your people."

"Here, in the town. Those I serve."

"Ah. You're interesting, Mr. Melchior."

"You also, is it—"

"Prioleau."

"But French?"

"My father, the white person."

"Naturally. Pree-o-leau."

The jeep's horn honked outside and Prioleau said, "See you again, maybe, Mr. Melchior. Robert Dander says he has got a line on the future of the Middle West."

"Of the entire large country, Mr. Prioleau. Maybe correct. We will discuss this?"

"It beats waiting for baseball season to begin."

"Yes?"

"Sure. We'll have a talk sometime."

"Yes, we will. *Au revoir.*"

"Sorry?"

"The French father."

"Gotcha. *Auf Wiedersehen.*"

"So."

Outside, Rita was dancing in place on the front of the jeep. Two wooden boxes were strapped on a mattress in the back. "Does he carry those French ticklers, Mr. Paloo?"

"You going to use them on Sergeant Amboise, Rita?"

"No, he does it with machine-gun barrels. I am preparing myself for the most energetic evening of my life. What's a foreign pastry called, Mr. Paloo?"

Prioleau sighed and said, "Probably, for you, a tart."

Rita laughed, then said, "Shh-*tru*del, mein Herr." He ground the gears and jittered them back to the base.

First Lieutenant Moffit and Bob Dander were smoking Wings and drinking tea laced with Johnnie Walker. Moffit, his stubby legs wound in a khaki blanket, sat on his desk and listened. Bob Dander, still wearing his camel-colored, double-breasted coat, stood periodically to light Moffit's cigarette, to pace the small office decorated, on one wall blackened by dry rot, with a large bright map of Europe and a small crude drawing labeled JAPAN. The light that came through Moffit's window was the hard, painful pearl-shimmer of the sky before sunset, and it played on his gold-rimmed eyeglasses and then slid away each time he swung the blanket-cocoon and flicked his cigarette or reached his face for Bob Dander's clacking Zippo. The same light stayed on Dander's face and in his blue eyes, and they looked moist with excitement. "It's pure future," he said. "It's what will be, I have got *no* doubts. Listen. We've got the skeleton—we've got the electricity, we've got the staff, we've got the studios. Oh, we'll invest. We'll have to invest. You have *got* to give if you want to get. But whatever we spend, and I'm talking *my* money now, and you don't see me crying, do you? Whatever we spend, we earn back double, quadruple! A small regional network is what I'm talking about. Me, and you if you want some, and that sad sack of yours, Purloo. What we want, you see, is his expertise. Starting soon. Starting *now*. And just as soon as there are enough television receiving sets on the market, and they'll be there and fast, why we're ready. We're on the air. KRBD, that's my name, you see, the Voice of the Center of America. Or something of that nature. I'm talking future, son, Lieutenant. Would you like a slice?"

"I'd need a job," the lieutenant said. "If wartime hasn't got me a captaincy, I can tell you peacetime won't."

"I'm *talking* job."

"And a title. In business—am I right?—you got to have a title."

"I'm talking *title*."

"And a significant amount of change."

"I'm talking job, I'm talking title, I'm talking salary. I'm talking *future*."

"We're talking the same talk, Bob."

"Oh, I thought we might be. Have some Scotch, Lieutenant. Have a cigarette, why don't you? Have yourself a vision of tomorrow. Isn't that what radio brought to the world? Well, isn't that what television is going to bring in *spades!*"

The lieutenant pulled his skirt of blankets tighter under his wide thighs and kicked. He nodded, looking at the map of Europe with its pins, indicating a progress in which he had no part. "There are an awful lot of details for us to worry about, though."

"No," Dander said. "*I* worry about the details. You deliver the services of one Purloo. I hear he's good at what we need him to be good at."

The lieutenant said, "He was a C.O., did you know that? He went into—I don't know, Europe someplace. A few years back? With a mixed detachment of limeys, something like that. I'll look it up. He was supposed to be a civilian

advisor, I think. Something happened. He killed somebody,
or somebody else killed somebody. They pulled him out
covered with his own puke and pretending he was crazy.
Blew the mission. I don't know if that was his fault. But
they blew it. Sent him home. Then they called him up from
his job, he was at the GE company doing radio work,
someplace out East. So he said he wouldn't go. His con-
science wouldn't let him, which you don't really want to
hear when people are killing you. So they sent him to New
York City, and he went to jail. Pretty cushy detail, I hear,
the prison they use in New York. Hot food and everything."
But Bob Dander wasn't listening. He was moving up to
Moffit's cigarettes and down to the folding wooden chair, he
was gathering the lapels of his coat and pushing up the
Windsor knot of his Marshall Field tie, he was sipping
Johnnie Walker-and-tea. He was looking into the light,
broadcast so glaringly down from the Illinois skies.

And after Bob Dander had left to be home before full
night, as the lieutenant sat in front of his desk, still wrapped
in khaki, and lit his own Wings with his own steel Zippo,
he wrote his daily letter home. It would go to St. Louis for
censoring, then be transmitted to Fargo, North Dakota,
where his wife would read the report aloud to their two-
year-old son:

My darling,
I can't discuss in very great detail the nature of our
hardships. Any slip can do us great damage. Just know
that we do our duty and daily hope to be called to the
front. Not because we wish to suffer or die, but because
we know what "duty" means. If I could describe this
place to you, I suppose I would call it "hard." But I had

*better say no more about it, for my purpose is not to
excite your fears. Morale is adequate. The men do their
best under trying circumstances.*

Lieutenant Moffit leaned back from his notepaper and blew
at the nib of his Parker, leaned down again to address a
few more lines to his wife and child, when Master Sergeant
Amboise knocked as he swung the door in, announcing, in
aggrieved tones, "There is quim on the post, sir. Would the
lieutenant care to see?"

"Quim, Sergeant?"

"Quim, sir."

"I'm sorry, Sergeant—"

"Begging the lieutenant's pardon, sir. There is cunt in a
smoking Dodge behind the civilian's quarters."

Up a road of frozen packed earth that was walled in
by oak stumps and pasture fence, leaving a long cloud of
greasy smoke, in the panic of being no place familiar at the
worst time, at first in search of a service station, and then
willing to settle for a human voice, with her fine red hair
hanging into her eyes, a loose beret scratching her ear,
Ellen LaRue Spencer drove the hot car in low gear, over
the whine of which she could hear herself humming a song
—it had no regular tune—about being very much lost. She
looked over the long hood of the Dodge and saw more
land, its greenness burning away in an early freeze. She
raised her knees until they struck the steering wheel, the car
slowed and stalled, and there she was, halfway or nearly so,
but no place she knew. "I'm not doing this very well," she
whispered.

Master Sergeant Amboise and his guns were swinging

around the installation's perimeter, looking for serious threats. Anthony Prioleau lay on his civilian bed in his shack of civilian furnishings, Corporal Prince having left after taking down the usual report—no progress. "I don't do this very well," he had said to Prince, who had shrugged, then thought to mention how, in his opinion, Ted Williams would never be the same after flying combat, but if they put a ball game on television and Williams played, and that transmission worked, he would watch it anyway.

Prioleau, still in his flight jacket, crossed his legs on the bouncy bed and closed his eyes. The coal stove poured heat, which was sucked away through chinks in the old walls. He pulled an army blanket over his legs and settled again, telling himself, The trouble is, you don't do anything that well. You're a fifth-rate technician at a fourth-rate post, failing at a job that doesn't need doing and can't be done anyway, and nobody much cares whether or not you do it, except the radio corporations who hornswoggled this whole project in case they need the research for after the war, which for all you know is over anyway.

Even when he was a boy, very strong, tall for his age. Even then, as his father moved them from school to school, his father settling in, ironing his own neckties flat and scrubbing the collars of his thick white shirts, buying or renting land, bargaining for lumber, leaving the little boys in a harsh clean boardinghouse in town (this was after Amanda), while, outside its limits, always on a plot screened off by low hills or trees, he and Tony built their new house. Even then, nailing plankwood floors, framing windows, hanging doors, even after the measuring and remeasuring, after studying his father's diagrams pressed deep into the cheap unfinished pine with thumb-thick carpenter's pencils, even then he would cut a board too short, bang ten-penny nails into horseshoe shapes, split casing, crush lath. "Tony, shit and goddamn," his father would say. Then: "Do it again, please. Do it right." And he never would. Until, at the third or fourth attempt, he would shy from the sound of his hammer, the bite of his saw, like a bird hunter with buck fever, scared of the noise he would make with his tool and the failure that would follow. Which was how his father would find him—arms dragged low by equipment, lips tight on one another, eyes burning, standing in slow panic before what he would ruin for this man. That was when he would cry and when his father, oily with sweat and smelling of stale bay rum, would hug him, and take the tools from his hands, and draw more diagrams, maps through imagined rooms and vacant doorways, for the frightened boy to follow.

At Tulane, too, on his football scholarship, when what he wanted to read was books about whole families, he would stand on the fenced field and stare down at diagrams of plays, hearing Coach Seager beg softly, "Prioleau, you got to lead the play. You got to pull to your right and *hit* the man. See, otherwise your halfback don't have no place to go. See? Then we lose yards. We lose enough yards, we lose the game. We lose enough games, we have a losing season. Then I lose my job, and *you* sure as shit lose your scholarship. You wanna go back to black beans, son? You wanna kick shit in the fields all your life or get an education? You got to pull right and hit a person's *body*. Understand?"

No. And Seager had lost his job, though Prioleau had kept the scholarship and had gone on to be the least successful guard at Tulane, distinguishing himself by tearing apart his own halfback's knee during an infamous game with TCU.

And he hadn't understood—no: hadn't *felt*—the new lightweight transceiver he was supposed to have helped design and produce for General Electric. Nor had he sensed the intricacies of his assignment when, in 1943, he and another technician had smuggled the parts, taped in crated saxophones and trumpets, into Lorient, on the French coast, traveling by boat, to deliver the radio that GE claimed would help to win the war. The advance post of Englishmen in neckties and Communists in filthy wool had welcomed them with coarse brandy and sour mutton, and then had reviled them, as Prioleau displayed his inefficiency, and his partner, Rosenthal, had fallen ill with typhus. The radio worked at twenty yards only, except once, when they had broadcast into a secret frequency used exclusively by Germans outside the submarine pens. Rosenthal and two of the Communists had been captured, and Prioleau had carried a wounded Montenegrin, educated at London University, who tried to sound like a Balliol scholar, for half a day to the boat that took them off. The Montenegrin had bled down Prioleau's back. Before he died on top of Prioleau, he had said, over and over, "You're really not good at this, are you? I must tell you. You're no bloody fucking good to us at all."

GE had taken him back long enough to pay a bonus and fire him. The Army had called him up, and he had told them how poor he was at war, and how sometimes he dreamed of the blood coating the back of his neck, coagulating between his shoulder blades, and how he smelled the rot in the Montenegrin's mouth as he started to die, and how there must be something else he could do in order not to smell that way himself, and bleed like that, and miss the nail, and miss the block, and kill those people with his well-intended blunders, and the eyes of the review board had narrowed as if all their lids had been hinged on the same steel pin, and they had sent him to prison, telling him the only favor they would do was call him Conscientious Objector instead of traitor or spy.

Why they had called him back, he couldn't tell. Perhaps while he was learning to fight with his hands to keep the counterfeiters and embezzlers from beating him daily, all the electrical engineers had been killed. Perhaps he was having a second chance. Perhaps the Army Air Corps had made a mistake: according to Moffit, an Army's only purpose was to make mistakes. But in spite of his fear of their uniforms, and in spite of his sorrow over being reminded each black November dawn of his unsuccess, he was lucky, he supposed, to be useful to anyone, even by failing again, and then again. And he remembered the happiest moments he had known, when he and his father, despite the boy's shuddering mistakes, had a house up and were laying tarpaper on the roof: the marshes of Florida, or one long absolutely glittering river in northern Louisiana, or a dozen miles of rich field in Tennessee would lie beneath them and before them, and in the cooling breeze under hottest sun they would pause as if signaled, and would look at each other over the peak of their roof, and they would laugh.

He was breathing evenly, conscious as he almost slept that his life, at that moment, wasn't awful in a world that was. His memory of their laughter brought another one, for Amanda and her geese. Amanda was the mother of Charles and Louis, his half brothers; she had loved them all, had brightened their poverty, and had died of something that came up out of Creevey's Swamp behind their house in Florida, chewing her kidneys and driving her into a long, final fever that left the rest of them untouched. When she came, she wanted animals, she said, because a house had to be full of life. That was before Charles and Louis, whose every year saw a reduction in livestock, for the sake of money and his father's illusion of peace. So there had been a small red mutt, which they called Fox, and an infinity of cats which surrounded the house each night, and turtles for Anthony, and geese, Amanda had insisted, to go with Fox, because of a song she used to sing about the fox in pursuit of a gray goose. But the geese liked the small front porch he and his father had built, and their long green turds were always squishing between Amanda's toes. And one night, as she drank wine on the porch and stood to welcome Tony and his father, up from a trip to the market, she stepped in a soft large dropping and shrieked long and loud enough to frighten the geese and wake the swamp.

"Are you all right?" his father had bellowed from the road they'd walked.

"Get them geese out of my *life!*" Amanda had screamed.

"She means it, Tony," his father had whispered. "She'll kill us, or them, or all of us. She can be mean, you know. Now, just go around the other side of the porch and flap about a good deal while I come up and jump on one or the other. If you do get the opportunity, pull the wings up over the head and grab for their legs, all right?" Tony had got that part wrong, but his father hadn't noticed. In the dark, with Amanda shouting and waving a lantern, his father crooning, "Here, goose, goose, goose, goose," and Tony whistling as much to calm himself as drive the geese, they had staggered and bumped and stumbled across the turd-strewn dooryard, geese wailing and hissing and thundering their wings, all of them lifting a mournful chorus to notions of order in a world full of shit. It was a long half hour's chase, and then ten minutes of panting laughter, and then hours, it seemed, of sitting on the front steps as his father and Amanda drank the wine and whispered, his father's voice hoarse and happy, Amanda's light and a little blurry with drink, and he had grown drowsy there, in as much happiness as he thought he should expect—those low voices, the chirr of cicadas, the gentle swamp-smelling wind—and in the certainty that somebody would touch him after a while with soft hands and lead him into sleep.

She said, "Hello? Can somebody come and help?"

He sat up in the dark and chilly room and held his hands before him, wrists bent hard and fingers stiff. "What? What?"

The woman on the other side of his door called from a darkness that was brighter than the dark inside—he saw through the window next to the door a final gray glow on the sky—and she sounded as frightened of the darkness on her side as he was of the dark that lay upon his cold pillow, on his hands and sleep-numbed face. The window lit up harsh and white, a motor roared up and then slid into a bronchitic idle. Master Sergeant Amboise called, "That's the cu—the qui—that's the one, Lieutenant. She was doing a little lurking, I'd call it, out behind the civilian's quarters."

"Stand to be recognized," sang First Lieutenant Moffit.

Prioleau, in front of his door now, heard the woman say, as if she talked to schoolchildren, "Don't be absurd. I don't lurk. I never lurk. And I don't need all that light to knock on a simple door. And I can't imagine why any of you should recognize me, or why I should let you try."

Prioleau opened the door, and the light drove him back a step. Over the chugging of the jeep came the *hump-drump* of the Morgue's generator. And into his shack came a woman little more than five feet tall, her face invisible in the jeep's lights, the thin shape of her head surrounded by fine hair that glowed. Two hands held his left hand and pumped it.

"Yes?" he said, pulling his hand away, blinking.

"Yes," she said. "My name is Ellen LaRue Spencer and I wonder if you could draw me an accurate map."

Prioleau laughed as he had laughed at the end of the Florida goose chase. He spread his arms wide and flapped them against his chest, then opened them again, saying, "Not a chance. I can get you as *lost* as you please, though."

She said, "I can do that perfectly well on my own. Now, I've got a shaky car, I'm only halfway to where I should be, and I need some help. And what could possibly be so funny?"

Prioleau sidestepped to the light switch, and she blinked in the glare of the service-issue lamp. He stared at her. He said, "Oh, my."

Carl Melchior's wide stucco house, painted yellow every year, was built for love. Melchior, who had come from stoking his furnace in the cellar, loved everything in it. Tall and tough-muscled, his big thighs jumping under the hems of his tight shorts, his long biceps shifting smoothly under his white golf shirt, long toes gripping the fronts of his sandals, even his long nose and chin holding on to the air he passed through, Melchior behind his tortoise-shell glasses —his eyes grabbed the space before him, cataloguing— Melchior was loving it all. This was his house, heated to 78 degrees. This was his crackling hearth and marble mantel, his Krieghoff shotgun hung above it. This was his wife, little Lotte, in her flounced blue peasant's dress with its navy-blue shoulder straps, her hair the shiniest gold, her small nails the same sunset-red as her lips, each cheek punctuated with a rouged circle. This was his daughter, Louisa: tall, wide-hipped, narrow-waisted, with her father's long, curved nose; the long, pointed, thick-nippled breasts, though proportionally larger, of her mother; and the long arms and legs and hands of her father, who watched her in her fitted gray flannel slacks and light-gray short-sleeved sweater. Louisa's lips always looked slightly swollen, and tonight they looked larger still. This was the soldier, Corporal Rita, sweating in his woolen khaki shirt and tie, his legs shifting as he sat on the green velvet love seat, studying Louisa's movements into the kitchen and back. This was Melchior's American house, and this was his healthy family, and this was their guest.

The smells were of onion zwiebelkuchen, with its sour cream and caraway seeds and bacon, and of red cabbage, and of beef brisket, somewhat inferior, but all that Lotte could find, enhanced by the chicken feet and necks with which it was boiling, and the carrots and onions, the celery and peppercorns and bay leaf—not elegant, but nourishing and appetizing, adequate for them, and surely for an Italian type with overly thick eyebrows and short fingers and a hint of uncleanliness about the wrists and neck.

From the Victrola came Bing Crosby singing "I'll Be Home for Christmas," saccharine sentimentality for the troops and for the families many would never return to. He saw Louisa smile at Corporal Rita, and Melchior's jowls tightened. She was setting a tray of highballs on the glass-and-chromium coffee table and Rita was staring at her all over. So. Melchior stood behind her, and as she straightened, while Rita sweated and watched, he placed his hands gently over her eyes and said, in his lowest dark voice, "Who can this be?"

Louisa leaned back into him. He felt her face move into a smile. "I'd never guess," she said.

Melchior circled her shoulders from behind and bent to kiss the top of her head. *"This,"* he told the soldier, "is my good daughter."

Rita nodded, his knees moved up and down. "Yeah," he said. "Right. Nice lady."

"Exactly," Melchior said. "A lady."

"Oh, Daddy," Louisa said.

Melchior straightened, releasing her. He took a deep breath, watching Rita watch his chest expand. He noticed that Rita also watched Louisa's chest expand. He moved around her to straighten the coffee table, permitting Rita to glimpse his strength.

And then, at the table, in the dining room lined with books from Dr. Eliot's Five-Foot Shelf, and in the radiance of the bright-green wallpaper with its repeated images of pioneers in furry hats marching through happy forests, at the cherrywood table, moving heavy silver and wide plates, they spoke of uncles and aunts, unseasonably cold weather, the coming redecoration of the shop for Christmas, and Melchior's experience as a manager, in Schweinfurt, of a metal-parts factory, the work of the Army Air Corps installation outside town.

"Television, you see," Melchior instructed them, "has much of Germany in its past."

"I thought we invented it," Rita said. Louisa smiled and he smiled back.

"You have done much," Melchior said. "But once, in a Germany about which Americans are told little—it would hurt the war effort, you see. Well. A Paul Nipkow, you know of him? No. Yes, Nipkow, long ago, 1880s or nineties, made what was called an electrical telescope. There was much of your telectroscopy—what you call television now.

He did much advancing in that area of the visual science. The picture, you see, must be separated into tiny little pieces—"

"Scanning," Rita said. Louisa smiled again. Melchior snapped at zwiebelkuchen and shoveled cabbage.

"Correct," Melchior said, as Lotte placed the beef beside his plate. "It was the old story. Money, funds—he lost the patent, poor man. Nobody would help him, it is the same all over the world. But what he did was impressive. It was *essential.* Of the essence. The Nipkow Disk was a revolving metal wheel that he had, you see, perforated at the edge with many little holes. *This* was the beginning of—you called it scanning? So. The separation process. Before he died, he was recognized. It was too late. But his country made him president of the German Television Society nevertheless. Then he died. Weiller's drum, a tube that turned with many little mirrors in it—that came after Nipkow. He was superseded by it. This happens all the time in science. This is life."

Lotte began eating again. Louisa poured more beer for them, inferior American beer, from the yellow Fiesta pitcher. Rita nodded and consumed. Melchior, swallowing a forkful of zwiebelkuchen and beef, said, "The Frenchman, Prioleau? It is apt that you employ him. Television is a French word. Perskyi, of Polish blood but a Frenchman, it was he who named it."

"Paloo's okay. You know him?" Rita asked.

"We have spoken together. He speaks only a little, I should say."

"He's got his own problems," Rita said.

"Poor man," Lotte said, then looked to Melchior, whose eyebrows were up. She cut her meat.

Louisa said, "He's cute."

"Not my type," Rita said, and he snorted; Louisa smiled.

"It is his work, probably," Melchior said. "His work is difficult. To make television work on an airplane, tch-tch. Not an easy task, eh?"

Rita said, "Oh, we're not gonna get it done. Forget it, if you know what I mean. They'll have to win the war without us." Then he looked up at Melchior: "That's okay to say?"

"Daddy's *American,*" Louisa said.

"Gotcha."

"We are all American, of course," Melchior said to Lotte, who smiled and nodded. So they spoke of the war, of General Patton and his tanks, of British night bombing, of Churchill's unpopularity, of the difficulty with which a television camera in the tail section of a four-engine bomber transmitted images over the engines' electrical broadcasts. And in spite of Melchior's efforts to delay them, they ate their dessert, and drank a glass of peppermint schnapps, and chatted the wispy end-of-dinner words, and stood so that Louisa could take a drive with sweating Rita in the Nash that Melchior had given her the week before when she became nineteen.

Melchior watched her shoulders arch, her breasts stand forth, as she slid on the navy-blue pea jacket. He also watched Rita. He swore her to return by ten o'clock and knew that she wouldn't. He chewed his lower lip. Then, slowly, he moved to stand before her, and slowly encircle her with his arms, and slowly hug her hard to his chest. "*Liebchen,* you will make your father proud?" And when she had kissed him on the cheek and had squeezed his hands, waved good night to her mother, gone out the door with Corporal Rita, who definitely generated a sour smell, he sat in the leather easy chair under the wide-shaded bridge lamp, removed his glasses, rubbed hard at his eyes, and mourned. Lotte washed the dishes, keeping silent. Melchior sat erect, opened a copy of *Collier's*, and waited.

Prioleau slammed the door against the sound of the generator and of the jeep, and against the headlights; the scene jumped again as different qualities of yellow-white threw changing shadows along the scuffed floor, and as the door he'd slammed caught Ellen LaRue Spencer in the shoulder and knocked her sideways. Prioleau reached for her, or for the door, but held on to her, and the door continued on its own to close. He held each of her shoulders and looked down onto the top of her head, and she looked up to say, "Are you assaulting me? I haven't got *time*."

He stepped backward and turned away, as if he knew she would stay, and he slid the partly filled kettle to an open burner on the stove, then with a folding field shovel threw coal onto the fire until it roared. "Here," he said, "get warm. I'm making some coffee if you'd like some. And I'm not dangerous. I'm not dangerous on purpose."

She stayed at the door, and they heard Moffit's voice over the idle of the jeep, and then the jeep's engine as Master Sergeant Amboise engaged the gears and the brighter light slid off the window and away. Then there was the gruff metronome of the generator, and the sizzle of fresh coal, the low huffing of heat up the rusted flue pipe.

"Could you tell me where I am? My name is Ellen LaRue Spencer, I'm from Philadelphia, I'm supposed to be going westward. I want to get to San Diego."

Prioleau stayed at the stove, showing her that she was safe. He studied her face, long and pale, flushed under the eyes with fatigue or anxiousness. She wore no lipstick and she bit her lips as she stood, hands folded before her. "You're a teacher, or a minister's wife," he said. "They're the only people I've seen who stand like that."

She nodded and smiled, and he saw that her eyes, so clear as to be nearly colorless now, would be blue under daylight. Her hair was wispy and red, mussed as if by hands. "I teach. I used to teach. I had to leave—I need to be in San Diego, fast."

"This isn't San Diego. This is Patoka Plains, Illinois, or that's the nearest town. This is no place. This is a U.S. Army Air Corps post."

"You're a soldier?"

"I'm a civilian who works for them. I'm Tony Prioleau. I'm completely at your service, Miss Spencer. What's in San Diego?"

"A fiancé. Kind of."

"It could snow. They get—I forget, tornadoes, hurricanes? They get terrible weather here. You could be stranded."

"I can't be stranded, Mr. Prioleau. I have to be in San Diego before somebody leaves for someplace. I can't tell you."

"Classified, huh?"

"Oh, it's not funny. It's serious. It's a matter of life and death. Obligations aren't a joke, you know."

"You're a teacher, all right. And I bet you San Diego is where they're marshaling one of the invasion groups, Marines and Rangers. He's a Marine, probably. Marines love redheads, according to a movie I saw. William Bendix said so. And you want to see him before he ships out. No, it was Lloyd Nolan who said that, about redheads. To marry him before he leaves?"

Her face went paler, and then the red beneath her cheeks poured over her face and she chopped with large teeth at her chapped lower lip. "Are you a fortune-teller, or what is it? A clairvoyant? Are you some kind of spy, knowing all that about San Diego and everything?"

"Miss Spencer, I heard it from somebody who heard it from somebody else who probably heard it in a letter from Japan. Like all the other secrets we're keeping, it's public information. We knew about Pearl Harbor almost for sure before it happened. All I am is a lousy electrician. I don't think there's a secret in this war. Could I give you a cup of coffee? Should we sit down and drink a cup of coffee together? The lieutenant's coming back with four armed men probably any minute now, to make sure you don't shatter the foundations of democracy and the American Way of Life as we know it today. Wouldn't you love to be drinking coffee and talking to me about the weather—because it could snow any hour of the night around here. Give a calm kind of quizzical glance when he busts in with his .45 waving?"

She stood at the side of the door with her hands folded in front of her. She stared at him, and then he was blushing. He turned to put coffee in the small enameled pot. Smoke began to run from the rust spots on the flue pipe and a small finger of fire jumped out at them. Prioleau, as if he always did this, poured water from the kettle onto the pipe —it hissed and steamed—and then banked the fire lower. He poured the rest of the water into the pot and turned to smile and shrug.

"They shouldn't leave you alone too long," she said. "Things happen to you, don't they?"

"And there's snow on the way," he said. "It could happen."

"Black," she said.

"What?"

"I'll drink it black, thank you."

"Good," he said. "Good."

"Prio-*leau!*" First Lieutenant Moffit cried from the window. They saw his face against the windowpane, and then Master Sergeant Amboise's. "I want that civilian to stand and be recognized, I want it *now*. There's a mission operating here, and nobody walks on this base without clearance. Understood?"

Prioleau went to the window and pushed his nose against the pane so that it met Moffit's own pink smear. Cupping his mouth with hands, Prioleau intoned, "Does that include Bob Dander and his quick money, Lieutenant?"

The nose went away. Master Sergeant Amboise's face still hung at the window, teeth bared. Moffit's face returned. "You're vouching for this woman?"

"Miss Spencer is my guest, Lieutenant. If she steals any secrets, however, I will not hesitate to turn her over to Sergeant Amboise for torture and interrogation."

Amboise's face moved, and his deep voice said, "I'll have your ass someday. I'll *bite* it if I have to."

Prioleau blew a kiss to him, and Amboise moved as if struck. Then Prioleau turned back to her and said, "It looks like snow any minute. You better think about staying. Really."

She was sitting in a white lawn chair, her coat was hung on his clothesline, her legs were crossed, her hands lay loose in her lap, on her dark woolen slacks. "Would you believe," she said calmly, "that I almost am?"

"Sure," he said. "I'd love to."

She took the heavy china mug and sipped and grimaced at the taste. "I mean I'm really comfortable. I'm not driving and I don't have to look at the road. Thank you. But I'm going to San Diego."

Prioleau sipped at his coffee, sneezed out smoke, spilled coffee on his flight jacket, and set the cup onto the stove top. "I'll make sure and draw you a map," he said. "You'll be back before you know it."

Corporal Prince was under the hood of Ellen Spencer's Dodge, dismantling the carburetor, shaking his head. Private Bagley, who held the flashlight for him, was shivering with cold and shaking his head, like a dog, to keep the fine, blowing snow from his eyes. Prince said, "I can't work under these conditions, Bagley."

"Nothing works under *no* conditions here, Corporal. Shit. I hate this."

"What, fixing some broad's car at ten o'clock at night in a snowstorm and we don't even know her name but we know she didn't come here out of love for you and me?"

Bagley turned the flashlight off, put it in his camouflage-coat pocket, blew on his hands, then walked away. Over his shoulder, in the invisible snow, he said, "Yeah, that too, Corporal. I quit."

Corporal Prince slammed the hood, knocking the air filter off the fender and chipping the condenser up and away, out of sight. "I herewith dismiss you," he said to Bagley's back. "She can stay the night. In the morning she can buy herself a car that runs. Let her boyfriend Prioleau buy her one. But that won't run, either. Nothing runs here except the goddamned generator."

He went off toward one of the lighted huts, and the snow began to collect on Ellen Spencer's car. Master Sergeant

Amboise, under a withered small ash tree behind Prioleau's shack, with a small mound of snow on his khaki helmet liner, noted Prince's departure and kept watch. He shuffled his feet and blew on his hands and touched his sidearm. Then, his footsteps deadened by the sporadic high winds and the steady beat of the generator squeezing out the margarine-colored light that pulsed from First Lieutenant Moffit's window, he dodged and sidled, like a man in a fire fight, to the rear boarded-up window of Prioleau's quarters. There he lay the side of his face on the gray rotted wood, found with his fingers the crack between board and window frame, pushed his ear there, and listened. He moved his head back soon and rubbed at his ear. He squeezed it, shook his expressionless face, leaned to listen further, then looked at the tops of his shoepacs, touched his sidearm with a gloved finger, walked off to sleep a little before resuming his protection of the smallest and least important and least successful operation of the armed forces in the continental United States and probably the world.

Ellen LaRue Spencer slept under Prioleau's khaki raincoat and blankets, her legs curled beneath her on the white iron chair. Prioleau, listening to the wind and the pounding of the generator, sat on his table and swung his legs and watched her. In sleep, her mouth was slightly open and he saw her nearly buck teeth, the tip of her tongue. When he instructed himself that he was privileged to witness such privacies, he tried to overrule his pleasure and he told himself, as he had so many times, on different roofs, over several hot new countrysides in his boyhood, to just hang on, hang on. The rest of her was invisible under the bedclothes he had piled upon her when he'd seen her drop into sleep, so he studied the neck, the chin, one ear visible through her hair; he studied the hair itself and even leaned forward as if he would jump from the table and walk on the tips of his toes to lift a handful and feel—he was certain he knew the sensation—its awful weightlessness. But, holding on like the frightened boy with his younger face, he stayed where he was, watching. Despite the uneven light and the cold hard shadows of his hut, the hair was brilliant and deep. In spite of the temperature—he was reluctant to feed the fire, he insisted upon silence for the sake of her sleep and in order to see unseen—her neck was unmottled and almost cream-colored, smooth. He looked at his right hand, its dirty fingernails and knuckles, and he saw it curve as if to settle on the surface of her neck. He imagined touching, with one frightened finger, the dry surface of her lower lip.

Her sudden pale eyes drove him back where he sat, and her smile changed his temperature. As if they had been speaking for an hour, she said, "How tall are you?"

"What?"

"How *tall* are you?"

"Five-eleven."

"I'd have said six feet even."

"I haven't been six feet since I was in college. When I played ball they called me six feet to scare the other team. But I'm really not."

"How much do you weigh?"

"Now? About two hundred pounds, I guess."

"You're big."

"I'm pretty big."

"You noticed I'm little?"

"God. Yes. Yes. I noticed."

"So how come you act like you're frightened of me?"

"*Me?*"

"Never mind. Can I use your bed? If you intend to be awake for a while?"

Wrapping the blankets and raincoat around her, dragging portions on the floor like a child in a grownup's bathrobe, she shuffled to his bed and crawled up onto it. She lay on her side and pulled the covers around her and curled back into sleep.

She murmured, "You and Mike would get along. He's scared of women, too."

Prioleau said, "I'm not scared," but she didn't reply, was already breathing evenly. Prioleau said, "I sure as hell wouldn't like him. *That's* the truth, anyway."

He stayed there, then moved to put coal in the stove, one lump at a time, as gently as if he wired circuits. She said, he thought she said, "I know."

He tiptoed to the iron chair, put his hands in his pockets, listened in case she spoke again, and stretched his legs out, closed his eyes, smiled an uncontrollable grin.

He didn't want to sleep; he wanted to study the pictures —what almost managed to become pictures. The electron gun scanned the mosaic, blowing electrical charges toward the cathode-ray tube. But the picture wouldn't reassemble. The picture scattered into hundreds of thousands of particles, and each one was a tiny interceptor firing aerial cannon, and each time they fired, Prioleau saw the rear turret shatter and heard the meat sound of bullets entering flesh. Because the engines broadcast to the *scanner*, he announced inside his head. We can do it, if you want. All you have to do is use gliders, and then you won't have interference from the engines, and then the image will reassemble, and then the gunner won't die and the plane won't fall out of the air. He saw the large kinescope magically begin to work. I'm flooding the turret with infrared rays, he told the lieutenant. But the lieutenant answered, So the gunner can see the darkness better? Prioleau said, It's for night bombing, it's a *contribution*, for godsakes. And the lieutenant screamed, But there is nothing on the kine-fucking-scope! Prioleau begged him: Stop the engines, then. All we have to do is stop the engines. And the lieutenant answered, You're supposed to do it *with* the engines, you jerk moron deserter! We don't *need* to know any more ways to kill our own people, we got that right already! And the Montenegrin said, You're no bloody fucking good to us at all.

Her cold hands on his cheeks woke him, and he looked up into her lips, which said, "It's all right. You were dreaming." He pushed his cheek against her hand, but she moved away. "I'll make some coffee," she said.

"What'd I say?"

"Nothing."

"Really?"

At the stove, sliding the pot, she said, "Maybe we'll write to each other. Maybe I'll stop back on my way home. Do you think that's possible?"

"Why would you do that?"

She turned, and her face was red, and the smile was helpless and wide. "Sometimes," she said, "you make me feel as if I'm still in a classroom."

"It's a deal. What should I learn?"

"Whatever's necessary—how to make good coffee, for example."

"*Coffee?*"

"And how to get to San Diego," she said, turning back to the stove.

He rubbed his face and watched her put his raincoat on, then roll up the sleeves and return to the stove. He sat back in his chair as if it were easy to do.

Then it was Sunday, and no imaginary aircraft flew. Master Sergeant Amboise, not yet on duty, studied *The Mastery of Life*, which he had received from the Rosicrucians (AMORC). Obeying the booklet's orders, he touched the mound of gristle beneath his thumb to feel "the long-forgotten secret beat of life." First Lieutenant Moffit wrote home to say that the war went with difficulty, but that men performed their duties without complaint even in tough going. Bob Dander's radio station, in the shell of a ruined bank, broadcast *Your Cathedral of the Air*, featuring an angry Missouri Synod Lutheran pastor named Dieterkorn, whose sermon was about "Failing the Test of Love." Then came the marching-off-to-battle rhythms of the Coe College Choir. Corporal Rita showed Corporal Prince how, with a little effort, you could do the rumba to their songs. He also explained how Louisa Melchior, possessed of a classical education, insisted upon coitus interruptus, fellatio and cunnilingus, but *not It all the way*, because she feared that theirs was a wartime romance and would close down with the installation's generator once the Germans had been defeated. "Tell me about how Germans do it," Private Bagley begged. But Rita, shortening his steps to the mambo, since the Coe College Choir had shifted to Bach, reminded him that soldiers have a code of honor on the subject of shagging ass. Lotte Melchior had coffee with an elementary-school principal named Palfrey to discuss the final adjustments they would make to costumes donated by Melchior's Pharmacy for Monday night's Victory Pageant. Carl Melchior stared at his daughter with a cuckold's eyes. And Bob Dander drove his Kaiser through frozen fog that hung on roadside trees, making them glint in the weak morning sun, as he journeyed to Patoka Plains in order to make further plans with First Lieutenant Moffit.

Ellen LaRue Spencer pretended to sleep. Tony Prioleau was taking a sponge bath at the stove, and she peeked through narrowed eyes and above an arm to watch his flanks, the silly wobbling penis, the goose-bumped thighs, as he scrubbed himself with a floral-pattern washcloth and shivered.

Mike's penis was longer, but not so thick. Mike himself was longer, but not so thick. Mike's hair was as curly as Prioleau's was heavy and coarse and straight, as blond as Prioleau's was black. Naked, Mike looked less capable than Prioleau, less bulky in the world. In bed, Mike had been efficient and insistent: not until she had shifted and shuddered would he roll away and say, "Ah." Prioleau, of course, remained a dozen feet from her, as if one or both of them were wired without a ground and might transmit electrical shocks. Prioleau's scrotum had shrunk in the cold—baby walnuts, she told herself. She permitted herself to giggle, and Prioleau pulled his trousers on so quickly he struck the pot of soapy water with his elbow, spilling enough to make the stove top hiss. Ellen made a sleep sound and turned beneath the covers, willing herself to stillness for the sake of his embarrassment. She felt him looking at her, and breathed as regularly as she could.

Mike had volunteered. Taking two weeks' leave from his job as teacher of woodworking, he had run around the Temple University gym, had punched the heavy bag, had practiced reading facsimile eye charts at long distance, and had presented himself to the officers and doctors in Center

City as something like a secret weapon, withheld until 1943, when he was needed. He had never been home since. After each rotation, he had written of strange places—Russell Islands, Choiseul Island, Gilbert Islands. He wrote of the earth-moving equipment he drove, and of the men he knew who had died. He wrote, always, with a happy firm stroke of the pen and something like a lilt in the tone of his sentences: somehow, no matter who was dead after however long under fire, "boys" were always "catching some sun," and "it could have been worse," he guessed.

Standing behind Uncle LaRue, waiting to interrupt his count of passing cars on the Pike, she had been very happy about her—lover? boyfriend?—probable fiancé, and the adventure of her trip had pleased her, she was understanding, as much as the imperative that she reach him before his new training was complete and he left to die, more than likely, among the cannibal Japanese. Pretending to sleep, she decided that what she had wanted was to volunteer. Making gestures toward teaching composition to the children of Higby & Madison plant workers, escorting Doris the Slut to the principal's office for smoking in the girls' room or offering her breasts to a circle of palms in the cloakroom—insufficient. Reading misspelled letters from a happy warrior whose body she had mildly enjoyed, but whose impending death she had terribly thrilled to—also insufficient. What she had pursued through Harrisburg and Terre Haute, on through Greenup, had been a sorrow she might appropriate: an anguish all her own in order that she not feel merely witness to the war but part of it, its victim. And knowing this, her waking to dress and drive without further rest or pleasure now became a duty. She was on the job.

Prioleau called her to coffee and local eggs, and she came

from the bed, still dressed in his raincoat, angry with him, as surly as he was happy to serve. For she was the person in this shabby hut—not this handsome boy of a clumsy man, but *she*—who had driven in a Dodge with no knob on the gearshift lever through Zanesville, Ohio. *Zanesville!* Not even in her classroom had she spoken a place in sounds like that. It was she who had wept, and now it was a pleasure better than sex to admit her tears. It was she on the road, weeping because she had no better reason for the journey than the journey itself. It was she who had wished, through the mists and traffic, that she might hear more from the little men in gas stations than "Lady, where did you get those tires with *treads?*" And it was she who fled with mouthfuls of peanut butter and saltines, too dry most of the time to spit at people like the Chiclets salesman at the Esso —"Honey, I'll put the oil in for you, and anything else you need put in"—after seeing a man off at 30th Street Station, and waiting to hear of his life or death, and knowing no more about either in spite of his letters, and understanding after not too long that while much of the world's life-and-death, and surely that robust, capable, and devoted man's, were subject to review each day and night, she was feeling neither under her housecoat or her jumper, her college-girl sweater or the lacy nightgown he had given her before departing. And that, then, was what she had been crying for, wasn't it? That, and not the broken windshield wiper, and not the coveting of her tires, not the mild interest—the one some men express for handsome hunting dogs, good tools, expensive liquor—so many men had told her she'd aroused. It was that sense of being stateless, a privileged refugee, loyal to less than nothing, for her fealty would not extend to even herself. And that was why she had wept so much of the way, wishing that on the seat beside her, instead of a

Boston bag filled with gas coupons, there had been a baby, a little person, two years old or three, with blond bangs, dressed in, say, a snowsuit and white woolen mittens and little rubber boots, and maybe sick—not awfully, but with something mild and finally curable—who needed her attention, whose flushed face and whimpers made her wild with worry and regret, and for whose sake this trip was being made, and in whose name a loud, and reasonable, and unembarrassed lamentation might be cried.

And that, then, is why she stood and, still in his raincoat, losing his face as she had lost the sight of Howard Johnsons and highway patrol cars, trailers shaped like bombs and diners shaped like airplanes, lone trees on lonely frosted soil, she walked outside to find her car and be away. The wide, uneven semicircle of huts reminded her of hulks at the Philadelphia docks. From one of them came the sounds of a church service; somebody changed the station, and a band played "You Are My Sunshine," and she moved more quickly in her bare feet, which were stung by the frozen earth and hard snow. A handsome, heavy car drew up to one of the little buildings and she ran around the corner of Prioleau's hut to see her dirt-gray car, its hood ajar, a long screwdriver sticking into the ground nearby like an exclamation point for some mechanic's statement of inability to repair it. She knew that she would not be leaving. She thought of Uncle LaRue, up and counting cars in which people *could* be leaving as they chose to. She thought of her father leaving her mother, living first in a roadside cabin he rented by the day in Mays Landing, New Jersey, where as a college girl she had driven to beg him home. She thought of him leaving New Jersey for New Mexico, from where he'd written them a largely incoherent letter, enclosing $57. She realized that she had driven in the same direction her father had traveled. She felt only envy that his car had carried him through Illinois. And, as she turned, returning in reaction, not through choice—essentially the way she'd started from Philadelphia—she thought of her mother, who had mourned in church, and then in cocktail lounges, and then with whiskey in bed, and then in Philadelphia General Hospital, pleading for a shot of Calvert's Reserve and crazy with the pain of a corroded liver, which was hard, the daughter thought, as a daughter's hardened heart. And here I am, she told herself: bitchy elf-girl on the road, wading through men without pleasure and going no place long before my wretched car gave up, and all the time I have a mission that's mine for accepting, the entire history of the world is conspiring to offer me a future and all I could ask for to remember when I'm old enough to want the memories. And all I can do is hum a stupid song and go inside and bother that man a little more.

So they sat again, he not asking questions, she offering no answers, and they drank reheated coffee and prodded scrambled eggs gone cold. Prioleau cleared the table, put more coal in the stove, rubbed his hands, put on a harsh brown sweater, put his hands in his trouser pockets, did half a deep-knee bend, forced his eyes—she could watch him push his face toward her—and said, "Did you check on your car?"

"They gave up."

"I'll get them to work on it some more. Maybe I can do something. Though if Prince and Bagley can't do it, I don't imagine I can do it."

"Because you foul up a lot?"

"I surely do. But also, they're experts, I'm not. I just do vacuum tubes and heavy wires and boring things like that. But I surely foul up a lot."

"That's what you told me."

"That's what I do."

"All right."

"Are we having a little war between us, Miss Spencer? Ellen?"

"Mr. Prioleau. We don't know each other well enough to have a war. Germany's having a war, and Japan is having a war, and England's having a war, and America's having a war. All we're having is somebody got lost and somebody thinks he found her."

"Now—I haven't been making overtures or anything, have I? Really: have I? You know I haven't."

"You've been polite about it. You've been a little gentleman. Your mother would be proud of you."

"My mother's dead."

"That's no cause to sound sulky. So's mine."

"I'm not sounding sulky."

"Yes, you are."

"Please. I'm thirty-two years old. I've had about four real girlfriends in my life. Probably average count, wouldn't you think? I messed around some too, but you wouldn't count that. No, listen. I had girlfriends like everybody else, and once I had a dog I really took care of for a while. But what I'd like to say is, I have no doubt that I've been waiting for you since puberty."

"Pewberty. Not pooberty; that sounds ugly and it's incorrect."

"Boy, you've got it in for me, haven't you? Why?"

"The word is incorrectly pronounced, the word is ugly the way you pronounce it, and your assumption—Mr. Prioleau—"

"—Tony—"

"—is plain damned wrong, juvenile. God. How can you stand there, pure victim, and make yourself so vulnerable to somebody you don't *know?*"

His face was naked as he shook his head.

"I'm going to San Diego," she said, tones as tough as those she used to batter through the noise in her classroom, calling her restless students to heel at their desks. "I am going to San Diego in that car. If all of you men can't repair one small car, I am walking to a bus station or a railroad terminal, and I'll get there that way. I'll walk all the way. I'll hitchhike. I'm going. I have a boyfriend in San Diego who is a war hero and he'll probably die within the month. Now, how can you stand there, with your face hanging out like a surrender flag, all white and waving around, and tell me you've been waiting for me? *Don't do that!* And you *don't* look like Joel McCrea posing up there at the stove, so you can cut it out. I apologize. I apologize. I apologize. But I would profit if you'd show some restraint. Maybe I could copy it, maybe I could act like a grownup if I tried a little harder. I'm sorry."

She saw his hands tremble slightly as he hooked his thumbs in his belt buckle and readjusted the position of his feet. "I don't think I look like Joel McCrea," he said. "I don't think I look like anybody. What I think is, I don't know anything about you, but that's all right. I didn't mean to offend you. Upset you. I should have better manners. I will. I'll get your car fixed for you, and I'll get somebody to show you how to go and you forget the rest. I apologize."

She was nodding her head. "Don't we apologize nicely?"

He said, too loudly, "We're mannerly folk."

She continued to nod. "Tell me about your life, Tony. Tell me a couple of sad stories about deprivation in the South—that's where you're from, right? You say *o* like a man from the South. *Aiow.* You tell me something with a little mournful tune to it, and then I'll tell you stories about city life."

"No," he said, "just save it," taking his flight jacket from the clothesline. "Tell your boyfriend. I can get patronized by a wide variety of strangers of my choice at convenient hours. Shit. I know songs about sadness that people really mean, and I can play them on the harmonica whenever I like. So shit on you. I'll get your car fixed."

And when he slammed the door, she threw her china coffee mug halfway across the room, where it spun on the floor and came to rest on its base as if someone had set it there. She smiled at that.

The wind was steady now, and it was knocking people over again. Private Bagley crawled in the powdery snow and rose to his knees and stood. He shouted to Prioleau, who acknowledged without hearing more than noise. Prioleau made steering motions, as if he gripped a wheel, and Bagley staggered to him, poured an unfresh breath into Prioleau's face to say, "Three, maybe four days to get parts, I'll bet you. I don't know how the hell she got it here. Anywhere. Gorgeous tires on it, Mr. Prioleau, but she shot the hell out of the car—the choke won't open up, the plugs are fouled to shit, she needs new points and a new condenser, and *that's* no good unless we get her a new carburetor. Prince tried to rebuild it, but he can't, and I can't either. We got to order her a new one, or pull one off a junker someplace. Except nobody around here junks anything, so we probably got to buy her a new one. Nobody knows where to send for one. So we got to find out where there's a big Dodge place and haul the car in, or buy stuff and try and do it ourselves. Tell her three, four, five days, okay?"

Prioleau wiped his face as if that motion would pull Bagley's breath from his flesh. He shook his head. "Tell Prince I'll pay fifty bucks if it runs tomorrow."

"You want to get *rid* of her?"

"Bagley: just make the car run."

"Tomorrow?"

"Anytime tomorrow. Seventy-five."

"A hundred." Bagley's face was that of a cunning boy. "A hundred and it goes if I have to push it to Montana."

"Missouri will do."

"Mr. Prioleau, we got a deal. Missouri by Monday night."

"Tuesday's fine. Never mind, Bagley. Monday, and a hundred bucks."

"You got the wartime-effort special, Mr. Prioleau."

"That's patriotism, Bagley, and we're all very impressed with your work." Prioleau was looking over Bagley's shoulder at First Lieutenant Moffit, who stood in his doorway and gestured. "General Eisenhower's calling me now, so I'm going to leave the mission in your hands, Bagley. I'll strike a medal if I get a chance, all right?"

In Moffit's hut, Bob Dander presented Prioleau and Moffit with gift-boxed Dunhill cigarette lighters. "They're windproof, boys. Straight from whatever's that street right in the middle of London, England. All the dukes and princes use them. And that's *gold* along the edge, in case you need to buy your way out of a Nazi prison or something. You know, that's how all the Jews escape. Gold on the scales and freedom around the corner. If it trades, your Jew's gonna carry it, your German's gonna make a deal. So let's do us some Jewry, if you get what I mean."

Moffit flicked his lighter several times, blew on the wick,

and a greasy yellow flame came up. "Bob," the lieutenant said, "Mr. Prioleau is part of the job here, and I don't think it's necessary to give him presents. That right, Prioleau?"

"Lieutenant, I'll give you my lighter so you can do cigars and cigarettes simultaneously, if that's what you mean." He threw the lighter onto Moffit's desk and looked at Dander, whose grin was fixed.

"Come on, boys," Dander cried. "I've got a rare opportunity cooking. The big name for it is *tomorrow*, pure and simple. The little name for it is Victory Pageant. Listen: the school over in Patoka Plains is performing a small war dance to help the Allied forces shove the flag up Hitler's ass. They'll recite and sing, and everybody in the village will be there because it means they're spies and quislings if they stay away. I believe we have an unparalleled opportunity tomorrow night to show some folks what television can do. It's a new force in the life of America, is what I intend to demonstrate. You truck in a few of your lights and one of those kinescopes, the biggest one you got. And a camera, of course. I don't know if they put out the right kind of juice for you at the school, but you've got a generator you can hitch to the truck, right?"

"This is a top-secret operation!" Moffit said, flicking his lighter in syncopation to the *hump-drump* of the generator.

"Only to seven Japanese soldiers in a tunnel someplace," Prioleau said.

"No," Moffit said. "I couldn't allow it."

"Sure you can," Dander crooned.

"Sure you will," Prioleau crooned back.

"Didn't you listen to what I've been telling you, Lieutenant? Network? Midwestern monopoly? Dollars and *cents*?"

"Oh, we're on the air, all right," Prioleau said.

"You'd do it?" the lieutenant said.

"Tomorrow night? Oh, you bet. How far away—in the village? Yeah. Tomorrow night in town, it's a deal."

"I been counting on you, Mr. Purloo," Dander called.

"Good community relations, Lieutenant," Prioleau told him.

"But what about secrecy?"

"Lieutenant," Prioleau explained, "that guy Melchior who runs a secret detachment of storm troopers out of his drugstore—he knows. Which means, probably, his family and all know too. I hear from Bagley and Prince that Corporal Rita spends more time inside Melchior's daughter than he spends in his socks, so *she* knows. So maybe her friends know too. And Melchior's wife and *her* friends. Mr. Dander here, the voice of America, seems to know more about the operation than I do—"

"With the results you're getting, that isn't too hard," the lieutenant said.

"Correct. Correct. So they all know, the Patoka Plains Volunteer Fire Department and Rotary Club, they are all informed. So what would you suppose we're hiding here?"

Moffit narrowed his brows in his fat face. "Why would you be so anxious to cooperate, Prioleau?"

"Good chance to get out and meet people, Lieutenant. I can show off my science and technology, too. And I think I need some rest and recreation off the base. Tomorrow night especially."

"Prioleau, I don't trust you."

"I never thought you should, Lieutenant."

"Boys," Bob Dander shouted, "this is the beginning of tomorrow."

"Ah!" the lieutenant said. "If you're coming on board with us, Prioleau, you kind of lose your lever to keep your piece of ass on a military base, don't you?"

"She'll be gone tomorrow, Lieutenant. That's a guarantee."

"You're going back to Washington in a briefcase if she isn't. And from there to New York City and your swanky jail."

"I can appreciate your patriotism, Lieutenant." Prioleau turned to Dander. "You're in business."

"Boys, we're *all* in business," Dander sang. Moffit flicked one of his Dunhills.

Louisa Melchior opened the pharmacy at ten-thirty, accepting prescriptions that her father would soon come to fill, selling a Baby Ruth and a small bottle of Bisodol. She practiced, each time she passed the small mirror near the pharmaceuticals counter, ducking her long neck gracefully while slightly pursing her lips—a gesture of submission and delicacy. She told a grumpy man in scarf and mittens that the Chicago *Tribune* was late again. She turned the radio on, and as Lionel Hampton rose to the occasion and Louisa began to swing her hips, Carl Melchior entered through the back door and stamped his galoshes. Their metal buckles dominated her dance because she turned off the Stromberg-Carlsen under the counter as soon as she heard the door and boots slam.

He walked into the store, still wearing his thick red hunting jacket with its black-cross motif, his brown hat with earlaps. His eyes were small behind his glasses, and his mouth was set hard. He bent to regard her, ducked his head in what was not a gesture of submission and delicacy, said, "Yes? All is well?" He studied her for too long.

She smiled impatiently, said, *"Yes."*

He stood ten seconds longer, then returned to the back

of the store, emerging again in oxford shoes, dry trousers, and a long, white pharmacist's coat.

Louisa said, "Mrs. DeLong needs the sulfa right away. Somebody's really sick."

Stooping to a shelf of bottles, Melchior said, "She would not need the medicine if somebody was really well, yes?"

"What's wrong, Daddy?"

He straightened, blew his chest up under the white coat, raised his chin. "Soldiers."

"*Daddy.*"

"Half the night outside like a whore with soldiers."

Louisa ducked her neck, but he didn't see her. She bit her lips and ducked again, but he was counting tablets. So she said, "I'm not a whore, Daddy," and she started to cry. He moved like a soldier in the field, low, fast, silent, to stand before her, above her, a man encircling someone without the use of arms.

He waited, she wiped her eyes. She leaned at him, then she rested her forehead on his chest. He closed his eyes and shook his head. Then he hugged her. Into her topknot he whispered, "A father must worry."

"I'm a girl, Daddy. It's fun to drive around with boys."

"You only drive?"

"I'm your *daughter.*"

"This I know." He smiled into her head, kissed the hair, said, "Yes. I must restrain my worries and my woes."

"Someday I'll get married."

"That is not a logical thought now."

"Well, you can't come on my honeymoon, Daddy."

He gave her a chortle, and then another one. "You are sure?" he said smoothly.

When Mrs. DeLong returned for her prescription, they both were laughing, and when Prioleau escorted Ellen

LaRue Spencer into the shop, Melchior was humming "The Stars and Stripes Forever" as he marched about, dusting.

Ellen bought a pair of sunglasses and some Hershey bars for the trip. "You travel?" Melchior asked her, wrapping the glasses as if they were half a pound of sirloin.

"I'm going to San Diego," Ellen said.

Prioleau sat on the edge of the shelf behind the front window, nudging with his back the apothecary jar filled with red-dyed water. He crossed his legs and watched Ellen, small in her big coat, her face lost in the dark scarf she wore over her head and ears, tied beneath her chin.

"That is far," Melchior said. "You have a dependable automobile?"

"No," Prioleau said.

"Ha. Then that is farther, yes?"

"Not to her," Prioleau said.

And then Ellen and Prioleau were in the jeep, she wrapped in blankets against the wind, removed from the long and very wide street of Patoka Plains, so tightly shut on Sunday, two walls of closed brick buildings seemingly long deserted. The sky was bright, the wind severe. Ice shone on the fields, the winds were constant and the jeep's exhaust blew about them, they traveled slowly in a dirty cloud.

"I'm leaving," she said.

"I'll make sure of it."

They passed a small child on the lawn of a white farmhouse. In his red snowsuit, he was grimly scraping snow with mittened hands, making a shapeless mound. Ellen waved to him. He studied her.

"What kind of baby were you?" Ellen said.

"The usual kind."

"I'm trying to know about you."

Prioleau said, "I can't imagine why."

"You are pouting," she said.

"And you're leaving."

"Are you asking for something? What are you asking for?"

Prioleau shifted down as the road dipped into a dark and icy patch. When they were out of the shade and running level again, he said, "Nothing. Not the way a dog asks for food. Nothing."

"In another way, then?"

"I don't know."

"Sure you do."

He blew a spume of breath into cloud. "Sure I do. Sure I am. So what."

"Private Bagley said you used to be in jail."

"I was a conscientious objector. And your boyfriend is a hero."

"I wasn't referring to that."

"Okay. I didn't want to be in the Army."

"That's all right."

"Thank you."

She pulled her scarf from her ears and redid the knot as she covered her nose and mouth with it. She spoke.

"You look like an outlaw," Prioleau said. "Which of course is the pot calling the whatchamacallit—"

She spoke again.

"I can't understand you," he said.

Ellen pulled the mask down. "I said different people have different commitments. That's all."

Prioleau looked at her and lifted his foot from the clutch. The jeep bucked, rolled, stalled, then stopped. In the crusted small road, bulky in his flight jacket as a baby in a snowsuit, nearly jumping over the gearshift lever, he moved toward Ellen and put his hands on the back of her neck and kissed her under the right cheekbone, just above the fabric of her scarf. He stayed there, his lips on her skin, leaning awkwardly in something of a crouch. He said, "I'm afraid to look at you."

Her lips made a dry parting sound. "It's all right," she said. "It was a beautiful kiss."

"I'll move back."

"All right."

"You think I should move back?"

"Yes," she said.

"But I could kiss you one more time."

"You could," she said.

He did it, as he had before, and then he fell backward into his seat, to look over the windshield at the huge sky and shining fields. He pumped the gas pedal and pushed the starter, and the flooded motor whined before it caught. Still not looking at her, Prioleau waved his hand at the horizon. He said, "Help yourself."

First Lieutenant Moffit wrote:

My idea of Sabbath dinners on Sunday nights is not working out. Because we are all specialists, there is no cook on the roster. So we've been taking turns at the cooking, and you know how I've felt about the meals. A good base is a well-fed base, and we just aren't. But we know also that there are men over there who haven't had a hot meal in weeks. We can't complain. But we do! The enlisted men do, anyway. One of the technicians, a corporal named Prince, spread his turnips all over the table last week, did I tell you this?, and he wrote a word in the mess that I simply couldn't tolerate. I gave him

*extra KP for that, but what a mistake it was! His cooking
was worse than his manners, and last Sunday we ate a
stew that was full of apples and olives that Prince had
stolen from someplace, and it had some kind of meat,
horse, if not worse. Tonight was another Sunday Night
Special, and our civilian, Prioleau, drew the rotation. He
made something he called "gumbo." It had pieces of
catfish in it! I didn't think you could catch fish in the
winter—don't they hibernate? If they don't, they should.
Horse is better than catfish, at least if Prioleau cooks it.
There was beer, donated by a businessman in the area.
We needed it. Corporal Rita, who is not military
material, tried to dance with a guest of Prioleau's. He
made lewd gestures, and I confined him to quarters. This
is what I have to work with. What's worse is that I need
Rita, so I had to rescind punishment, which is intolerable
for discipline. Nobody ever said war was easy. I know
that. And nobody ever said command was easy. I know
that too. My prayer is that the war will end soon and that
we will be together.* Perhaps in a new place with new
opportunities!

Lieutenant Moffit lit another Wings with his Dunhill, flexed
his writing hand, then wrote:

> *Please tell my little Dickle-Dockle that Daddy wants him
> to be a big good soldier and do everything Mommy tells
> him to. Tell him Daddy never lets his soldier-men go
> dee-dee in their pants.*

Moffit stared through the shadows of his hut at the map of
Europe. His round face wrinkled as if the cheeks were

sucked in by a vacuum; if he had been smaller, he would have looked like a boy on the verge of tears. He sighed and sipped his Johnnie Walker, then sipped more, then sighed, and dipped his face toward the page.

Prioleau had carried in her Boston bag and suitcase, then had gone for a cot. It was little more than a piece of canvas which, when the folding wooden legs were locked into place, became a sleeping platform. He'd hung blankets on his clothesline, dividing the room in two, and on the darker side he was kneeling to assemble his bed. He heard snaps and the soft slap of clothing, an occasional scrape of leather. She was humming. It was simple: you straightened a corner leg and closed the metal brace, then you did the opposite leg and brace. But the first brace wouldn't lock. He crawled to the far end of the rolled-out canvas and worked on another leg, which did work properly, and then he crawled back to a middle leg, which did not. He heard the bed creak, then he heard her sigh. He crawled across the canvas to the opposite middle leg, but it didn't work either, and when she came through the hanging clothes and wrinkled khaki blankets he'd hung, he was sitting on his haunches in a nest of canvas and broken-looking wooden legs, his fists knotted and his lips sucked in.

"I thought you were going to sleep in the—where we ate."

"Oh."

"But I guess you're not."

"Well, I could. I suppose I should, shouldn't I?"

"I think so, yes."

She was wearing heavy blue pajamas under his raincoat, and her feet were in white socks.

"You look nice," he said.

"Thank you. I didn't bring a bathrobe along. You don't mind if I wear your coat?"

He squatted, looking at her, and after a while his fists opened. He breathed out hard, as if he were blowing cigarette smoke, then he shook his head.

"What I still don't understand," she said, pointing at the wreckage of the cot, "is how they could want you here as a scientist or whatever it is, seeing how you can't *do* anything."

"No," he said.

"Because television must be complicated."

"Television is simple," he said. "You're pretending you're an eye. There's a camera, Zworykin's camera, you get 50-line definition with it, which is okay. Hell, there's a guy at Bell Telephone who knows how to transmit in *color*. Definition, scanning, we've got it all. It's just, what they *want* here is what nobody knows how to do. They should have found a genius, or a real technician anyway. There are thousands of them. Getting *me* was the mistake."

"You spill things."

"I do?"

"In that store? Where we went when you kissed me?"

Prioleau was crimson. He stared at the one locked leg of the cot.

"Before we left," she said, "you were sitting on the edge of the window, then you walked outside and waited for me. You knocked a jar of colored water over—one of those drugstore things they all have? You just stood up and walked outside, and it fell over and red water spilled all over the ledge and the floor. That man went *wild*. And you nearly set your stove on fire. And you cook like a mass murderer. I wonder if you might not want to turn your talents in the direction of chemical warfare."

"Mustard gas instead of mustard," Prioleau murmured.

"Exactly. And where are your blankets?"

"On the bed, where they should be. I'm not exactly that dumb."

"That's right," she said. "There are blankets on the bed and blankets on your little clothesline. But what did *you* propose to sleep beneath tonight?"

"Oh. Well. I'll sleep in my jacket, I guess."

"You guess. And you can't even put a cot together, which Boy Scouts do in their sleep."

"Okay," Prioleau said. "I can't make food and I can't make beds."

She waited. Then she whipped through the blankets to the other side of the room. "You Sad Sack," she said. "You can't reach conclusions either, can you?"

No, he couldn't, he told himself, and he pulled at a wooden leg and hit a brace with the side of his hand until the brace clicked home and his hand was scraped. He sucked at the blood and remembered how, his mouth bloody, he had offered a tooth to his father and how his father had assured him that the tooth fairy would come. That night, a hot night in northern Louisiana, a woman had come. Prioleau, seven years old, too grown-up for Santa Claus and tooth fairies, but willing for his faith to be renewed, had stirred and wakened to the footsteps. A flicker passed inside his eyes, something with long gauzy wings and his dead mother's face. But then he'd recognized the sound as high-heeled shoes, the kind his father's women wore, and in the small shed behind the kitchen, where he slept among boxes and sacks of onions and tools and the dresser on which his father had laid cowboy decals for him, he had burrowed into the damp flat pillow with a frown of disappointment. Half sleeping, he heard his father's rumbling voice, and then a strange woman's smothered laugh. And then the heels had slowly tapped from the front of the little house and through the kitchen and into his room. As the light rolled in, he had closed his eyes, pretending to sleep. His heart beat hard. Dry lips, a woman's, kissed him on the bridge of the nose. He smelled sweat and a wonderful perfume. There was a chink of coins at the edge of his pillow, and then the footsteps moved away, then the light, then the footsteps again. And as he sat beside the useless cot, he told himself: Yes, he *could*.

When he stood, he realized that she had stopped moving. The hut was silent, except for the sound of the stove, except for the beating of the generator, except for the sound of something—hard wind? blown snow?—rustling against the rear wall. In the morning, he would rise to Corporal Rita's knock, and he would carry with him the portfolio of charts he hadn't looked at since his failure on Saturday. But it would be Monday, dawn, and he would be transmitting darkness through four Flying Fortress engines, and then he would close down again, and Moffit would sneer, Rita would shrug, his stomach would tighten, the sun would come up, and some time during that day he would pay Private Bagley and Corporal Prince their hundred dollars and Ellen LaRue Spencer would drive to St. Louis, catch Route 66, and eventually find a properly made bed, with a full consignment of heavy blankets, and sleep under or beside a man who went to war. Yes, he could reach conclusions.

So he walked through the blankets, pushing them hard, but becoming fouled in their folds anyway, needing to unwind himself too energetically for the silence or dignity he sought. Knees up under his covers, her pajamas buttoned to the neck, her red hair down along the sides of her pale face, teeth slightly protruding, and laughing hard, Ellen called, "Oh—wait: I've *got* it! Bela Lugosi as Dracula. Right?"

But he didn't stop for long. He went to the side of the bed and pulled the covers back. She said nothing, she watched. In his mind, he swore viciously each time he moved—to unzip the flying jacket, pull his sweater over his head, unbutton his shirt, tear at boot laces, pull off his pants. But he said nothing. He looked at her as though she dared him not to. As if into cold water, he dived into bed and pulled the covers up. And now he didn't know where to look.

Ellen moved to the other side of the bed and propped herself on an elbow. She undid the top pajama button. Her face was calm, and she contemplated him—he felt this, resented it, and resented his pleasure—as if he were a slow student whose long-expected progress had begun. "Shall I unbutton the rest?" she said.

"If you would," he said, "lest I tear something."

So with her right hand she unbuttoned, her left hand still propping her, and finally, when the pajama jacket was undone, she closed her eyes. "I've never done it with the lights on," she said.

He moved in the bed and kissed her stomach. It was soft, and it smelled of something warm he couldn't name. He kissed her there again and her breath hissed. And then he moved, too suddenly, she made a sharp sound of surprise, he was kissing her small breasts, nuzzling them, and then he stopped—"I haven't shaved," he said.

Her eyes were open, and she was laughing again. "I

noticed, but for heaven's sake, don't *try*. You'll bleed to death before I can get you into bed again. Come here." She arched her back and pulled the pajama bottoms down. And this time it was he whose eyes closed, because she was moving his hand between her legs, guiding his large hand with her small ones, setting up a rhythm and moving into it, whispering sounds to which she moved alone. She said, "Oh," and then pushed his hand away, then retrieved it, lay back pulling him, and he went where he was led—upon her, and into her, then out again. "What *now*," she snapped, the teacher. "What?"

"I don't have anything."

"I don't care."

"Yes, you do," he said. "Yes. You will. You can't get yourself pregnant going West to get married, for godsakes."

She pulled his penis, then her hands were tenderer, and she guided him in. He moved his head back, stilled his body's lurches, and, as he was about to speak, she pulled him by the ears, pulled his face into hers, and kissed him so long that he became breathless, then forgot to breathe. She pushed his head back by the ears and whispered, "Stop thinking about me like that. Stop being considerate. Stop being a gentleman. Stop." As if his head were an earthen vessel to pour from, she pulled his face down, and they began to move together again.

She was stronger than he, her thin, downy arms were locked behind his neck, and her legs held him. He reached and bent and took one of her wrists and forced it to the bed, and then he forced the other. He leaned above her, holding her in this parody of rape, and her head whipped back and forth. Then, still holding her arms, he fell upon her, and she battered at him with her groin, and he held on, insensibly, hoping to finally be useful, but letting go of everything and

crying out in a higher voice—he heard it, he despised it—
than he had wanted to.

I̲t was when she was wading in the Wissahickon with
Mike, as he told her that the war would end within a year,
and as he tried to teach her to smoke his Camels—"You
pretend it's a straw, then when you feel the smoke in your
mouth you pretend it's not"—that she understood how her
father "fixed" the cars he brought home. Make believe it's
a straw, he'd told her, parking the car he'd driven home
from the lot, angling it so that she could bring the siphon
tube to her mouth and suck the gasoline up, almost into her
mouth, then aim the tube into their own car's filling pipe.
That's how it had gone: Daddy parking the car for her after
dinner, Ellen siphoning gas—"Just enough, Pumpkin, not
all of it, now"—while Daddy worked with his screwdriver
to remove the speedometer and sit on the running board to
make adjustments. As he had taken small amounts of gas
each day, she'd understood, standing on hot flat rocks while
the Wissahickon ran around Mike's ankles, so he had un-
wound miles from the cars on the lot to make them easier to
sell. She remembered her father's long, almost simian arms,
thin and muscular and flexible, the long flat fingers, the
easy sureness with which he "fixed." She had sat down, that
summer afternoon, to watch Mike's hands as they fiddled
with small rocks, skipped flat ones, dropped big ones just
to see them splash. He had done what all boys do, she
remembered, when there's something small enough to hurl
through the air: he had aimed and thrown, carelessly at
first, then at last with determination, working for distance,
accuracy—*that* cattail *there*—repeating and repeating the
throw. His hands seemed so certain in their economy of twist

and flex and heft. But that was too simple. She would not permit herself to believe it. No one, not Miss Ellen LaRue Spencer, for sure, would spend the next twenty, the next forty, years of her life in pursuit of hands, ten flat fingers, with which she had passed the first twenty-odd. Fixing: winding back the distances passed by strangers over strange roads.

For a while, hearing her stories about the long-distance searches for her fled father, Mike had tried to call her Pumpkin. He had done it once too often, at McGillen's Bar, after ordering the liverwurst she hated, with onions she didn't want, the ale she found bitter. He had clasped her hand across the table and called her from thought. "Pumpkin," he had said, making his lips soft, running a hand through his curly hair, smiling gently. And she had walked out. Because she would *not*, she told him, be taught to bark at someone's signal.

Nor would she tell him any more stories—about the time her father borrowed a customer's boat and ran them aground off Mays Landing, New Jersey, so that they had to eat cold, canned Dinty Moore beef stew washed down, by her parents, with warm whiskey, waiting for the tide to turn; about the time her mother, searching for the fled husband, had driven into a traffic-light stanchion, bringing much of the traffic near Fair Isle Avenue to a halt; about her own trips to motor courts, driving alone at seventeen. Mike had stopped asking, and he'd paid attention to what she was then: a young teacher of kids who were taller than she, a lady who lived alone with mad, gentle Uncle LaRue, who counted the cars on the White Horse Pike. That had been satisfactory. And Mike had made a silverware box for her, and a long, oblong container for her jewelry—she had little enough to put inside it—and lacquered rings, for which she had cut and hemmed a set of bright-red napkins. At the lathe, or with a coping saw, his hands had seemed to grow larger. While he worked, she watched the tendons protrude, the muscle between thumb and forefinger swell.

What was she doing, then, in the presence of *these* particular hands? They were wide, almost square, and the fingers, though heavy and muscled, were rather short. They dropped small objects, prodded stationary matter from tables, became tangled in anything more complex than flat boards. How did he make a radio work? Those television things he was supposed to wire to something warlike and secret? "A slip of the lip can sink a ship," Uncle LaRue had told her. And she remembered a song, then—some band on a radio in some service station on Route 40, and a man singing about slips of the lip. She had smiled at that, then had retreated into her car from the one-armed Sinclair man's confused stare. But there it was, and she was proof, going from hand to capable hand, until now, in Illinois, surrounded by hapless soldiers doing something mechanical under the direction of a man whose hands were frail for all their bulk, and not much good, really, to anyone. Except when they touched her skin as if it were hot.

It had gone on for a month, the coming home from high school, checking the mail, sometimes in cold weather drinking some cocoa, then backing out the Chevrolet they had bought for $75 when her father left with the Buick, and driving—into Germantown one afternoon, Quakertown another, even to the fringes of Chestnut Hill, and returning, often, to the same neighborhoods, sometimes to the same rooming houses or salesmen's hotels. "Hello, my name is Ellen LaRue Spencer, and I wonder if you've seen my father? He's kind of tall, he has red hair just like mine, and he wears good suits."

Once she had driven out to King of Prussia and had stopped at a large white sign that said TOURIST CABINS! It was the exclamation point that pulled her in, up the graveled drive to the top of the small hill. She thought that anyone who could paint a sign with such excitement would be hospitable to a girl who was looking for her father. There were eight cabins marching in a straight line along the crest; each was clean white with dark-green trim at the windows, and each had a name over the door: Poinsettia, Daisy, Morning Glory, Rose. The office was in a huge white gabled house with a porchful of tubular metal chairs that sat in a row, evenly spaced, looking off the porch and down the hill toward the White Rock factory. Dusk had fallen, and the house was dark, and so were the cabins, and Ellen couldn't see if there were cars parked behind the house. A man answered the bell beside the heavy carved door. "She don't want to rent no more," he said.

He was shorter than she was, not much heavier, completely bald except for his ears and nostrils. She felt her lip pull back as she studied the sprouting dark hair. He was dressed in dark-blue pants and shirt, and his little hands fiddled at the collar of his shirt, directing her attention to the red and white enameled pin: a drop of blood, a tiny cross. Watching her eyes move from his ears to his nose to the pin, he pushed at it again and said, "Blood. I give more pints last year than anybody alive in King of Prussia. *You* give it?"

"I'm Ellen LaRue Spencer," she'd said, "and I wonder if you've seen my father? He's kind of tall—"

"Taller than me?" he said, looking almost across. His face was very wrinkled, she could see now, and she wanted desperately to laugh and cup her mouth and shout *Call-for-Philip-Mor-rees!*

"He's got real red hair, like me? And he wears really good suits. He's a salesman, you see."

"We get some of them," the little man said. "But my mom, she don't want to rent no more. She's too tired. Her joints get froze when it's damp. When this batch moves out, we ain't renting no more."

"But you have some salesmen now?"

"Upstairs. First door on the right, second door on the right, last door on the right. All the doors on the right. But no women—you ain't a woman, you're nothing but a kid, but we got the same rules for any kind of woman flesh: stay outside the door of the room. Come down real soon or my mom'll throw your body out."

So she had gone into the dark house on a carpet that seemed to be covered with gritty powder. The light of dusk struck through a blue-and-yellow-stained window on the landing of the stairs, showing the ash-colored powder. The room to the left of the vestibule was sealed by wooden sliding doors, and the room behind the stairs was closed off, too. There was a smell of many flowers, and then a harsher smell, as if the flowers were in foul water, rotting. As usual, she was frightened of the door, of the knock, of the pause, and then her little speech. Her stomach hurt as it always did on these errands. Another tinted window at the end of the narrow hall threw blue and yellow light onto the dark carpet, and her feet felt, through her saddle shoes, as if she were crushing tiny shells or bones.

The man who answered her knock was running with sweat. His perfectly round face gleamed in the light of his room. She smelled his sweat, and it was old; she stepped back. He wore no shirt, and there was so much hair on his chest and stomach—it poured over the waistband of his gray trousers—that the perspiration was lost, like puddles in a forest. "Oh," she said. "No. I'm sorry. Wrong number, wrong *room*, I'm sorry." He quickly closed the door.

No one answered her knocking on the second door, but as she turned from it, the third door down, near the blue-and-yellow window, opened in, and a very young man dressed in brown tweed looked around the edge at her. His hair was brushed flat, and she could smell his after-shave lotion, something to do with cloves. He prodded at the knot of his shiny brown tie and on his hand a ring with bright stones took the light. His smile was for someone else, and when he had seen her long enough, it vanished. *"What?"* he demanded. "What *now?*" Behind him, an infant started to cry, and she knew at once that it was sick.

"I'm—"

"No," he said, "I mean what now? It's a simple question. Are you an immigrant? Do you speaka da language? You can answer that even if you're some horrible kind of *Greek*. What do you want of us *now?*"

She had skipped into a run, then had forced herself to walk calmly down the steps, into the smell of old roots going mushy in stale water. The little man waited for her at the radiator in the hall. He held a card in his hand: "Prize Donor," he said, "see?"

"God," she said.

"Is your father up there?"

"No. No, he isn't. Thank you very much. Wait—the cabins. Is there someone in the cabins? Would you—"

"I know something about parents, see? Your father ain't in the cabins."

"There *is* someone there?"

"Not your father."

"Please show me. Please. If I looked upstairs, I should look in the cabins. That's the way I do it. Would you show me?"

And walking on his toes, little hands in his pockets, he had led her out the door and down the side steps of the white porch, across the gravel and then grass, past Daisy and Rose to Chrysanthemum. She saw the long nose of a Buick coupe behind the cabin. "You go home after this," he said. "My mom wants you to go home as soon as I can shoo you away. That's what she said."

"Yes," she said, "goodbye." As he mooched back to the house on the balls of his tiny feet, she took a breath so deep she thought she would faint. For two seconds or three, it was like listening to a seashell at Mays Landing: everything roared. Then she knocked twice, hard, blinking her eyes until the spots were gone.

Nobody answered, and she knew that her father was hiding from her. She knocked again, telling herself that she was no kind of daughter if she didn't arrive with her father on her arm—didn't sail in to present her mother with this gift. When she knocked for the third time and shook the doorknob of Chrysanthemum, she knew that she was stealing her father back for herself. She heard cars down the hill, and a lone angry sputtering single-engined plane from the training station at Willow Grove. Then the door swung back and a woman in a black slip stood in front of her. The woman's arms were at her sides, as if she expected to be helpless. She was pale in the pink light of the cabin, and in the mirror behind her Ellen saw a small suitcase with very little in it. They looked at each other. The woman, as if so tired she might not stand for long, said, "What."

"Hello," Ellen said, looking at the tangled long brown

hair and then at the bruises under one ear: they were the colors, though muted, of the stained windows upstairs in the house. "I'm looking for my father. His name is Spencer."

When she looked at the woman's arms, she saw the bruises repeated, and then on her long, bony chest. The woman permitted her to look, then said, "I'm not your father."

"No," Ellen said, but the door had closed, and she was on a hill in King of Prussia, looking down at dark factories and open countryside behind them, and the traffic on three roads, each of which was lined with cabins where salesmen might stay after leaving their family, unless they chose to drive to New York, or Ambler, or Maryland, or Texas, or every place else in the world. She went back to the Chevrolet to drive home, cook them some kind of supper, stay in her room, do her homework, and listen to bottle and glass and ice, the sentimental radio songs that would help her mother to cry before early bed and then a morning's hangover at the shoe factory. Trigonometry and blended whiskey, she thought, looking into occasional lights on the road through Conshohocken. It was then that she might have started traveling, Ellen LaRue Spencer told herself, lying with her nose near the arm of snoring Anthony Prioleau; it might have been then, on that little trip or another like it, driving on a mission. It might have been then that she started, nine years before, heading west to Mike, or to this big uneasy man in his bed that smelled like coal.

Prioleau lay motionless, and he pretended to sleep. He said goodbye to Ellen, didn't know what she would say if they agreed to give up shamming and talk about today: how in two hours he would dress and carry wiring diagrams and circuit testers to the truck, and drive out with Moffit and the others with the tarpaulin cover flapping in the high winds spiraling downdrafts, blowing coal smoke back into rooms; how sometime later, when the test had failed and the engines were shut down, he would give to Bagley or Prince a handful of cash and hear from them that the Dodge would run; how Amboise would study the plains, searching for any Midwestern maniac whose ambition it was to kill someone, or everyone, at the base; how in the early evening they would haul equipment to the red brick school and watch the children's play, and then show the wonders of television to hog farmers and soybean shippers; and how sometime during those hours—they appeared to him like bricks of the school—in-between them, in some interstice small as the half inch of mortar separating bricks, this woman would pack her car, accept or reject a thermos of coffee and some sandwiches, kiss him goodbye or shake his hand, give him her San Diego address, or promise to write him in Illinois, or neither, and then drive away in a high-tailed, long-nosed, dirty gray Dodge, going to California to marry a Marine who would support them, if he lived through the war, by teaching mouth-breathers how to fasten dowels and miter corners. He saw Ellen tucked against a bulky ex-Marine in bed. He saw her teaching in a high school and looking, sometime, at a nervous kid with black hair, finding him familiar but not sure why she did. He said goodbye, naming the ways in which he took on loss with her leaving. Naming the ways—protect me from *this* memory, please; protect me from *that*—did as little good as prayer. So, feeling her breath on his bare arm, he said only goodbye.

When the project was closed down, and when the war

was over, he would probably be sent back to West Street in New York, and then, whenever someone thought of it, released: he, and the few other conscientious objectors, and perhaps a crook or two on parole. He would find work. Television or radio, the ignitions of cars, control panels for planes—someone would need what it was assumed he could do: channel current, make things work on command. He would become a middle-aged man whom certain women found interesting and whom men disliked. And one year or the other, in no hurry, he would buy a car or take a train and go back South. In warm country, someplace dry and hilly, among high pines, he would buy land and build a house—tilting, errant-windowed, slope-porched—and live in it a little of every year, playing bluff host for his brothers and their wives and children. They'd bring their broken RCA Victors, and he would drive to town for tubes, and he would tinker, and sometimes they would leave with memories of sour mash, and of static hissing through the house their big half brother Anthony had built, just like he used to when they were small, but not so good, but what the hell, and that's old Anthony, the friendly bear.

Ellen would be a crooked foot or missing earlobe—an undisabling, healed wound. And what would remain would be a secret incredulity, to sometimes be confessed and examined, while breaking an alligator clamp or running a hundred and ten volts through his body by mistake: that after *this*, tongue and buttocks, slick crotch and wrenched banging bed, her pale hand and his dry fingers around it, she could separate her life from his, require of him some sort of forbearance, assume that he would see it as clearly as a ground wire separates from each of the rest, that she went in a direction different from his, that she *could*.

And this: that she had happened to him. The loss would

be his pain. But the amazement would remain in that she had ever arrived in order that, on a Monday in November, from a bleak flat field in Illinois, she might feel able to depart. From Philadelphia, where he had never been to leave his spoor, to plant the most minute cause for this effect; from Philadelphia, about which he knew only two facts concerning Benjamin Franklin; from Philadelphia, through which neither his father nor his stepmother had even passed, about which he might have spoken a dozen times in his life—from there, with no need for him, no suspicion of his breath or footsteps, this small woman with red hair and giant clear eyes had started traveling and had slid, from the map, from her life, into this base, the Morgue, and into this hut, and then this bed.

War makes strange bedfellows, he would drawl, and then he would smile. Or: *Take it easy, kid.* Or—surely this was being filmed, this random wartime romance, and surely someone might write a final line for him, redolent of grace and giving comfort she might one day need, a courage through such giving which he could bank against his own days on West Street and some ozone-smelling factory in an alien city—*What a hell of a time we had, eh?* Or: *Easy come, easy go,* and a walking away as if pain, like distance and the hours of a Sunday night, were relative and therefore susceptible to management through thought.

But, knowing himself as he did, as he suspected he did, he wanted to keep her, to own her, to engulf her, to fight with her for as many years as he could over which mattered more—her life, or his possession of her life. And he did not love her selflessly enough to be nourished by her pleasures with a handsome Marine, or to see her free for some other, possibly more pleasant, love with someone other than Mike. He wanted her as selfishly as he had wanted Amanda to

live, as he had wished for his mother, as he had prayed for
his father to this time—time after time—*not* require that he
make lines plumb and floors dead level.

What he would say, he knew, would be a useless *Goodbye.*

"What'd you say?" Ellen whispered.

"Oh. You're awake."

"Just woke up."

"Me too."

"Is it time for you to go to work?"

"No," he said, "we've got a while."

"That's nice." She turned and sighed.

"Nice?"

She lay with her arms at her sides, outside the covers.

He listened to the wind and the generator, the growling
jeep on patrol.

It wasn't until she was a freshman at Kutztown, at-
tending on the commonwealth's generosity and with the
aid of a loan from the Rotary, driving to school every morning at five, returning late at night because she couldn't
afford to live in the dormitory, accepting the black bubbles
of fatigue beneath her eyes but also, on Saturday mornings,
hanging before the bathroom mirror to lament that she
couldn't be young anymore—it wasn't until then that she
said to herself, driving home from school, "Mays *Landing!"*
And as surely as if he had sent for her, she drove south
without pausing at home to tell her mother where he was.

It was a warm October day, but the shore was cold when
she arrived. The summer homes were closed, and some of
the shops, and when she parked near the hummocks of
weed that separated the cracked sidewalk from the beach,
she began to shiver in spite of the sunlight. For a while she

walked near the turreted white homes, where in summer the tourists rented rooms; at night they stood around player pianos or the radio, then went to bed early, so that in the morning they could leave first thing for the beach or the old piers. There was no one about who remembered her from past Augusts, and she was grateful. She walked back toward the beach, climbed the dunes, and was lost. The beach was endless, white and straight, and with the tide out the ocean looked miles distant. The low sun looked distant too, as if it couldn't warm the sea it floated over. She hugged herself and pushed off at the sand, skating clumsily until she saw the broken pier where they had tied the dinghy of the borrowed boat. This was the only place she had seen her father shirtless, the place that made him smile and tell them to breathe, as if he had invented the air. This was where he had fixed nothing but had sat on the steps of their rented one-story beach house, grinning into the sun.

And this was where he had taught her to bait the eel trap with stinking chum, and how to hold the menacing heavy eels without being bitten, and how to skin and dry them; this was where he had showed her how to swim through surf, and how to fish from a boat, and how to cook red snapper; this was where he forgot about fixing cars and selling cars, and his dead mother, his father, who already insisted on calling himself Uncle LaRue; this was where he remembered his medals for track-and-field—she thought of his skinny calves, long arms, strong hands—and the bathtub gin he'd driven to Westchester in long, heavy cars when he was a boy.

So, as she had done at hotels and tourist cabins and boardinghouses, she walked up to the door of the summer place—it was two rooms and a bathroom, it had always smelled of suntan oil and mildewed cloth, it had always been dark and cool and sandy to the bare foot—and she knocked. She knew without looking that his car would be behind the house, that he would be inside. She knocked again, and he said, opening the door, smiling but not happily, "Hi, Pumpkin." And that was when, after the fights and the breaking glasses and the slamming doors, after the nights with her mother's weeping and mornings when her mother coughed herself awake, she cried for the first time since he'd left.

She sat at the table covered with yellow oilcloth as if it were a summer ten years before. And he told her, as he had so many times, "Gosh, you look terrible when you cry. Your face gets all red and spotty, doesn't it? And your eyes get that slitty look."

He sat across from her, waiting as she blew her nose loudly and apologized for making him nervous, and as he insisted that he was glad to see her.

"You are?" she said.

"I didn't run away from *you*, Pumpkin."

"Daddy, yes, you did. I've been looking for you."

"Almost found me, once. In Norristown. They told me you were there."

"And you left again? To get away from me?"

She saw how bald he was, how the dark-red hair was thin at the front, a crust of pomade. His big eyes looked naked because his eyebrows were sparse, and his small Irish nose, wide at the nostrils—suddenly she knew why old Negro men made her sad—looked bare also, and she realized that he had shaved the little mustache he'd always insisted would convince his customers that he was really William Powell. "No," he said in his soft voice, "just to get away."

She folded her hands on the sticky oilcloth. "From what, Daddy? Because Mother drinks so much?"

"I'm selling DeSotos," he said. "Malloy DeSoto, in Cape May. I wish I could send you some money—"

"Your shirt's dirty," she said, pointing at his cuffs. "Would you like me to do a wash for you?"

"No, Pumpkin. Thank you very much. I'm fine."

"Are you—you know—coming home?"

He shook his head, and she nodded back, to assure him of no more tears, and the adult understanding she should have, which she didn't, which she was certain he knew.

"Oh," she said. "Well. You're okay, though?"

"I'm fine. I miss you. I miss your mother too, you might want to tell her that."

He lit a cigarette with a small pocket lighter, and she sniffed in deeply as the smoke blew past her. "But you don't think you could sort of come home and we could all, I don't know, *talk*? About what Mom and I are doing wrong?"

"Pumpkin, you aren't doing anything wrong. You're my girl and I love you. Don't say that. Please."

She smiled and made a laugh sound. "I was just trying you out a little. I was just trying to make you feel like you should come back."

"I taught you too much about clinching a deal," he said, matching her laugh with his parody of smile. He put the cigarette out in an ashtray which came from a roadhouse near Ocean City. He lit another cigarette, then stood to switch on a pinup lamp above the table. The light was warm and brown, and she remembered chilly summer nights when the house smelled of fried fish and bacon fat, when they would play cards and he would instruct them in how to get rich. As he sat and hunched forward to speak, she studied his hands: they looked thin tonight, and she knew that they would be thinner, and weak, and that she would have to live a lot of her life alone.

"Tell me, Daddy."

He stared down at the thick yellow lines on the lighter yellow background of the cloth she had often enough scraped free of crumbs after meals. He lit another cigarette, it hung in the corner of his mouth and wobbled there when he said, as if ashamed, "I just thought I might die if I stayed there."

"I don't understand that!"

"I know."

"And you can't tell me any more?"

"I can't tell myself any more."

"Who's the lady?" He looked up. "You always carried the big gold Ronson with your initials on it. Now you have that little thing—did you run away with a woman?"

He shook his head. The smoke hung around them in the beige light. The surf beat. "I met her later on, a little while ago. She's out buying eggs. You remember the egg farm?"

"Do you love her?"

"No."

"Daddy: what do you love now?"

He looked at her over the ash of his cigarette, over the long flat fingers that held it. His eyes were stricken, and in the corners they pulsed. A word seized him, lay around him like another skin; it defined him and he couldn't tell it to her. Then he started to breathe again, then smoke, and she wanted to drive home.

"I love you," she said. "Bye-bye, Daddy." She didn't try to control the crying now, and neither did he. They stood and hugged, and she smelled his sweat and his dirty shirt, old cigarettes—her father had always been so *clean*—and he kissed the side of her neck, where he had never kissed her. "Bye-bye, Daddy," she said. She knew that when she was in the car and going too quickly, she would want to turn around and come to ask for something more. But she also knew that there was nothing more she could have, and she hated it that she could think clearly, could tell herself anything so cold as what was probably the truth.

He didn't call her Pumpkin. He held her, then released her, then lit another cigarette with the woman's lighter. She backed from the table, went out to the beach without turning again to see whether he watched her. She went down to the tide flat and walked over seaweed and shells and driftwood, ignoring the light on the sea and the sharp wind. Back at the car, she stopped crying. And on the long drive home she forgot nearly all they had said. Some of their words had returned on the drive West, and the rest came back now, in the Morgue, in bed with Anthony Prioleau, who—she wondered about telling him—had a lot less courage in saying goodbye than a skinny girl of eighteen had shown. Curling away from him beneath his blankets, she fell asleep again, and she knew in her dreamless sleep that she would not cry, and that Anthony might, and that when she left she would offer him no comfort.

İt became a matter of flesh to him. As if his brain bled into the bed, he became unable to think in terms of future or past, and what he felt, aside from strong loss, was the surface of his skin. His arm, on which she had breathed, felt irritated now, as if he suffered an allergy; he was sure that a mottling rash ran up the upper arm. His hip, into which her hip had curved before she rolled away, was cold.

His toes grew numb, and he wanted to slide his feet beneath her for heat. He thought of plunging his feet between her legs, prodding her with his toes until she was damp. He grew erect, and with his left hand, on the further side of the bed from her, he made a fist, relaxed it, sidled it over his stomach to cup his scrotum. He rocked gently up, then stopped himself. But everything now was concentrated in the nerves. He felt that he must be enormous, that he would explode up onto the top sheet and soak through the blankets. He tightened his lips and whistled breath out, softly, but nothing would remain compressed, and he turned as slowly and gently as he could.

The hand needed, and the awkward fingers touched her back and trembled away, then settled damply between her shoulder blades. With his wrist bent uncomfortably, he slid the fingers down to the cleft in her buttocks, far away in the darkness of the covers. Then he trailed his fingers up, then slid them down again. They lay like that, she unmoving, but far away from him, he, pushing his paw against the cold bony back, trailing after her as though her spine were a road on a map.

His eyes squeezed shut, he'd caught up with her and didn't know it. She turned, she trapped his hand between her legs, then released it as she threw a leg over his. She seized his neck with a strong arm and pulled his face down and in, uncomfortably, so that he breathed with difficulty the smells of harsh soap and heating skin—it was like smelling bread, finally, and his mouth opened to receive the skin at the base of her neck, he lapped at her. And then she ducked to kiss him, and as he kissed back, as their lips banged hard and teeth clicked, she threw him down and over, mounted him, lifted to fumble and slide his penis into her, then descended as he rose. She lifted and sank, she rode him until, closing his eyes, he felt himself riding too, the room upside down, one on top, then the other, they pistoned and spun in a slippery free-fall, gravity gone; then even the sense of friction gone, they rode each other up, gasping and sweat-wet and crying out, first he, who started to descend, then she, following, until she was beside him again, panting on his face, kissing his eyes. She lay still soon, as if he were the ground she came to rest on.

He knew how to think again. He held her and rolled her off, sat to pull the covers over them, slid an arm beneath and around her shoulders, hugged her hard, then loosened, but didn't let go. They breathed into each other's face, tangled their legs together, smiled onto each other's skin. He knew to stay that way and say nothing. When Corporal Rita knocked and called, "Here we go, Mr. Paloo. You awake?" he kissed her and she let him go.

No snow, dying winds, a gentleness to the dark morning, and a light shadow behind the black sky gave a feeling of fullness to Monday's dawn: sun would pour on them all, in time, and even Moffit gamboled, raising his carbine as if to fire at Rita, who turned his imaginary rudder to fire wing guns at the lieutenant. Amboise patrolled. Grim and dirty and in his jeep's orbit, far off, he was not so much a reminder that acts of war had been committed in the world as a circling fetish: he was all the war there was, and he wasn't of them now. Prioleau and Prince plugged cables into the kinescope receiver while Private Bagley settled the camera onto its padded mount in the make-believe tail turret of the make-believe plane. Another private aimed the lights on their high tripods while Prince, finished with the receiver, hauled the starter motor out to engine number 1, on the invisible starboard wing. The camp's generator chugged, and a blue jay cried into the general noise.

Moffit told Prioleau, "Tonight could be very important to us. Matter of fact, I would say it's all you've got going for yourself. Because this is bullshit. Nothing happens here. We do something tonight, though, we get some bucks in the beanbag and you could possibly even have a future."

"Don't step on the cable," Prioleau said.

Moffit stumbled over a thick black tape-encrusted cable, and it pulled out of its unfastened join. "Can't you just plug something *in* the right way?" he said. Then: "Or do I misspeak, since you probably *have* been doing some plugging for most of the night?"

"I've been selling her military secrets," Prioleau said.

"If you knew any, I'd believe it."

"If we had any, you'd be somebody else. And *he'd* most likely be a major, don't you think?"

Prioleau put his fingers in his ears as the engines, fed from a four-pipe fuel tank, started one by one to roar, drowning out the generator and whatever Moffit replied. On the blue-gray screen, a storm of white spots raced and flared. Prioleau made adjustments. Bagley crawled behind the camera and the kinescope screen pulsed, the static brightened in flurries. Pieces of sticky black tape, small bits of wood, the tops of frozen weeds, all blew up into the air, their clothing flapped, and Corporal Rita, this morning's Messerschmitt, made faces and flew at the Midwestern B–17. Before Prioleau could make a sign, Moffit squeezed off two rounds, and Rita landed, while Prince shut the outboard engines down, then the inboard engines; the generator's rhythms marched in over the whine of Amboise's jeep.

"Gosh," First Lieutenant Moffit said, "we're doing won-

derfully, aren't we? Pack your stuff away, Prioleau, you've
done another morning's miracle." And Prioleau, trying to
get used to it, obeyed orders.

It was the finally believing in what someone else decided,
for the first time since he had left the jail on West Street in
New York; it was having to listen, now, for the sake of the
next moment, knowing that if he didn't live this minute
according to her wishes, he would lose the minute after that
—no matter that soon enough he would say goodbye and
watch her drive the Dodge away. Quite like being a kid
again, he thought, knowing so little about your daily fate—
having a motherly woman to hug you, having a father's
smile—that you give the life around you whatever it com-
mands in order that it just treat you gently for a bit. That
was what made him think of Ellen's lover, Mike.

He didn't think of them as married, and he couldn't
imagine the sound of Mike's voice. He thought of Mike at
war in the Pacific. Amboise was the only one of them who
had seen regular combat, and that was in the European
theater, for a month, before he was sent home with a
herniated bowel and, Prioleau suspected, a platoon leader's
urgent recommendation that he be kept away from action
on grounds of mental incompetence. But Amboise never
talked about being under assault, and the rest of them knew
nothing on the subject of open war. What he knew was
night and small-arms fire, failed radios, a dead man carried
to a boat. What else he knew he had seen in newspapers
and magazines and grainy newsreel films full of speeches
on freedom and death. He had seen pictures of men in torn
combat gear, staring into the recent past with blackened,
hollow eyes, and he had seen pictures of row upon row of
the tattered dead. So Mike became for him a large man
with horrified eyes, his battle dress flecked with blood, his

future more actual in Ellen's mind than in Mike's own. Prioleau didn't know whether he was in the Philippines or in San Diego now, or on a ship approaching the States, or dead. He wished Mike were dead. Knowing how treasonous such thoughts were to Ellen's obligations and possible—probable?—desires, he wished him alive again, and un-wounded. But he really wished the man dead. His corpse moved, jerkily, like a picture in the little coarse paper books, the pages of which they had flicked with their thumbs as children—Mike was prone and curled, shot with puckered holes, then standing and entire, arms wide for Ellen, who ran from her car, jumping awkwardly on the rippled pages. He didn't get to the last picture because he didn't want to. He walked slowly back behind the truck loaded with men and equipment. Soon the truck was small, then gone, and Prioleau bent into his coat beneath the lightening Illinois sky, squinting against hard gray light. You're no bloody fucking good to us, the Montenegrin had said, and Prioleau, again, agreed.

O PPORTUNITY, Moffit wrote large. Then he begged his Dickle-Dockle to listen to Mommy like a good soldier, and signed off with love. He reread his letter and approved. He was drunk on Bob Dander's presentation bottle of twelve-year-old Scotch whiskey. He listened to the pounding of the generator, the cursing of Corporal Rita as he tried to hook the generator trolley to the rusty hitch of a truck—"Mother-lapping pig bastard scumbag *tit!*"—and above those sounds was the voice of the civilian's quim, and then the bass solemnity of Prioleau, instrument of their exile, and then Bagley's shrill cry of triumph as a motor coughed like a chain-smoker, long and weak and gagging, then caught. It could have been a patrol making ready for something worthy, Moffit told the bottle's black label, his map of a distant war. But what we have here instead is a bunch of rejects getting ready for a grade-school play about what *Life* magazine says the war is supposed to be, plus a civilian's quim shoving off while the civilian goes into mourning. "What you do," Moffit announced, "is you drink to that."

Amboise sat in the lead jeep. The flap to his belt holster was open, and the grease gun lay on the seat beside him. He had a private in the back, and a belt in the light MG, and there would be no ambush perpetrated on the convoy as it rode into Patoka Plains. Amboise signaled his readiness by turning on the jeep's headlights. No one responded.

Prioleau counted money into Bagley's dirty hand, and Bagley counted half into Rita's. Each doffed his campaign hat to Ellen, who curtsied and laughed. Prioleau walked to her Dodge, which rocked and throbbed, and which would carry her now. He looked in at her Boston bag, then turned to say something about the dangers of glare ice and driving at dusk. She was behind him, and she put her hands, as he turned, onto his coat, almost holding.

Her eyes were excited, her face pale, and he saw that she already was on her way.

She grinned, and he knew that he had pleased her by saying nothing. This is what it's like to be in a cowboy movie, he decided. When you're the girl and Buck sits high in the saddle, aiming toward sunset and motion. You're the one who waves goodbye. Which you are no bloody fucking good at.

She pulled at his coat and he bent so that she could kiss him. Women leaving his father had kissed him like that. She sat in the car and closed the door. He watched through

the window as she repeated to herself instructions for finding Route 40 and eventually Mike, the handsome soldier.
She turned and shrugged, so he did too, and then she put
the Dodge in gear and she left. He looked in a different
direction.

There was a certain amount of difficulty because he pic-
tured her saying goodbye to Mike, in Philadelphia, and
that led to his seeing her say hello to him in San Diego.
That image, as the trucks followed the jeep, as the portable
generator followed the second truck, like a baby elephant
holding its mother's tail with its trunk in a small-town
circus parade; as Amboise, up front, his machine gun erect
like a parade marshal's baton, aimed them toward the
school—that image hung ahead of Prioleau, who squatted
in coils of cable. Then Prioleau, in turn, held the image on
his own as the cables shifted like eels at his ankles. There
was some difficulty. She kissed Mike on the lips. Mike bent
down to cover her mouth with his. Mike held her, his
thumbs at the sides of her breasts, his fingers curved under
her arms, and lifted her against him. She clasped her hands
behind Mike's neck and pulled herself onto him. She slid
down his body to stand and touch. She held his belt and
bent her head, leaning on him, silent. They stood, touching,
and Prioleau was in the truck as the cables crawled over his
legs, and there was a certain amount of difficulty.

The convoy went slowly in low gear and Prioleau, alone
with transmission apparatus, could have seen just the little
generator bobbing behind him and the lilac-tinged, pigeon-
gray sky, if he had looked at either, and the icy brown road.
He saw none of them. He sent and received the same pictures, over and over: Mike holding Ellen, Ellen holding
Mike. He interrupted them to show himself how he might

have said goodbye in such a way as to keep her from going. But the picture of that success was as blank and blue as the daily dawn reception on the kinescope at the make-believe plane.

What you ought to do, Prioleau tutored himself, is learn some gratitude. The war absolved you, maybe, from a prison term. It put you smack in front of her car, and you had a lucky collision. You didn't get smeared in your own blood across a Midwestern highway, either. You managed to get yourself seduced and abandoned, which, as people will tell you, is as good a way of learning as any. And you don't die from it, and you're not required to kill or maim. And tonight you will be the most famous television broadcaster in the Patoka Plains school system. And she will probably name a dog, most likely a large and shaggy dog, in honor of your bed and board. You'll live beyond your abilities, your namesake pissing posts and hydrants. You're almost immortal. And the picture will slowly drift from focus, and one year you'll forget the large and slightly prominent teeth, and then the bright hair, and possibly, though there will be a certain amount of difficulty, the way you were taken to bed and screwed to confusion by a woman half your size.

He looked away—as if the small pale teacher from Philadelphia were projected onto one square foot, and only that one, of the canvas cover of the truck—and he found that the low sun had laid an orange shimmer onto the ice behind the convoy. The cables tightened around his legs, and Prioleau dropped to his knees and wrestled with them, grunting, as he tugged their cold heavy coils. He was on his side, kicking and pulling, making unwelcome sounds, as the jeep's horn sounded and the truck braked hard, throwing him loose. He was sweating, it was night, and Ellen, if she drove hard enough and long enough, would see the sun go all the way down before he did.

His father had taught in a school like this; they had driven for days to get to it, they had built another house for themselves, and his father had gone every day to teach in the high granite-and-brick building—make-believe miniature castle, probably built from discarded blueprints for a runt armory—with hard yellow light from classroom windows glowing on the parking lot and playground, the monkey bars shining, swings drifting as the wind blew, the bright-painted wooden seats hanging in light, then blowing into darkness. Children dismounted from farm trucks and cars, and so did the soldiers. The older ones stood to watch the equipment unloaded, and the younger ones held their nervous parents' hands. One boy climbed the monkey bars and shouted into the darkness while his mother stamped her icy boots. Amboise, on foot, patrolled their perimeter as if he were his own jeep, circling against ambush. Rita worked at the generator's hitch, and Prioleau watched Bagley instruct the other privates in what to haul out first. Moffit leaned against a truck and slowly shook his head.

And out the door, in a thud of wood and clang of latch bar, in an explosion of light and waving arms, came Bob Dander, bearing the American future. "All right, boys, you're late, but that's all right. I can't ever see how you can be *too* late if you show up at all. Glad to see you, Mr. Purloo, delighted you're aboard. How-do, Lieutenant—let me, why don't you, call you *Captain* tonight. I'm talking captain of industry, and that's what we're unveiling tonight, whether anybody knows it or not. Well, they *will*. This little show is the first local transmission of the most important industry in the U.S.A., I promise you that. Boys," he called, waving to the privates winding cable and carrying gear, "you're luckier than you know. You're in at the start of something big." He led them, talking about the stand he'd ordered built for the kinescope and the sites he'd cleared backstage for the generator and cable, for Prioleau's switchboard, and for the fire extinguishers Prioleau had insisted they position near the equipment. Mike hugged Ellen and told her hello, and Prioleau's mouth closed on itself in what Dander took for a smile, so he smiled back, holding Prioleau's shoulder, pulling him on.

Children in uniforms watched the grownups in uniforms. Teachers in hissing dresses and starched-looking suits walked back and forth, holding thin scripts. A pink-faced boy under a bowl of brown hair looked into a small room backstage of the auditorium that smelled of steam, and he cried, "Mr. Palfrey! Mr. Palfrey! Roger is doing something unusual!" They heard the retching as Palfrey, the principal, wearing a navy-blue suit so large that First Lieutenant Moffit might have got inside it with him, clopped across the floorboards in heavy cordovan brogues.

"Oh, boy," Palfrey said. Then he coughed, and the cough became a gag, and Mr. Palfrey started to throw up in honor of stage fright in Patoka Plains. The boy with the bowl of brown hair, wearing a dark-brown uniform over black rubber boots, looked around the corner, ducked back, then started to retch. A girl in a pink dotted-swiss dress and brown Mary Janes caught his rhythm and picked it up and passed it along, and soon the smell of vomit weighed on the smell of hot pipes and floor wax, and children everywhere behind the fireproof curtain were clutching their bellies and crying and throwing up, while a teacher in brown tweed ran away, and a teacher in blue-and-white polka dots, her hair the same range of blue as her dress, stayed to help by shouting and breathing through her mouth. Rita said, "Fuck it," and abandoned his pliers and walked outside. First Lieutenant Moffit vomited tomato sauce and Johnnie Walker in a puddle on his combat boots. The teacher with blue hair stopped shouting and, holding a wad of brown paper towels, went from child to child, accompanied now by two mothers and an old thin man in a Boy Scout uniform, wiping faces and hugging little shoulders and smiling courage to them all.

A stumpy janitor smoking a pipe, the sweet tobacco smell seizing Moffit's stomach again, strewed sawdust and mopped. Bob Dander stood near a pulley with a large red handkerchief over his mouth and nostrils. Prioleau finished Rita's work, making connections, making little jokes to himself about making connections, while the old man in Boy Scout shorts and high khaki socks assembled his color guard: a very tall boy who insisted on wearing a target pistol in his belt, despite the Scoutmaster's objections; a tall but very fat boy whose knees seemed to blush, and who carried an American flag on a short wooden pole; and a boy who looked to Prioleau like Prioleau twenty years before, broad-chested and lean-flanked, pale with fright, and gripping a cornet with white knuckles. Prioleau nodded to him and said, "Go get 'em," but the boy could only nod and lick his lips.

Rita deigned to return and start the generator, which was so noisy that the murmuring audience in narrow wooden seats that held them buttock to buttock went suddenly silent; the silence prevailed when Prioleau had Rita turn the motor off and get two privates to help him wheel it farther backstage, into the cafeteria, and extend the generator cable. The silence held, though, and everyone worked in whispers, even the sobbing children.

Of course, it was possible that she might tell Mike about him right away, and that Mike would coil with fury and jealousy and send her off. He saw the overheated Dodge on a two-lane highway, rocking with its faulty camber, swaying back toward him on a dark night. But that was to suppose that Ellen LaRue Spencer was in need of a man whose expertise was incomplete missions and failed assignments and the transmission of blankness in Illinois. She had no cause to tell Mike, anyway. What swaggering adventurer comes home to speak of anything but high seas and warring tribes? The unassailing passage and the easy lay are what you recall far later, when you lack for a story but still need to tell. The ones who remember in detail and with pain are the ones you meet along the way.

And then Mr. Palfrey, his chin scrubbed red and his suit gone shapeless, went through the safety curtain and the stage-front curtain. "Ladies and gentlemen," he said in a high wobbly voice, "welcome to our second annual Victory Pageant. This year, grades K through Four are happy to present an original play, written by our own Miss Louisa Melchior, who graduated it only seems like yesterday, and who after a year in St. Louis has come home to help her folks with their business, and grace our town, and stay where she belongs." A murmur of laughter. "It's a pride and a pleasure for us to present something by a local authoress. She entitles her play *Victory*. And after the colors are presented by Troop 8, under the direction of the man who steers the snowplow, otherwise known as Scoutmaster Rudy Champlain"—clapping of six hands, a hoot of laughter, the sounds of people relaxing in their seats and moving their shoes on the smooth floor—"we'll turn the lights down and think about our fighting men, some of them, two, I guess, now, from our own Patoka Plains, and we'll pray together—no, we'll pray *first*, I mean, with Reverend Duykinck, we'll pray for victory and salute the flag, and then watch our own kids in action."

As Mr. Palfrey fought his way backstage through the curtain, a sound of shoes on the wooden stage preceded a long low "*O* God. Thou who makest war on Thine enemies and givest peace to those Thou lovest in Thy mercy and tenderness. Grant safety to those we love who wage war in Thy name on alien soil. Comfort those who fret upon their return and those who suffer their loss. Turn the minds of Thine enemies from hatred and greed. Show us, that we may beat our swords into plowshares and study war no more. And bless these children, who are tomorrow. In Thy image and Thy name. Amen."

And grant that Ellen LaRue Spencer hath forgotten her toothbrush and returneth for it. And that though she will not, she recalleth, when Thy clumsy servant is crippled or dead, how once she clasped his body in what he took to be love.

The color guard tore slowly through the curtain and marched in several directions, then marked time in place. Scoutmaster Rudy Champlain shouted orders—they made Bagley snicker and Rita hold his nose—and then the nervous boy, under his tangled forest of black hair, his knuckles no doubt white, played long, pure notes as the soft thunder came up: people rising in song. "God Bless America," they called, and in their choir Prioleau heard the voices of men threatening him, in the name of a fat boy's low-slung flag, with broken bones. But in the sad, tinny tones of cornet and off-key farm-supply clerks in harsh ironed shirts and housewives in baggy sweaters, and in the high voices of children singing words they didn't understand—"from the *mount*ain's toe the *fair*ies"—he also heard an assumption:

that they were, in fact, blessed, and were deserving of the favor, and that the long various landscape, crossed at this instant by a dark hot car crawling through darkness into its light, was also his—was being *made* his, by the boy's earnest music, and by the men and women whose now fervent singing made the fervor actual, and by the woman who carried his story over black flat fields and into her life.

The generator chugged its cycles over and over, the Boy Scouts marched off the stage, and teachers herded the soldiers into the wings as children softly stampeded into place, everyone hushing everyone else. Next to him stood Louisa Melchior, her heavy perfume overcoming the stink of dried vomit and rotten mops. She squeezed his arm with both hands, and he blushed for his continuing boyhood as he made a muscle that she might feel. Her breast was against his arm; he stood very still. She said, "Oh!" and moved a pace away. "I'm sorry," she said, "I'm scared."

"*That's* okay," Prioleau told her, making what felt like a fangy smile. Rita, across the stage near the small lighting board, raised his eyebrows at Prioleau and moved his lips to fit what was probably a snicker.

The curtain rose. The nine-year-old girl in the pink dress was now powdered and rouged so that she looked like a parody of children's thoughts about aging. She was bent, she moaned a good deal even as the parents applauded the paintings on the wall, the dark coffee table, the fake fireplace with its mantel adorned by a huge shining candelabrum.

"Oy vey!" the girl shouted, leaning on her cane. "Dey voodn't leave us alone, we should live so long!"

A woman in the audience cackled. Another woman said, "Shut up!"

In skipped another girl, younger and meant to look her

age. Imitating the older one's lilt, but not pronunciation, she said, "What's the matter, Grandma?"

From the painted window, gray as a late Midwestern dawn, the older one cried, "You know vat I mean, darlink. Dey took avay two more Jewish men last night! Dese Nazis voodn't let us live in peace!"

The audience burbled now, their whispers and murmurs collided and ran through the room like streams against stone. There was a sound of heavy footsteps at the back of the auditorium; they coincided with steps on the stage.

As the younger one moaned, shaking her head, "I know, Grandma. It's horrible! I just wish our friends in America could know this!"

Grandma nodded, and the footsteps became the feet of a tall, slender boy whose freckles were covered with a patina of dark makeup: an unshaved man, his shirtsleeves gathered with a mother's garters, a long-billed accountant's eyeshade on his head, corduroy knickers billowing on his lean legs. "Have you heard, Greta?" he said to the young one.

She nodded. Grandma nodded. Father nodded to them both. They stood, a posed picture: *The Forgotten Line*. From backstage, next to Prioleau, Louisa Melchior whispered hoarsely, "We must tell Mother!"

"We must tell Mother!" the boy and girl cried simultaneously.

The girl covered her mouth. The boy looked at Louisa.

Grandma then shouted, "We must tell Mother!"

They began to breathe again, and the girl said, "Here she comes now."

Mr. Palfrey, near Rita, slammed a piece of wood against another piece of wood. There was silence on the stage.

"Here she comes *now*," the girl said. And the teacher

with blue hair pushed Mother, in her black shawl, through the door, which already had slammed.

"Mother," the boy-father said, "did you hear what Grandma told us? I learned it downstairs, in the shop. Those Nazis are at it again."

"When will it stop?" the mother said, raising her arms, shaking them once, losing her shawl and stooping for it.

"They'll stop soon," Father said.

"No, they won't," the daughter said.

"We must be patient," Father said.

"We must pray for our friends from America," the daughter said.

"Ven de American boys come marching—" Grandma said.

"Through the cities and the towns of Europe," Mother said.

"The American warriors will rescue us!" keened the daughter.

From the back of the auditorium, a cornet in a high sharp single note shrieked warning. Someone in the audience angrily said, "Jesus!" Mr. Palfrey slammed the wood against wood, and in the door stood three boys in dark-brown uniforms and black galoshes. Their hands were on their hips, their little legs were planted wide.

"You," one of them piped. "You and you and you—come mit us!"

Grandma screamed in imitation of the cornet, which picked up the note and sounded it again. Grandma screamed again. "Jesus!" the same man said. Father cowered.

"Fight them!" the daughter cried.

But Father, cowardly Jew, covered his face with his hands. The men in the doorway goosestepped forward and seized the mother and grandmother. Father dropped to one knee. The daughter hurled herself against the Nazis. The cornet screamed once more. They threw the daughter to the floor. The stage went black.

As children whispered and giggled, as teachers prodded and metal scraped against wood, Louisa Melchior stood next to Prioleau, shaking.

Mr. Palfrey threw the light switch and four small boys in miniature American uniforms, carrying Daisy BB guns and knapsacks, crawled slowly forward from stage left. The GIs were coming, and in the audience a parent started to applaud.

"Hey, Joe," one of the soldiers said, "you see any Krauts?"

"They're out there somewhere," another replied.

The third, wearing sergeant's stripes on his little sleeve, said, "Pipe down, you fellas. This is war. We're here to save some people, not to have a—a—conver*sation.*"

The spotlight moved crookedly and clumsily across to stage right. The Nazis, holding shiny cap guns, menaced the family of Jews, who sat on chairs, their hands behind them as if bound. The head Nazi snarled, "Tell us where you keep your gold!"

"Ve are poor shopkeepers," Grandma said.

"We have no gold," Mother said.

"And if we did, we wouldn't give it to you so you could use it to make bombs and guns!" the daughter declaimed.

"Don't hurt me, please," Father whined.

The spotlight jumped across the floorboards to the GIs crawling to the rescue. "Look, you guys," the sergeant said. "Over there—isn't that a torture chamber?"

"Je-*sus!*" the chorus in the audience said.

"I say we go in and save whoever the Krauts are holding there, Sarge!"

"Me too!"

"Okay, fellas! When I count to three!"

The spotlight wobbled and drifted back to the Jews in their plight. The Nazis mouthed as if shouting; they shook their fingers and waved their arms, miming a cruel interrogation.

"Hold it right there!" an American voice called from the darkness.

The Germans turned and crouched, pointing their guns toward the voice.

"It's our Allies!" cried the daughter.

"I wasn't frightened," said Father. The audience roared.

And then the spotlight widened and the GIs rushed in, rifles at the ready. The Germans, with one exception, threw their guns to the ground and placed their hands behind their heads, just as in the newsreels. The audience cheered. The Nazi leader pointed his gun at the Americans. Mr. Palfrey slammed the wood against wood. The Storm Trooper fell in his tracks.

And as one of the GIs held his rifle on the Germans, as another untied the smiling Jews, who murmured their thanks, the little sergeant stepped to the edge of the light and, waiting until the cornet began to softly play "America," said, through the sweet notes, "And this is what we must be doing all over the world. For wherever there are those who —who, *oh!* Oh. Who will not be ruled by, uh, compassion and the American belief in fair play and freedom, then we must be there. And we *will* be there. Sure, I'd rather, uh, be home in the bosom of my loved ones." At *bosom*, one of the Nazis began to giggle; he hung his head and shook with laughter. "Sure, I'd rather—um—I'd—"

"Rather be in St. Louis eating hot dogs in the ball park," Louisa hissed.

"*Sure*, I'd rather be in St. Louis eating hot dogs in the

ball park. But we've got a job to do. We're cleaning the world up. We're scrubbing out the dirt called Nazi-is-im. We're—"

As if Mr. Palfrey had slammed wood upon wood, heavy footsteps banged on stage left, beyond the light. Carl Melchior, in his red wool hunting coat, wearing his brown hat with earlaps, carrying his shotgun, ran from the darkness into the spotlight, then ran off. Master Sergeant Amboise followed, his grease gun in his hand, running from darkness into light and then out of it, stage right.

"—justice and the American way."

The lights went out, then came on, and the cast were assembled at the front of the closed curtain. Prioleau held Louisa's shoulders while she shook. They watched around the edge of the curtain as the cast bowed to the applause and cheers that rolled in. Then Mr. Palfrey and the blue-haired teacher came forward, and there was more applause. A woman in the audience called, "Author!" and then Louisa, her hips rolling under her dark skirt, came on from stage left, and the heavy clapping of the men increased.

Backstage, the slamming of footsteps rang again, and Moffit, his .45 in his hand, drew aim but didn't fire on Melchior, who, pursued by Amboise, ran out the emergency exit.

The children and teachers came backstage, and the audience began to move. Bob Dander, flying through the curtains like a champagne cork, ran onstage and called, "Folks! *Folks!* We ain't done yet! Robert 'Bob' Dander's my name, and when you listen to KRBD you are listening to me. That's my station, where you turn to for the best prayers, and *Helen Trent,* and all the news you want to know. And what we got to offer you now is a taste of the future. Something you'll be seeing—you got that right: *seeing,* not just hearing, when tomorrow comes around the corner and into your houses. Bear with us, folks!"

The curtains drew back, and soldiers, big ones this time, in actual uniforms, moved a wooden platform, five feet wide and six feet high, onto the front center of the stage. The audience sat in stillness. Rita and Prince carried out the kinescope and gently fitted it onto the platform's top. Then Bagley dragged out a thick cable and Prioleau, feeling himself blush even at this attention, came forward to check the coupling. Soldiers hauled out tripods and small field lights, screwing them into place and snaking out loops of wire. Backstage, Prince and Dander supervised the general plugging in. And then, on a cafeteria dolly which squeaked as they pushed it, Corporal Rita and Private Bagley brought forward the bulky, long-snouted camera. Prioleau, backstage again, walked over each line and stooped to inspect each connection. He pointed to the main panel, small and gray and dull, and Rita nodded. Prioleau walked off the side of the stage and, crouching on one knee in front of a row of parents, who watched him as much as they watched the activities onstage, he waited for Bob Dander's show to begin.

A humming sound came from the panel as Rita threw a small fork switch. The generator chugged. Bagley turned a rheostat. The screen of the kinescope went blue-gray, and snow streaked across it. Then the houselights dimmed, and portable field lights glared into the eyes of the audience. Prince went from light to light, making minor adjustments. Prioleau crouched, breathing shallowly.

The hum went louder, then soft, there was a tinkle of expanding filaments in vacuum tubes, and on the screen of the kinescope appeared an audience in Illinois, waiting for the show. The same choric voice called, "Oh, my sweet Jesus,

I'll be damned." There they were, in starched shirts and short broad woolen ties, in loose cardigans and ironed shirt-waists, in heavy open-mouthed faces with small bright eyes: there they were, themselves.

From the darkness behind the field lights, Bob Dander called, "That's what I'm promising you, folks, KRBD Television, right there, soon enough, on your very own dials. That's the future, folks. And you're watching it tonight."

"Be-Jesus," the voice exclaimed.

Someone started to clap. A man stood, peering, and they saw him, on the screen, stand to peer, and then he clapped, too. Others stood. Others clapped. Then more of them stood. Prioleau, crouching, heard their clumsy movements and saw them on the screen. They were all standing now, some holding overcoats, some wearing winter caps, arrested on their way back into their lives, half dressed for the world outside, standing, now dropping coats behind them onto the small folding wooden seats of the auditorium, and all of them applauding. Their hands were up before them, they were smiling into the camera and clapping for what they saw: themselves, crowding into the small, blue-gray screen, clapping back at themselves. The applause grew denser as they leaned to watch their bodies lean, clapping. And in the lower-right-hand corner of the screen, as they greeted the American future in Illinois, at night, in the Patoka Plains school, Prioleau, on one knee, spotted movement.

Maybe this was the happy end of the program: Ellen walking through the school doors to announce that she would stay. Afraid to look back at her, he scuttled closer to the edge of the stage and studied the screen, squinting, as the audience cheered. But the figure wasn't a woman, he saw. It was big, and bulky, and armed—a man with a shotgun, the fight scene with which this program had to conclude. Ellen was away in her future, bearing him as past, and this—they clapped mechanically now, but with gladness, staring at their faces in the gray light—this was Melchior, the town magician, helmeted in earlaps and raising his long weapon. The first shot missed everything. Applause stopped, the screaming began, the camera caught it all. The second shot took out a spotlight. The grease gun chattered as Amboise came through the auditorium doors. But Melchior had reloaded, and his next shot buckled the right side of the kinescope platform. On the screen, Prioleau saw Amboise stumble or slip on the waxy floor, and fall backward, sending six rounds into the ceiling. Rita ran onstage to rescue the kinescope, and Melchior's shot took it dead center, blowing the video tube in a glassy sizzle. Prioleau, on his stomach, covering his head, closed his eyes. Rita bellowed his fear from the floor of the stage. Moffit and Bob Dander hurled execrations at one another. Children, some of them, cried out delight. Parents called their children's names. Prioleau, as Louisa screamed *Daddy!*, saw the Dodge crawling over the country into its lights.

1956

The bus stop at the Drug Fair was new; there were new book racks in the Food-O-Matic, itself a recent addition to the wide street of red brick shops with apartments or empty lofts above them. And from across the street, leaving the diner next to Gene's Bar at 8 a.m. after coffee and eggs, with men off to deliver oil for Phillips or to sell hardware or hoist sacks of feed, Prioleau paused to look at the other store. Where apothecary jars of colored water had stood in the window there were wide wooden TV sets, small clock radios, record players with automatic changers. The window's lettering said TELEVISION CENTRE. It had been Louisa's idea, when he bought the store from her and her mother, that he spell the last word as the English would, since television itself was regarded by some as vulgar, she'd told him. So Prioleau studied his classy operation, but stayed away from it.

He walked slowly toward the tracks and past the chromium-and-glass Drug Fair and its little bus station. He had never traveled from there, had never smelled the dead air inside or watched people he loved go up the steps of a bus, carrying paper bags of lunch and underwear, but the little building with its concrete apron made him sad, always, as if he were about to suffer a loss. Prioleau patrolled the business street's perimeter to be certain that Melchior wasn't about; his absence made for tranquillity, and Prioleau then felt he could walk back, this time along his side of the street, to open the store, start coffee, and begin to solder and splice, making it possible for *Hopalong Cassidy* to travel from New York to Chicago to Patoka Plains.

In the back, along with his coffee-and-chicory blend, there were mystery novels and Winston filtered cigarettes, and hours, because there was little urgent business, of reading polite British novels about the deaths of strangers. On the air this morning, in the glare of an overcast springtime sky, there was the smell of grain, as if the crops of rye and soy were fermenting. There was a gentle wind, fresh and wet, and there wasn't anything wrong.

Across the street from the Greyhound stop, he watched the long silver bus drift in. Its brakes hissed, its door thudded back, and faces he knew bobbed down, and then a face he knew but didn't want to, and everything, possibly, was wrong. But this was a boy, and his hair was dark; the resemblance was only superficial. He was tall and slender, and even from where he stood, Prioleau could see that the boy's eyes were light and very wide. A hand was at his mouth, the nervous lips sought something to bite at. Prioleau slowly crossed the street. He realized that this anxious boy might think he was being met, so Prioleau stopped, turned to walk back, then turned—as if the boy *were* to be met, and by him—and went to the bus, around its dark smell of hot rubber, and toward the door. When he saw the face, and the long bitten fingers, the dark, dense, curling hair, the eyes so large in the narrow face, he lost control of his own face and stood before the child, peering.

When the boy spoke, his lips stuck and his voice was whispery. He looked at Prioleau, smiled the half smile of which only a child, in such circumstances, could be capable —believing that, out of a whole country of strange adults, this one had come forward to gentle the rigors of traveling alone in strange places. "Did you use to wear a lot more hair on your head?" the boy said.

"What?"

"I think I heard about you."

"Me?"

"If you used to wear more hair hanging in your eyes. Your hair was shiny, right? Like a crow's wing?"

"I'm just going past here, son. I'm not here to meet you. Tell me their name and I'll see if I can help, but we don't know each other."

"No," the boy said, serious and scared, but somehow confident that stepping from a bus and talking to a man who gulped air and stared could be as simple as that. "No, I think I heard about you. From my mom. I heard you were my father."

As the boy said "Mom," Prioleau thought of the woman he knew who looked most like a mother—Louisa Melchior, with her swollen lips, breasts with wide brown aureoles, the small mound of stomach that he cupped. He felt defended by the thought. And his next, or its next helpless segment—the second half of a stagger when you've caught yourself but know you'll go gracelessly down—was of the only woman who could be this lean child's mom.

So he did what he had done in half-made houses, or in towns where he stayed because there weren't towns elsewhere which obliged his presence, or in a TV shop, or in town meetings at which the specter of Communist conspiracy was raised: he nodded, stayed silent, acquiesced, waited for events to tell him what to do. He led the boy to the side of the bus, where, at the open cargo hatch, they retrieved a scuffed overnight bag. Then Prioleau crossed the tracks, and the boy, carrying his bag, followed. They went past Railroad Street and then the GLF, with its sacks of feed, neither speaking. At the Television Centre, Prioleau led the boy to the side entrance, off the alley where his truck was parked, and into the back of the store, where he lived and worked, sometimes—less and less frequently—made dull love with a lush woman who more and more sat up all night writing scripts for television programs which never used them. "Home," he said, not declaring whose as he shut the door behind them.

He had cleared the front of the store so that it was a large square, with no obstructions in the center. On his right, as he came from the back, were shelves with radios and appliances on them. On his left were television sets, all sizes, new and old, some to be repaired, some already fixed. As he had done each working day, he turned the new sets on, showing in his window and in his shop the same silent picture. There was a high hum he lived in, as fishermen live in the sound of the sea. The boy was standing near him, in the middle of the store, looking at the pictures that shivered from set to set. Prioleau went to the back and started coffee. From the little refrigerator in which

Melchior had stored perishable drugs, Prioleau took a quart of milk and half a cherry pie. He knew to place all of it, with a hotel fork and a tin cup of milk, in front of the rocker on the broken-backed kitchen chair where he propped his feet as he sat in the back and read mysteries, smoking. The boy followed him, touching loops of solder and burned-out tubes, rubber-grip pliers, strips of antenna lead.

"Eat something, son."

The first word or the last was magical, because the boy took Prioleau's rocker, perched on the edge, leaned forward with a hand in his lap—Prioleau tore a piece of paper towel to set on the boy's thin thigh for a napkin—and in what was one long slow motion, without pause, he ate the pie, drank the milk, wiped his mouth, said "Excuse me," and rose to set the empty pie plate and cup on the littered work counter.

"I could find you something else," Prioleau said from the hot plate, where he'd stood to give the boy some room.

"No, thank you."

Prioleau made a lot of noise and motion, rinsing the boy's cup, pouring coffee into it, sipping, wincing at the heat, sighing as the coffee went down, lighting a cigarette, moving things at the counter and the sink.

"Could we talk about it?" the boy finally said.

"I'm going to help you all I can, I promise. But I think you should understand something. I'm not anybody's father. Nothing *wrong* with being a father, understand. I just don't happen to be one. I never was. I haven't hardly been a son for years and years."

The boy watched him—his hands, his coffee cup, the motion of the cigarette down into the ashtray and back up to Prioleau's mouth—and he didn't smile. He nibbled at his long fingers and waited. "He used to be Howdy Doody's clown, Clarabelle."

The boy was pointing at Captain Kangaroo, on the sets out front. "I didn't know that," Prioleau said.

"My father told me."

"Then there are two fathers?"

The boy's face was red now, the freckles around his nose melting into the blush. His eyes filled, and the bottom of his face thickened as he held himself. Prioleau said, "Tell me your name?"

"Gus Spencer Eewald."

"Spencer."

"Yes, sir. It's my mother's maiden name. From before she got married."

"Right. Right. And you're about eleven years old."

"I'm ten years old."

"You're a big ten, aren't you. Do you know my name?"

"Pree-oh-loh," he said.

"And you heard about me from your mom."

"I heard her telling my father about you."

"You want some more milk, Gus?"

"They were having a discussion. It was at night. They were having this discussion"—Prioleau heard *discussion* as the word they would use when interrupted during a fight: he saw the tall boy standing around a corner and bracing himself to enter the room to witness a battle which his parents would think to make less frightening by naming it talk—"and I guess what happened was my mom told my father this thing about something that happened before I was born. About how she met you around here. There were soldiers and some kind of airplane you were building with these soldiers who worked for you, and you and my mom fell in love."

Prioleau knew that his face looked as red and clenched as Gus's. He looked at this boy in jeans and sneakers and red turtleneck shirt, the long bones and muscles beneath it. He drank coffee and smoked, staring. "Would you mind telling me your father's name? The, um, the father in—where are you from, Gus?"

"Kimball? Wyoming?"

"*Wyoming?* You came all that way, alone, from Wyoming?"

"I wanted to talk to you."

"Sure," he said, trying to talk the red swelling out of the delicate face, the slender, slightly turned nose, cleft chin. "Sure, I guess I can see that, hearing something like— hearing that. Would you tell me your father in Wyoming's name?"

"Michael. His name is Michael Eewald."

"Mike. And"—he blew out smoke, and his breath kept going, it felt as though his face shrank as the air escaped, as if his lungs hung empty and his ribs fell in—"and your mom is named—"

"Ellen LaRue Spencer Eewald."

"Ellen."

"Yes, sir. Did I come to the right place?"

What Prioleau wanted to do was walk in close and kiss the boy and take him back to the bus station. That no longer was possible. So he tried to look through Ellen's face, which rode on the bony shoulders, and see his own. Looking for himself in the boy, he spoke before he knew he would. He said, "Yes."

And then the boy nodded, with the embarrassed assent

which grownups give to hard news—you need a new roof; your mortgage is raised; you might die—hiding fright by placating the awful event. And then Gus dropped his chewed hands to his sides, long wrists showing from the outgrown cuffs, and he closed his eyes and started to cry. Prioleau stepped up to a ghost and leaned down to hug himself. Gus felt like someone else, however, as well as a terrified Prioleau thirty-four years younger, and no matter how hard he tried, and though his arms went around the boy's thin arms and shoulders to meet in the small of his back as he squeezed, there was too much to hold. He was on his knees, resting his chin beside the boy's neck. He moved to kiss Gus's hair, smelled dust and sweat and maybe a sweet shampoo swiped two days ago from the mother's shelf in preparation for a journey. He held on, embracing what he could, and pinning Gus's arms to his sides so that he couldn't, in turn, reach and hold.

Louisa was in the Melchior house, on the narrow walk which separated the northern part of Railroad Street from the large back lot which ran west behind the GLF and Steen's, the old boardinghouse, and then the Television Centre. She was thirty; she lived on the mortgage Prioleau paid on the store, and on her father's disability, and on the Lutheran Brothers life insurance her mother had taken out when they moved to Patoka Plains and joined the American institutions nearest to hand—Lutheran Church, Parent-Teacher Association, Rotary, Daughters of Rebecca; Louisa was tall and handsome, the author of a play about the Holocaust, performed first and last in 1944, when she was a prodigy; and she was thirty, she was typing alone in the house, and springtime felt hard.

Louisa was finishing a revision of her new TV play for
The Edge of Night, and she was typing up the cruelest part:

(*Extreme closeup*)
FATHER
I am not a Communist! I am not a traitor!
DAUGHTER
No, Daddy. You are not a Communist. You know it,
and I know it. The town knows it. But you are a traitor.
(*Camera withdraws to medium range, showing two
tense figures*)
FATHER
Then?
DAUGHTER
Then.
(*Two beats*)
But you are a traitor.
(*Short pause*)
To me.
(*Camera withdraws to long range:* FATHER *and*
DAUGHTER *in tableau*)
To me.
(*Camera holds, then blackout*)

Louisa said, singing it nearly, "To me." She reread parts
of *Love and Betrayal* and snorted as her eyes filled. "This
is ridiculous," she said. Then: "Well, so is *The Bachelor
Party,* if you think about it." Then: "I'm not going to think
about it."

The script went into an envelope, along with a folded
envelope with stamps on it. Then Louisa composed her letter
to the CBS producers in New York, who, according to the
papers, were looking for fresh material.

Dear Sirs,

I am a Midwestern author, my most recent script having been produced by local players a year or two back. It was about the persecution of the Jews. I enclose for your consideration Love and Betrayal, *a contemporary drama on the theme of Communist infiltration and family turmoil. It asks the question, Who can you trust? Perhaps you will have time to read the script and even comment on it. I will be happy to make any revisions you care to suggest. I think it can be adapted to your program's needs.*

Yours sincerely,
(Miss) Louisa Melchior

She said, "Hopeless," as she signed the letter and slid it into the large brown envelope.

At her desk, in the room she'd worked in since she was a child, staring at file folders and stacks of magazines and a Chicago phone directory she used for characters' names and the Webster's Unabridged, half a ream of white paper, a bowl of sharpened pencils, Louisa shook her head, then laid it a moment against the keys of the typewriter. She looked up and out of her window, which gave her a view of a corner of the bus stop, and of Railroad Street, and of the town garage behind it on the side of the westbound tracks. She saw Prioleau walking up Railroad Street onto Main, and beside him a tall young boy. A wood-sided station wagon passed them, and Prioleau put his hand on the back of the boy's neck to caution him. Something in the gesture brought her up and into a half crouch over the Olympia. It was how he might caution her, or surely how he once did. He watched the street like a soldier on the lookout. He was protecting something, maybe the strange child, and

Louisa leaned her pelvis on the machine to follow them as they turned up Main toward the store; she pushed her forehead at the glass, and then her cheek, and then she lost them to the bulk of buildings and probably, she thought, to something else.

O n Channel 9, on KRBD, Lester Beere, who once was Bob Dander's advertising manager, and who now bought time from Dander, was introducing the morning's guest on *You and Your God*. In the Television Centre the sound was off, and Beere's lips flapped in silence like the wings of a distant bird. In Henry Watervliet's small house, set behind the park at the western edge of Patoka Plains, the set was on, and loud, so that Henry in the kitchen, cooking beans for the evening meal, could hear. He shuffled, he staggered, his long, backless slippers caught on torn linoleum and stuck in the narrow curved legs of aluminum tubing on which the kitchen table stood. Sweating, red-faced from steam and the sweats of drinking, his hands delicate as he sipped his pure wood-grain alcohol just mildly tinctured with orange juice, his lips as soft and delicate as a child's, his swollen nose running, his hair in front of his eyes like a dirty curtain, his cracked knuckles swollen, his feet so clumsy they might have belonged to someone different from the man with the dextrous hands, his yellow teeth clacking and his large hairy ears redder than his nose, moon-faced Henry Watervliet laughed silently when Lester Beere handed the airways over to the Reverend Billy Horsefall. "Give 'em hell, you mean son of a bitch," Henry called. "Give 'em more shit than they know how to handle. And you *know* he will."

Melchior, in the brown leather easy chair, sitting broken

in the lightless shade-drawn room which was the rest of the house, didn't move. His khaki trousers were washed and wrinkled beyond shape, his feet in striped socks were motionless, as if he were paralyzed. His large hands in his empty-looking lap lay still. The flesh had fallen away from his throat and his cheeks and his temples. He looked like the father of the Melchior who had, at the circuit court's insistence, been kept at the bar-windowed hospital near Centralia until the shocks and the hot baths and the icy drugs had made him calm.

"I said, give 'em *shit*," Henry called again.

And as Reverend Billy Horsefall started to chant of danger in the waters they drank and the very air they breathed, Melchior slowly lifted his left hand before him, three long fingers pale in the grainy dark. Pointing to the index finger, he told the television set, "This is the father. He needs our help. This is the mother. She needs our help." He tried to hold the fourth finger high, but his fisted fingers dragged it forward, nearly down. "This is my baby, who always lies down. *She* is the helpless one." He lifted the fingers again and with his right hand he cradled them.

"Beans, old buddy," cried Watervliet from the kitchen.

Holding his family in his hand, Melchior whispered.

"You holding your hand again, buddy? Best you hold your old peter, if you need comfort nowadays. Nobody *I* know gonna hold it for you." Henry laughed and, with his pinky outstanding, as if urged to be sociable, drank a little 200-proof wood-grain spirit while he stirred his beans.

The Reverend Billy Horsefall was enlisting the aid of all the decent proud Christian Americans within the sound of his voice to send a nickel, send a dime, send the most or send the least, but send with your heart, with your *soul*, send faithfully, and that means with confidence, dear friends, with knowledge of the right and abhorrence of the wrong, but *send*, learn giving as Our Lord gave, for as He gave His only Son, we must give with *our* all as well, which means your dimes, which means your nickels, why pennies'll do— listen to this letter from a totally paralyzed boy in Ohio whose parents, at his *own* direction, sent the pennies from his piggy bank: *I* want to fight the anti-Christ Communist dictators, Reverend Billy, *I* want to do my part, and if I can't move, why then I reckon you'll have to do my moving for me, won't you? And that, my friends, is *real* charity, that's giving from the bottom of the most oppressed of souls. And remember what you're giving for. You're gonna buy ten thousand Bibles with that money. You're gonna send these strapping young men, each one a veteran and each one a *hero*, into that Sodom of West Berlin. And in your name, a Bible will be tied to one of these red and white and blue balloons. And in your name, each balloon will be carried to the city's edge. And in your very *name*, a balloon will be released to the Communist-dominated, God-thirsting minions of Russian tyranny and atheism. In your name. In *Christ's* name. We *will* spread the *Word*. Give what you can.

"She is the helpless one," Melchior said, finishing again, again becoming motionless.

"Don't he do just one goddamn *hell* of a job on the bastards?" Henry called.

The little park was at the southern end of town, near the school. A big black Labrador retriever stalked leaves blown under the trees at the park's edge, near Henry Watervliet's house. Prioleau looked at the weathered clapboard and shaded windows, the paintless door, as if Melchior might emerge from it to carry his fingers into the world.

But no one came, and the dog lay down to pant at the leaves, and Gus Eewald sat on one of the slatted benches, next to Prioleau, his chewed fingers wrapped around one another in a knot of knuckles.

"Gus, I wonder if maybe your mother said those things to your dad, you know, the way you'd hit out at somebody in an argument—a *discussion*. Just to be mean? Are you cold? We get a bit of wind here, even in the spring. You want a sweater or something?"

Gus looked across the street, toward the Television Centre and Steen's, where boarders used to stay and which now was locked and abandoned. The sun was diluted-looking, as if water surrounded it, though the sky was clear and cloudbanks distant. They squinted at each other in the aqueous light. He said, not looking at Prioleau, "You think I'm adopted?"

"I could fetch a sweatshirt from the store."

"I should probably go home."

"Well, I could help you do that," Prioleau said gratefully. "Hell, I'll drive you there. Most of the way there. If that's what you'd like."

"You think they adopted me?"

"No. I think you're their kid, and they love you, they probably called out the state police and the national guard —no, I mean it. They probably figure you're kidnapped."

Gus's head turned, and he smiled; it was the smile children use for fire engines and emergencies requiring uniforms and exotic machines. "My mom knows."

"You told her?"

"She knows what I do, she always does."

"Because you're her son. *Not* adopted. Right?"

"I think probably, Mr. Prioleau."

"Tony."

"But what if you're my real father?"

"You can still call me Tony."

"You *are* my real father?"

"How could I be, if you're so damned much smarter than I am? You keep arguing me back into the same hole, and I can't keep up with you. I'm *not* a father, and I don't hang around with children, and I don't know what to say. I don't know how to talk with you. What do you know about —this is what I mean: what do you know about babies? Where they come from and everything?"

"Making love?"

Prioleau covered his mouth with a hand, rubbed at his lip, then folded his hands together. Gus's were still folded, too. "Yeah."

"I know about that."

"And how sometimes babies get born because two people make love?"

"Only if they love each other tremendously."

"Ah. Right. Right."

"I know about that."

"Well, what if there was a war going on, and everything was crazy, and everybody was frightened—of almost everything. And two people met each other, and they loved each other." His hand came up though he ordered it down, floating like the moist air in front of "And they made love." Then his hand dropped. "But they couldn't stay together because of things that were going on, on account of the war. Understand?"

"You and my mom slept together in the same bed?"

"Oh, Gus. Boy. All right. Yes. And your mom had to leave here, and she and your dad, who loved each other terrifically, right? You know, they got married, and you were born, and they loved *you* so terrifically—"

"Excuse me, doesn't that mean I come from a different father than the father in my family? So I *am* adopted? I think I'm *part* adopted. If your and my mom's sperm and eggs met."

Prioleau's voice dropped into a growl he couldn't help: "It means they love you and you're their son."

Gus's face stilled at the petulant tone.

Prioleau held his hands out and hated them, because they contained nothing for the boy.

"I don't really know why I came here," Gus said. His eyes were flooding, his face was crimson, but he was holding himself tight on the bench. The Labrador walked past them, wagged once, circled the bench, sniffed, walked away.

"If— Listen, I'd always want to talk to you, now that we know each other. Whether or not—"

"What?"

"Whether or *not*."

The boy nodded. "My mom said you were shy."

"She did?"

"And I was wondering who I was supposed to live with, in case you were my real father."

"Mike's your real father."

"Even if you and my mom made love and slept in the same bed?"

"You don't always have babies when you make love."

Gus crossed his long legs and smoothed his jeans. His face became pedagogical; he earnestly gestured and explained: "Tony, my mom never lies to me. So if she said you're my real father—"

"Ah!" Prioleau pounced, as the dog pounced on scuttling

leaves. "Yeah, but she was talking to your *dad*. You see what I'm saying, Gus? So maybe she wasn't tell—she maybe wasn't *sure*."

Gus looked away again, following an oil truck up the street and out of town. He continued to look south, away, as he spoke. "No, she was right, Tony. From the way you looked at me and everything. I mean, *maybe*. But I think she was right. You hugged me like a father. I think we look like each other a little, don't you?"

Prioleau was guessing at the bus schedule, wondering when the next westbound bus came through. A passing freight went slowly across the north end of Patoka Plains, blowing long impatient blasts of Midwestern music, hoarse whistles. As if to echo them, the siren on top of the town office and fire-engine garage began its single long shriek to signal noon. And the school doors slammed, the Labrador howled at the siren, and children covered the high grass of the playground. Gus turned to watch them throw softballs and fall from the monkey bars as the Labrador raced between thrower and catcher, chasing back and forth in lopes and leaps.

"Here's what we do," Prioleau said, turning to Gus. "You hang around with me today, I'll put you up tonight. I'll take care of you."

"Thank you."

"Would you please not thank me."

"Yes."

"Thank you. In the morning, we talk again—I mean, we can talk all the *time*, you understand. But we make sure we get up early and talk once more, hard. Then we make some plans."

"About what?"

"I don't know, Gus. That's why I'm sitting here like an idiot saying these idiotic things to you."

"No," Gus said, "I think you're doing fine."

"I am?"

"Considering everything, sure."

"Thank you."

"Thank you, too."

"For what, Gus?"

The boy shrugged his shoulders and grinned his big teeth. "I don't know," he said. "I'm just trying to sound grown-up."

Prioleau was flooded with gratitude. He put a hand on the bony shoulder next to him and nodded, said, "Me too."

Louisa, in a wide bright peasant skirt, a tight white blouse, espadrilles with thongs that went up the calf, carrying a string bag as if to shop, drifted from Railroad Street around the town at four in the afternoon. She crossed to the diner and saw through its plate-glass window that Prioleau wasn't there, and he wasn't in the dry-goods store or Gene's Bar. She went next door, into the Food-O-Matic, and walked its few aisles, lifting round cartons of oatmeal and a five-pound bag of sugar, replacing them when she saw that he wasn't there either. Back across the street, and past the GLF, the Steen house, not seeing him, she walked in front of the Television Centre, as if she intended to pass the alley where his truck was parked and go on out of town. Then she made a smile appear, as if thinking she might visit him, and with the easy steps of almost-accidental entry, she went into the shop and said, "Hi!"

On a broken kitchen chair in front of the bank of television consoles the tall boy sat, his hands at his mouth, nibbling, as he watched *The Swiss Family Robinson.*

"*Hel*-lo," Louisa called over the sound of a gray-blue young man telling his stocky father that they'd never be able to build a raft to carry them all to someplace civilized.

The tall boy in the chair looked at her, a finger still on his lips, and he offered a widening of the mouth she took for a smile. So she put a hand out, club woman at the orphanage, and introduced herself. The boy nodded and blushed, and then Prioleau came from the back, holding a channel selector in his hand, to rescue them. He said their names; the boy blushed again, then sat to watch the program. Prioleau beckoned Louisa to the back of the store. The father patiently explained that if you weave the logs with green vines, the raft will hold.

Prioleau returned to his work, and Louisa leaned against his back, stood on her toes, kissed him behind the ear, and wandered to his rocker, sat. "Who's your new friend?" she said.

He bent closer to the TV chassis.

"Tony?"

"Hmh?"

"Tony!"

"Oh. Yeah, he's—what he is, old pal, is, he's the son of somebody I used to know. People I used to know just about when you and I started to know each other. Son of old friends."

"You don't have old friends."

"Sure I do. He's the son of two of them."

"Gus is his name? Nice name. What's his last name?"

"Eewald. Not from around here. They live out West. He decided to come and visit me."

"Good. Nice. A cousin?"

"Maybe more like a nephew or something."

"Good. I admire precision."

"Bastard!" Prioleau held the splintered tuner in the palm of his hand. "I'll have to order a new one, it'll take a month to get here because they don't make the goddamned set anymore, and I'll end up giving them a new one. Terrific."

He threw the shattered parts of the tuner over his shoulder and lit a Winston. The mother on the island on the set in the front of the shop was screaming at dreadful danger. Louisa stood to put her hands lightly on his chest, remove the cigarette from his lips, lean in to brush him with her breasts and kiss each corner of his mouth, replace the cigarette, sit and slowly rock.

Prioleau said, "He's my son."

She stopped rocking.

"Half my son."

She said, "All *that* means is you let some woman give birth to him instead of doing it yourself."

"A long time ago, there was this woman I met."

"Where?"

"Here. Out of town, at the Morgue."

"When?"

"While you were dancing the carnal waltz with Corporal Rita. I was seduced and abandoned."

"That's not funny," Louisa said, sitting forward on the rocker. "That's the tone of voice you use when your joke's not a joke. Wait! Wait. She bought something in the store once? A little short girl?"

"And she had to leave. She wanted to leave. So she left." He was on his knees, feeling through the rubble of parts on the floor near the counter. "Maybe I can glue it so they won't notice."

"Why's he *here*, Tony?"

On his knees, holding one piece of broken brown plastic, he said, "Gus heard about me. He wondered what he should do about me."

"And the mother?"

"Married."

"And the husband?"

"Apparently he heard the news at roughly the same time."

"And you?"

"I was in the audience, too."

"You never *knew* about it?"

He slowly climbed to stand and hold to the edge of the work counter. "Can you think of any other way I'd have a kid," he said, "except to do it by accident and be the last to know?"

"And me?"

"What?"

"What about me?"

"My old friend. The finest flesh and ablest playwright in Patoka Plains. And my old friend. You're in for it just like the rest of us. So stay tuned." He shrugged and looked, at last, into her eyes. "Don't ask any more questions, because the next ones—I know you. You'll wonder, no, you're already wondering: how do I feel about everything, the boy, the mother, I know you. No more questions. No more answers. I don't know. You and I have got enough history between us." He stepped one long pace to pluck her sweating hand from the arm of the rocker and, a shade too roughly for the courtliness he sought, lifted it and pressed it to his mouth, replaced it on the chair, lifted his cigarette, and drew long, hissed smoke. He shook his head and tilted it back against the stiff hard muscles of his neck. "Stay tuned."

They ate in the diner with long-distance truck drivers and a highway patrolman who smoked cigarettes and drank coffee and fiddled with his Sam Browne belt, staring at Gus and Prioleau. Mr. Palfrey, from the school, came in with his always-outraged wife to eat strawberry ice cream. Prioleau and Gus ate hamburgers and french fries and Jell-O with cream poured over it, and they ate in silence, once Prioleau had anxiously inquired after the state of the chopped meat and the consistency of the catsup. Gus drank two Cokes, and Prioleau felt beneficent, a conspirator after the malnutrition for which, he thought he remembered, boys hungered.

They walked the western side of the street, strolling quietly out past the little park, to the low fields, a water tower, a farmhouse more than a mile back from the town shining its living-room lights. They went, in silence, as far as the three-rail fence which surrounded the long dooryard of the farm. Prioleau leaned against it, and Gus climbed to balance himself, sitting on the top rung. Gathering darkness made the fields a still ocean, the lighted house a beacon against shoals.

A cow bellowed, then went silent. The insects and doves chirred and crooned. Someplace distant, a car started. Though he never had been there, didn't know how to find it even on a map, Prioleau said, "Does it remind you of Wyoming?"

The white face above his nodded.

"Does it make you homesick?"

"That doesn't matter," Gus said. And Prioleau was so moved by his seriousness—the sense of mission: he had met with it years before—that he couldn't reply any more than he could calculate what he might offer to someone on such a hunt.

Later, he hauled from the loft, where his bed was, a moldy extra mattress which had been there when he moved in and found wrinkled clean sheets and an extra blanket. And something required that, dropping the dusty venetian blinds on the Centre's windows, he turn the front-room lights off, prop pillows on the mattress, leave the back room lit, and, turning on a set, lie before it with a cellophane bag of pretzels, waiting for Gus to lie beside him in the dark.

After a while, he did. They were careful not to touch. They wrinkled the cellophane and crunched the pretzels loudly, watched Gregory Peck direct bombing runs from England, while his Flying Fortress pilots, bound for German targets, were crushed by the pressure of their war. And something required that, after a long silence, as they were told that Lucky Strike Means Fine Tobacco, Prioleau let his arm slide from his side to barely touch the arm beside him.

The boy's arm lay heavier against his, then, as if it had been there all night, stringy and small, it lay against him and might as well have lain across his chest or legs. It was there, and there they were, as Dean Jagger watched the pilots sing, for their lives, "Bless them all! Bless them all! Bless the long and the short and the tall!"

The boy moved, away and over onto the sack of pretzels. Prioleau heard the bag rustle, like a letter in a corner, wadded and thrown, releasing from itself, unwrapping. Breathing so deeply he almost snored, Gus curled in his sleep, on his side, his legs drawn slightly up and in, his hands beneath his head, the fair cheeks and dark lips rippled by the flickering light and noises of the war, as Prioleau, on one arm, watched, and one by one the B–17s roared behind him.

Henry Watervliet snored and issued small moans in a coma of alcohol, his little cries bubbling into the dense stench of the house. He sweated while he slept, radiated heat, plucked with dainty fingers at the unraveling hem of the gray wool blanket he gave scent to. He was chanting nonsense under his nightmare noises, and their rhythm was the song of the Reverend Billy Horsefall: give a nickel, give a dime, give what you can, though the TV set was soundless and devoid of face, only a bright rectangle which pulsed dead light to show Melchior, in his backless bedroom slippers and huge khaki pants, as he shuffled from the care of his roommate and guardian out and into the tremendous clarity of an Illinois dawn.

Melchior was in the outer air again. His large hands moved from his beltless waist to the sleeves of his red flannel shirt to his pockets to his jaw. He peered through his tortoise-rimmed glasses as if the impacted atmosphere of Watervliet's rooms surrounded him. An early freight made slow thunder at the other end of the town, and its whistle spoke, and Melchior nodded in reply. He walked, looking as if he leaned into hard winds, studying the empty concrete bus apron and the dark closed Drug Fair. At the westbound tracks, now vacant, still smelling of diesel fuel, he stared above him, at empty glitter. The sky was five miles high.

From where he stood, Melchior could see three houses on the macadam walk off Railroad Street. The middle house was awake, its upper-story shades askew, one window open, a figure moving before it, then away.

The hand came up, and he cradled it, for this is the

father who needs our help, and this is the mother, she needs our help, and this, the baby, always lying down, is the helpless one. He was lost inside the loose fist before him, and he stood at the tracks beneath a high damp sun until his hand led him back past the Television Centre with its drawn venetian blinds and across the park and into Henry Watervliet's dream.

Hours later, Prioleau and Gus walked from the diner to cross to the Centre and open it for the day. They had eaten hashed-browns together, chewing with their mouths open and their elbows on the table, smearing catsup on small paper napkins, and pushing potatoes to their forks with their fingers, needing to smear more catsup onto napkins again. This quiet conspiracy to violate their table manners had been cheering to Prioleau, and had sufficed as talk between them until, on the street, Gus said, "I guess we have to decide now."

"I think you should call home, buddy."

"I told you, Tony. She knows where I am."

"Maybe what I mean is, how about going back home? Isn't *that* what we have to decide?"

"First you have to tell me."

"Mike's your real father. I told you."

"I didn't come out of your sperm and egg?"

"The father just supplies the sperm. Where'd you learn that?"

"Kids know that stuff now, Tony."

"Oh."

"Just the sperm, then. Is that where I started?"

"Gus."

Prioleau lit a cigarette earlier than he'd planned to, and he hissed at Gus, who turned his face from the smoke, then said, "Well?"

"Well, what if I said yes?"

"That I came from you?"

"Yeah: what *if*, I'm saying."

"Do you love me?"

Prioleau pulled on the cigarette again, and then again, his dizziness growing with each drag. He threw the cigarette down and stepped on it, grinding his shoe back and forth, envying his foot, which didn't have to answer any questions. "Do I love you."

"Fathers don't have to love their kids, I guess. Do they?"

He reached for Gus's shoulders and pulled, but the boy stayed in place, his thin pale face red from the chin to the nose, the lips hard against each other, the eyes now red also as the flush went up to the hairline. Prioleau looked into the wide eyes for clues, and then answered hard, as if he struck, or were himself struck: "Yes."

"Yes?" Gus asked.

"Yes! Yes." Prioleau dropped his hands to his sides. "So now what? Who told you that solves so terribly much?"

Gus, still looking past him, across the street, pointed. "Her. She did."

And Prioleau, only now registering the long, silver shape which had passed, and the sound of air brakes, turned to meet the rest of his life. This time her skin was white, as if clear glass had fogged, or in breaking had gone milky. She was close enough by then for him to see that the rims of her eyes were red, her lips a paler red. The skin had shrunk back on her bones, which mounded up under the eyes to give the impression of rawness at the ridges, as though her face might feel sore. She wore her hair in a heavy long braid down the back. Her eyebrows looked darker, less red, and the high forehead, with hair straining back to the braid, looked like a little map with creases from folding.

Carrying a small hard-sided suitcase—Prioleau looked at the other hand for the Boston bag, but the hand was closed upon itself—she walked the rest of the way to them as she had walked years before when he watched: hips controlled, the torso balanced on the waist, the head held still as if it had to keep something fragile from falling.

When she stopped a few paces from them, Gus went over, head down, as if embarrassed, and hugged her as she bent to him.

"You're okay?"

"Tony took care of me."

"Yes," she said, standing, but keeping a hand on Gus. "Yes." Then she brought her gaze up. "Hi Tony."

"Ellen."

"Long—" She managed to get that out before her face broke into semicircles at the corners of the mouth and folds at the edges of the eyes. "Long time no see, I was going to say. Whee!" She laughed so hard that she couldn't say more, and Prioleau laughed, too. Gus watched them.

She left the suitcase at the curb and stepped up, then over to Prioleau. She stopped before him, raised onto her toes, put her hands on either side of his neck, just the fingertips, and kissed him a while on the mouth. He leaned down farther, but by then she'd stepped back.

"Hello," she said.

Prioleau said, "Dear God."

"What happened—I should explain this to you, Tony. I had no idea of bothering you. But Mike—I married Mike? We were—Tony: I used your name, hard. The way you'd use a gun. I said some things to Mike about you, and Gus heard us, and I guess he wanted to find out from *you* or something."

Prioleau said, "We've been talking some."

"I'm very sorry."

"You are?"

The smile remained, and she stood before him, looking up.

"Oh, my," Prioleau said.

Ellen sat on the rocker and Gus sat on the broken-backed chair and Prioleau crouched on a crate. Reaching with a wooden fork for pasta, Prioleau stopped and asked Ellen, "Do you say grace?"

"Daddy does," Gus said.

Ellen said, "Well—"

And Prioleau said, "You go ahead and do it, Gus."

Gus went red, looked at his plate, said, "Father—" And then he said, "Thanks for the food, God."

Prioleau looked to Ellen, who was also red and was looking only at Gus. Prioleau said, "Fair enough." He forked spaghetti, ladled sauce, and they ate. They were silent. Tin mugs of wine went up and down, food went up and down, Gus belched from a throatful of Dr Pepper.

Eventually, Ellen said, "You're a pretty good cook."

Gus said, "This is good."

Prioleau said, "Thank you."

"Thank you," Ellen said.

Gus finished quickly and excused himself and escaped. He pulled his chair to the farthest TV console and turned it on, very low, and sat Indian-fashion on the seat, biting his fingers, sealed away from them by the gray-blue light of early-evening programs. Only then did Ellen slump slightly in her rocker and pour more wine for them each. She told him the wine was good. He told her that he had a friend who liked good wine. She raised her eyebrows and then looked down into her mug, then sipped. They were silent, and then she shared what was left in the bottle between their cups, and then it began.

"Gus is a nice boy," Prioleau said.

She nodded.

"He's brave."

"He's foolish," she said.

"Look who's talking, eh? Long-distance travel must be a tradition in your family. Look at you. He said you always knew what he was thinking, and you sure must have—to show up so fast. I'm willing to bet something precious that you have to halfway approve."

"I did use to get around, Tony."

"Hell, you're still doing it."

"I am, aren't I?"

He leaned forward suddenly and whispered, "Ellen, is he mine? Was he right about that? Is he *mine?*"

She leaned forward, too. "Half of him. Yes. I'm sorry I never told you. But then I never told Mike either. Or Gus."

"Well, if anybody ever asks you, I don't think you owed that to any of us."

The smile split her face and disappeared.

"Mike doesn't think so, does he?" Prioleau said.

"Mike feels incredibly betrayed."

"Sure."

"You're right," she said. "He's right. Except, I always told myself, *That was your time, and no one else's.* Of course, I was wrong. Because that left you out of it. And it was your time, too."

"I felt that way when you left, I can tell you."

"Your face was so sad."

"I tried to look happy."

"You looked like a puppy with worms."

"Felt like it."

"Yes. I knew how you felt. Not right away. I made about fifty or sixty miles, and all of a sudden it was like someone else was driving. I pulled over to the side and I cried and cried. It wasn't even missing you. It was, all of a sudden, I felt what I thought you were feeling. I was some tough traveling adventure-bitch, wasn't I? Gave you the generosities of my flat little body and considered it a favor, I imagine. And then took off. And you were so sad. All the time. You were—you wanted me to stay. Is that right?"

"It's true."

"Tony, would you tell me if you loved me? I don't mean now. I wonder if you loved me then."

He closed his eyes and said, "I did."

"That's why Gus is such a nice kid. His parents loved each other. Isn't that what we're saying?"

His eyes were still closed. "You did, too?"

"I think so," she said. "Yes."

He opened his eyes. She moved back in the rocker; it started to swing and she went rigid. He said, "Then what you did was desert me, dear friend. You—" He stopped, made his teeth and lips meet, stared unblinking at her. "Never mind. Never mind. I apologize."

"But why?"

"You want more? You like this? Well, forget it. Anything I say now—what I want to do is wipe out eleven years."

"Nearly twelve."

"Yeah. And a little boy. And a man you went a couple of thousand miles for, after you smirked on out of here. And a generous woman. I won't say it. I won't say it."

"No, do say it. Stop being *fair*."

He clasped his hands at his chest. He was shivering. They leaned toward one another under a yellow bulb, and Gus leaned toward the gray light fifteen feet away.

"You love me," she said.

He shook his head in wide swings, once to each side.

She said, "You do."

He sat as still as he could, though the shivering continued. He reached for cigarettes and matches, and he needed both hands to bring the flame up, so he threw the match across the table at her, and then the cigarette. She didn't flinch. The match landed on the collar of her plaid shirt and the cigarette went past her. The match lay there, burning a brown spot on her shirt, and she simply looked at him. He stood, finally, to reach across and pluck the fire. She moved her face up as his came down. They could have kissed. He drew jerkily back and sat again.

"I'm sorry, Ellen."

"I'm sorrier."

"Will you take him home tomorrow, please?"

"To Mike? I don't know. I don't know if Mike and I have too much of a future." She giggled. "You and I don't have one either. Everybody just gets to keep their past around here. This is the history depot."

"Gus has a future."

"We have to figure out where it is, don't we?"

"We?" He got a cigarette lit, still using two hands for the lifting of the match. "I feel like all we're saying is so long."

She said, "If you'd stop being so strong and proud and vengeful. Not that you aren't right to be mad. But you love me."

"Yes?"

"I'm not saying it's fair you do. But you do. Please. I want you to."

"Yes?"

"Hey, you guys," Gus called. "Look at this!"

"That's part of it, too," Ellen said.

"You wouldn't have come, if he hadn't," Prioleau said.

"That's right."

"Wait a minute."

"You always were very, very slow about things like this."

"You *sent* him?"

"Not like that. He's my baby. He's my little boy."

"You did."

"Not just like that. It isn't that simple."

"You sent him."

"He took off on his own."

"Yeah. I wonder how he found out how to get here."

"Nothing's that simple," she said.

"Look!" Gus cried.

Henry Watervliet was up and cleaning his kitchen for Sunday when Louisa walked through the park, brushing against lilac trees, the clustered petals of which had gone from dark violet to pink and which now were turning brown to drop, like dirty snow, into a ring around each tree. A young maple which was the height of Henry's roof had iridescent red rashes on the lower leaves. The grass beneath the tree looked sour. Louisa looked healthy, tall and red-faced, sweaty from her walk. She stood outside Henry's door and started to wilt. And inside, in his septic kitchen, Henry was singing along with the Reverend Billy Horsefall's American Youth Choir as they asked the timeless question "Were You There When They Crucified My Lord?" And Melchior, addressing his fingers, sat in the living room, staring beyond his hand, beyond the hand which held it, beyond the television set against the wall, and past the wall.

The knock came, lower than Reverend Billy's swelling chant—And do they have the presence of Christ in their lives? In their *lives*, my friends. Not in their Bibles, if their dictatorial leaders permit them a glimpse, from time to time, at the Good Book, oh, the Best Book. Which, I can tell you, they do *not*. And not on the walls of their churches, long abandoned, guarded by ugly men with ugly weapons of destruction. The churches they may not *approach*, much less enter. Is the Son of Man in their *lives*? Is He often on their *lips?*—and Henry called to Melchior, cautioning him to listen.

Melchior addressed himself to his hand.

Louisa pounded, hard, at the door of the shack. Henry called, "Sunday-morning company. Spruce up! Act alert! And keep an ear open, Billy's gonna give 'em a *shit*load."

"Daddy," Louisa called.

Melchior looked up, stood up, was younger at once. His feet moved, he held himself ready.

"What's that?" Henry called from the kitchen, clinking objects of glass.

"What," Melchior said.

But Louisa was walking, by then. And when Henry had shuffled to the door, plugging a fist ahead of him to encourage Reverend Billy's major service of the week, he found empty air, the hard yellow light, a figure at the park which then disappeared.

Sat*anic* forces! Reverend Billy cried.

"You know it," Henry answered. "Pure forces of Satan. I'm about to drink your health, Billy."

Forces which can take control of a man, of a woman too, and shape their lives, manage their destinies, and leave them in the dark world of choicelessness. You want a choice, my friends? You want a vote about your final days? You desire to take a hand, to *raise* a hand, to seize the seconds left to you and have a *say*? You do. Of course you do. We are all of us hoping to have a say. We are all of us looking ahead to that day. We are pilgrims on the long voyage. We are journeying on. The hours are numbered. And the day of decision is close to hand. Communists offer no vote. Their victims cannot speak about their fate. But *you* can. *You* can vote for life. You can enable *them* to vote for life. As the pilgrims sailed on to found this great nation, making crucial decisions about navigation and seamanship, so you, dear friends, sail on such a journey. And now you must make *your* decisions. You must make them for yourselves, and for those minions of militancy and malignant misery who cannot make their own decisions. Do it for them. Do it for yourselves. Do it for *Christ*, who suffered that we *all* may choose. Help to reach our brothers and sisters in their affliction. Help to send my voice, and the Lord's message, along to them. Help to keep it coming to *you*. We need your dollars. We need your small coins. Send us a nickel, send a dime, send what you can, send the *Word*, friends, and you're piloting the pilgrim ship, you're casting a vote, you're making a choice, but you need to send—send a nickel, send a dime, serve *Christ!*

"Don't he do it, though?"

"This is the father," Melchior said, holding his finger, "he needs our help."

"Well, he sure as shit does," Henry sang.

Louisa, at home, upstairs, was at her typewriter. She was writing about her father and the man her father lived with. She was typing rapidly, running the letter *x* through her mistakes, putting it down: about a father in his madness who chose to live with a drunken indigent; about a daughter who permitted him to do so; about the checks she mailed. Each time she went beyond description, each time she speculated on the reactions of people in Patoka Plains who thought her neglectful and hard of heart, each time she portrayed him as a new father, a no-longer-father, a strange person with a changed mind, each time she wrote of living forever little more than a quarter of a mile from her former father, who was still her father, and each time, soon, that she typed *father*, the letter *x* stained her page until she sat back to look at a page of *x*'s, a homework page of algebra offered by a fool who was failing. "I do want it to be better than this," she told herself calmly. "I do want it all to be better." And hearing her voice, its hearty false control, she bent her forehead to the letters before her.

Standing at the white van, watching Ellen stow bags among metal tool chests and racked spare parts, and the skeleton of an antenna, Gus said, "Which father do we live with, Mom?"

The little carillon peeped its call for second service. A blue jay nagged. Prioleau, inside, shoved something heavy along the wooden floor, and it shrieked its weight.

"Mom?"

A nation of artisans in trucks, Louisa decided, walking slowly from the town offices on Monday afternoon, having stood with other oglers on the frost-heaved, sun-cracked sidewalk as a highway patrolman marched Henry Watervliet back out of the town supervisor's office to take him home. The old Dodge truck, dark green and scuffed, with WOODWORKING—CABINETS lettered on its side, drove past for the second time. Instead of tinkers in wooden-wheeled carts, there were large grim men in weather-beaten trucks who travel the roads, fixing. And there was Henry, drunk as ever, somehow dressed in bedroom slippers and a Norfolk jacket of thick corduroy wrestled on over farmer's overalls, loony and smiling, arrested for putting two charges of bird shot into the air above his house and crying self-defense— something about the Communists were floating through the air, the patrolman had quoted, when Louisa, summoned by the town supervisor's laughing secretary, had come to take responsibility. Which was why she strolled the streets in thongs and billowy cotton, carrying a very old and greasy shotgun, cutting down the alley between the civic offices and the church, going past the pastor's house, near the school's parking lot, to walk through high grass toward Watervliet's house, where she would meet the trooper, assure him once more that Henry was only mad, not dangerous, and carry the gun away for good. She looked across the park as she went, and the dirty green truck, with its high tail fins, which made it look like a rocket, slowed to stop at the street side of the park.

Melchior was at the door when they assembled there, Henry laughing with the highway patrolman, saying, "It was a hell of a warning volley, wasn't it? Wasn't it?"

Still smiling, the patrolman said, "Not near a school, Henry. Never near a school."

Slyly, the old man leaned his head near his shoulder and said, "The Russians don't go near schools, then?"

"They live in bottles, Henry," the patrolman said. "I should take the gun," he told Louisa.

"You can have it," she said.

"Right to bear arms," Henry said. "Right to assemble in free speech bearing arms. Constitution. Bill of Rights. Declaration of fucking Inde*pen*dence."

"Take it," the patrolman said. "Keep it." As if Henry were deaf, he shouted, "But don't let the old man near it again."

"Right to carry small-bore weapons and not to quarter soldiers in your goddamned *house*."

The patrolman shook Louisa's hand, waved his palm at Henry, and left. Holding the gun, Louisa looked up at Melchior, who stood in the doorway, tall and healthy-looking that minute, smiling, younger, full of comprehension and as lucid as he'd been eleven years before.

"Darling girl," he crooned in his deep voice.

"Daddy?" She turned, walked toward him, the shotgun at port arms.

Her face, or the gun, or the sudden step—something dropped him two inches and crumpled his face, leeched blood from his flesh. He went old once more, and frightened. His hand came up. She stopped. He held his hand. She stepped backward. "This," he said in his whisper, "is the father."

But she was turning, still holding the shotgun up before her, and she was marching through the park. She was reminding herself how independent she was, and how she had grown over recent years by not permitting Anthony

Prioleau to be a necessity—how, in disciplined allotments of hours and sometimes days, he was a pleasure, somehow a surprise, once in a while a tedium or chore, occasionally a responsibility—when he became undecipherable in silence, his sealed interiorness. But, like chocolate or expensive meat or the new long-playing records that cost too much, he was not—had not been—a habit. This would be a usefulness to her. She would become fat suddenly, she expected. She might become promiscuous, or find that she had acquired a reputation—all that the men in Gene's Bar needed was to see a large pair of breasts on a body which didn't sport a wedding ring. Their small boy's needy dreaming required no more than that excuse, bosoms or thighs. Prioleau had protected her for years from that. Surely they had snickered or remarked, but not too long or loud. The men at Gene's had grown used to the two of them. Now that would end, now the other would begin as she was formally available and therefore prey to dreams and randy wishes. Or, if not fat, if not wasted on bad men, she could go as mad as her father—surely it might run in the blood. And if none of these, there was always the sadness which fell on her like early-morning cobwebs, stretched between trees, into which she blundered, not knowing she was unhappy until, suddenly, she was. It all had somehow to be written down. But she was really not the person to do that. She wasn't nearly good enough: that admission crouched, like the spider, out of sight. This wasn't going to be fun, living a long life.

Upstairs, having showered and changed, Louisa sat at her desk and looked over it to the window through which she had seen the van—TELEVISION CENTRE—driving east through failing light. Prioleau, behind the wheel, might have looked back along the difficult angle to her house. He might have. She would, not knowing for certain, decide for herself one day. But he had driven, that was certainty, and there were two smaller shapes beside him. The shotgun lay on the floor downstairs, where once there had been umbrellas, in the hallway closet.

Walking in front of the green truck parked near Gene's Bar, tall in spiked heels, wearing a blue high-necked dress with three-quarter sleeves, with gloves in her dark leather handbag, squinting into the streetlights, she entered the smell of beer and tobacco. The bar was longer than she'd recalled, and the counter was higher. Baseball banners were on the wall behind the bar, and in the back, a shadow, was the pool table at which no one played. A woman wearing a man's cardigan sweater sat at the far end of the bar and drank something from a shot glass which she chased with what looked like Seven-Up or soda water. Two men talked to Gene, who smoked his pipe. He wiped his hands on his shirt and, calling her ma'am, inquired after her father and asked what she wished. He smiled helplessly when she asked for a banana daquiri, so she told him rum-and-Coke. She didn't look down the bar again, nor did she take her notebook from the bag as she had planned to. She removed money from the bag instead, slid awkwardly from the stool, and walked out, saying nothing.

On the street, she took a breath, which left her dizzy, and she walked toward home. The ground still shook from a passing train, and she heard its whistle and bell. She was not crying, she noted. She was powdered and perfumed and dressed very well. She had gone to Gene's and had been noticed. She lived in a house that she owned, and surely Prioleau would make the proper financial arrangements about mortgage payments for the store, and she could afford to spend the next year recalling how to drive a car, and she would take budgeted trips to cities where she would go to civic theater again and listen to music and meet people. She would not starve to death, and she would not languish. She would not live like a nun. And on some other night, she would enter Gene's and smile, and people would smile back, and she would not sweat under her dress so that her ribs itched.

The man walking on heavy feet behind her called, "Miss?" He was tall and his hair was tousled, curly. His thick lips smiled. In his khaki fatigue jacket and dark trousers he looked like something she remembered from years before—an enlisted man on the loose. As he moved closer, she saw that he had been sitting at the bar in Gene's. "Miss Melchior?"

So she'd told him where to park his truck, on Railroad Street, and she had sat him in the rarely used living room, feeding him coffee and cheese sandwiches, watching him lean in his exhaustion on a fat pillow her mother had covered with crewelwork, and she had listened to his story about his child's flight, and then—he had blushed—his wife's, their *misunderstanding*, he called it, their *discussion*, and there was a man called Prioleau, he said, they—she—no, the boy too—somehow they had sought him, and he understood that she—Prioleau was a friend of hers, he'd been told in the town, and could she offer him directions and advice, could she help?

"Miss Melchior, we've been married for ten and a half years, a little more than that, really. Ellen, my wife, Ellen is not a fidgety person. She never takes off. She leaves messages on the table for me if she runs out to the store. She's pretty careful about herself. And she really takes care of old Gus. She takes care of me. She always says we're a two-boy family." He begged, with his big smile, for nothing-wrong.

"She came here?" Louisa said.

"Now, we all know that, Miss Melchior."

"Yes. Of course. She did come here. Apparently Gus, your boy. Your son Gus. Apparently. Yes, Gus came here, he took the bus. It must have been a frightful trip for a little boy. He came here, and then Mrs. Eewald followed him. She knew Tony."

He closed his eyes. "As you say, 'apparently.' Boy, did she know him. You heard the story from him, didn't you? The barkeep said you and he are old friends."

"For almost as long as you and Mrs. Eewald, I imagine."

"You were married?"

"Friends. Friends."

"Well."

"It's all right, Mr. Eewald. Half of the twentieth century's gone. Friends."

"Yes, ma'am. So you know the story, is all I mean."

"What I don't know, I can imagine." She moved her head forward on her neck in a way she hadn't done for a long time, and she smiled her best smile. Eewald stared, as if waiting for her to be comprehensible. So she said, "I know they met one another at an Army post here during the war. Near the end of the war."

He closed his eyes again and wriggled into the cushion. He looked as though he were settling down to sleep. He looked like a big blond dog. When he opened his eyes they were gluey-looking and very red. He looked like a bird dog cringing obedience. "You ask me what to do with needle rasps or a router. A sash clamp. Okay." He held up long-fingered, square-palmed hands which were chopped and rough and strong-looking. "Ask me about dovetailing a cabinet drawer made from antique cherrywood. You understand? I'm competent, believe me, ma'am. I am extremely competent. I'm what you might call a master craftsman. But I am ignorant as hell, I beg your pardon. I am, though, if you're asking me to comprehend what drives a woman to send her child on a bus to no place, like he's a package, and then follow it up by sending herself, and leave no word, and go to bed with a *stranger*. Ma'am, I don't care what part of what century it is, either. That was wrong. Every part of it. Though I'll take her back."

"Will you?"

"Good Lord, yes. She's my wife. Gus's my son."

"Yes?"

"You heard what she said about that? That's just cruelty and anger." His eyes flickered. "You know what I hate about the movies and what's on TV? Every time they show a play about somebody wanting someone's wife, they're on *his* side. They never side with the husband. I keep thinking about that. I feel like an Indian in a cowboy picture. Who's on the Indian's side?"

"Would you like some more coffee?"

"She hasn't really *left* me, of course." He shook his head rapidly, and she leaned forward to hear the flapping of canine ears, the jingle of a collar. He smiled a wonderful young grin. The reddened eyes dominated his face again. "This is hard times, Miss Melchior."

"How much do you love your wife, Mr. Eewald?"

"Michael. Mike, if you want. She's my wife. Gus's my son. We're having a terrible time right now. But we're a family."

"Do you know anything about Tennessee Williams?"

"No. Should I? Would it help?"

"No."

"Then I'd just as soon not. I've had enough bad news.

And enough driving. Can I sleep here? Would it be a bother if I did?"

"Mike, it won't feel better in the morning. I'm sorry."

"You're pretty cut up, too."

She nodded, stood, beckoned him to the stairs. No clean towels, and no discussions about the bathroom and an extra toothbrush: a finger pointing at the door, the finger waving to acknowledge his good night, and then the trip down the hall to her room, the undressing in the dark, the long slow collapse into bed, and instant sleep.

It lasted a few hours, and then she was awake—dry-mouthed, headachy, sore at the shoulders as if she'd carried considerable weight, and wholly awake. She realized that some of Tony's clothes were in her closet, that some of his foolish mystery books were on her shelves, that if it were possible, physically possible, some of his body might still be clinging to some of hers, hidden away and living the life of the invader, rowdy drunken cells kicking over furniture and calling for food. She went downstairs on her toes in the dark, holding her nightgown so that it wouldn't whisper on the railing or the steps. When she came up, she went directly to the bathroom and locked herself inside. She guessed at the measurements and ran the tap at a trickle. And then, with her nightgown hiked to her waist, she sat on the toilet and, the rubber bag suspended from the shower-curtain railing, she flushed him, her membranes' memories of him, away. She gasped at the bite of too much vinegar. She pressed the snaky tube too hard against herself and kept it there, burning at her body, and she wept in open-mouthed gulps.

After too long, she went to the sink and rinsed the douche, rinsed again, filled the bag with lukewarm water, went back to the toilet and laved herself, again and again, until the burning was lessened. But when the pain had decreased, she couldn't release herself. She sealed off the flow and then, her mind floating up and away against the top of her skull as if she were smoke rising to a ceiling, she moved a hand between her legs and leaned back. The hand loved her. Slowly, and with light pressure, the hand was constant. "This is—" The hand continued, and she permitted it, then encouraged it, then instructed it. "This is—" She wasn't awfully dextrous, and she was alarmed, but nothing, finally, was easier than loving herself, and she wondered, even as she shook in her own grip, if this was another of the ways she would be living in the years ahead.

Louisa was aware, then, of the cold flush box, of the pressure of her thighs against the toilet seat. She made herself stand, and heard footsteps. Perhaps she'd been hearing them. The steps went up and down the hallway, as if searching, and she stood with her hand in the air. The steps moved away, and then clumsily down the narrow stairs. Louisa thought of soap operas on the radio, and films with Katharine Hepburn, and she intoned, inside, with Hepburn's clipped voice: The program that asks the immortal question: *Can* an immigrant's daughter who has been abandoned in a hick town by a sad and clumsy man find peace and happiness with the first three fingers of her left hand? She rubbed at her stomach. She smiled sleepily and didn't like her contentment.

This is the father, he needs our help. This is—

Mike stood with his hands extended to the blue flame under the kettle, rubbing his palms as if he warmed himself. In the light of the stove, flickering, and in the dim light of the fluorescent bulb behind the stove, he looked less like a puppy and more like a kid—curly, sleepy, still red-eyed: a kid on the edge of illness. He still wore the olive-green fatigue jacket, zipped up, and the dark-green work pants. He looked like a soldier she had dated years before. His feet were bare; they were long feet, high at the instep, darkly veined and very wide. They looked almost like his hands. When she paused in the doorway he looked up and he spoke, as if they were in mid-conversation: "I always had a tough time understanding people. Not just women. Isn't that a stupid thing to say? But I did. I once taught shop. Woodworking shop. They called it woodshop. I got the kids, boys, who didn't want to go to college. Prevocational students, we called them. Big guys, and most of them with no hands for wood. I got a few good ones, but most of them wanted to spend the rest of their lives driving cars and drinking beer. And every time, I'd get some guy who thought just because he was a boy he could handle wood. And sure enough, he'd be the one to snap a molding strip or gouge a nice piece of pine. We had them working mostly with pine, because it was cheaper. And every time, I lost my temper. I'd get angry. Because of the wood. Boy, I was a terrible teacher. You'd think I'd of learned, but I never did. Not any more than they did. I couldn't understand it, not being careful with wood.

"So, if you're talking about understanding *women*, begging your pardon. But I really never did. And Ellen—I knew her for a while. It really stopped when she came to San Diego. See, we thought I'd be shipped out soon. We thought they were invading Japan. We overlooked by a year how long it would take us to clean the Nips out of the Philippines. So she steamed on out there—did I tell you we were supposed to be married? Back in Philly? She was my fiancée. She came out there—well, there was a stop along the way, wasn't there?" He poured the hot water through the grounds. His fingers were certain on the handle of the kettle and the neck of the filter jug. He spilled nothing. "Anyway, we lived there. Maybe two months, three. We shared this cabin with another couple. A lot of leave, a lot of dancing in roadhouses, probably too much booze: wartime, you know. I started knowing I didn't understand her there. She was really nice to me, mind you. She was sad. I mean, I could tell she felt sad sometimes. But I didn't know why. I thought it was the war. You want some of this?"

They sat in the dim kitchen across from one another, Louisa saying nothing. And Michael Eewald gabbled, gobbled, the words rolled on: new equipment, retraining, gas masks, livelier ammunition, the politics of off-base living, venereal disease in bars, the black market in rubber tires, vodka, weak beer, the new-model jeeps. "When she told me she was pregnant, I got worried. About the war, and money and everything. I remembered I yelled about how careless she was. Boy. I should of known, huh? But then I got glad, because, you know, you don't produce too much that lasts. Nobody takes care of wood, and it rots or gets busted up. Carelessness. But a *kid*. Well. So then they restricted us to the base, good food and everything, but staying there all the time with the snakes and all that dust. So I went AWOL a couple of times, I got away with it. I mean, most of the boys went once or twice. If they'd of called us into action without warning, they'd of needed a week just to round us up. But the sneaking got on her nerves, she was upset all the time. So we decided for her to go back, and she said she wasn't going all the way to Philly again and stay there. So what she did, she hitched a ride on a transport plane, and she got this grandfather of hers. She got him and they took a train back West. I had folks in Wyoming, and she decided that's where she wanted to live.

Never even saw the place before. Just a rinky-dink town like this, begging your pardon. That's where she stayed. That's where I went back to her. That's where we live. That's where we've been living. I don't know if we still live there."

"You do understand her," Louisa said. "It sounds as if you do."

His head rocked back and his eyes were wide. "No, I don't," he said. "Leaving her job? She's a teacher, you know. She just substitutes now and then. I figured Gus needed her at home. But she owes the school. And her home? Her fam—*me?* Leaving like that? No, I couldn't say I understand that kind of behavior. Aren't you nice, letting me go on like this?"

"Mike," Louisa said, folding her hands beside the cup, "what about when she was on her way through Patoka Plains? When she stopped here."

"I understand that. Anybody can understand *that*. She was unfaithful with your friend. They made my baby. I understand that."

"As you say, wartime."

"That's not wartime. That happens *all* the time. That's just wrong, war or peace, that's all it is. Wrong. It's immoral. It's unfaithful. But you can forgive that. You really can." He smiled and his eyebrows rose. He looked as though he were explaining how a card game would finish. Then the brows fell, his hands fell onto the table, his voice fell: "It's being disloyal. Not being loyal to your family. That's the sinful part. You understand this?"

Louisa said, "I'm not very good at understanding people either."

"Oh, you are. I can tell you are. You haven't complained once about him yet, you know."

"Him?"

"You know. Wasn't he your man?"

"That sounds a little bit like a song."

"But he was, wasn't he?"

Louisa went to the stove for more coffee, topped up both cups, replaced the jug on the stove, stood there watching the tiny blue flame, the steam rising from the jug. "These things happen," she said.

"They happened while I was in the service. I saw big feisty men crying. But I don't know about peacetime."

"Maybe there isn't any peacetime," she said. "Maybe it's really all the same."

"I wouldn't know about that. All I know, I'm missing a little boy and a wife. I don't know where to find them."

She said, "Don't."

"*No.*"

"Don't."

"Live alone? For the rest of my life? And my little son, growing up with a stranger? Never *see* him? He still kisses me good night before he goes to bed. Never see him?"

"Don't."

"What are you trying to *give* him?" Mike stood and pushed from the table, and the chair scraped backward toward the sink. "You feel like you owe him that much? *I* don't. No, ma'am. He owes *me*: one wife, one baby. I want 'em. I want 'em."

"Don't."

In the silence, then, with only the sound of their breathing, the echo of the chair and their voices, in the hushed house, they heard the click of metal, the depression of old wooden boards beneath carpeting, the pivot of a door on a hinge.

Mike said, "Ah."

"Oh, no," Louisa said.

"It's them. It's her. Would they come here?"

She shook her head.

He put his finger to his lips to silence her, but she was saying nothing. In his bare feet, he tiptoed the length of the kitchen toward the hallway, his teeth showing. He looked like a soldier.

Louisa opened her mouth, but there was nothing to say about this, and she put her own finger on her lips, as if she instructed herself to be still.

Mike was at the doorway, and then in the hall. She followed, a hand on each cheek, the pinkies meeting in front of her mouth. Mike's hand rubbed against the vinyl wall covering in the hallway, found the light switch, and pushed it up. The chandelier glowed, the dark hall jumped into smallness, crowding at them—closet door, metal-framed mirror, wooden bench, dull rug, the shiny gray-and-blue walls. Mike stayed still, crouched, on his toes. Louisa, behind him, held her face.

Very slowly, Melchior's frozen face came around the closet door, and then his open plaid bathrobe, tan pants, Henry Watervliet's bedroom slippers. His eyes were small and they didn't blink much. His mouth was tight, something scribbled onto his pale smooth face. He slid in the backless slippers to the center of the hall, staring at Mike's service-issue jacket and dark trousers, looking at his face, ignoring Louisa. He lifted Henry Watervliet's confiscated shotgun, and each hand pulled itself a little lower than the hand beneath it as he raised the gun, his hands going down from the muzzle and along the barrels, over the pump and down the checkered wood and over the ejection slide to the grip and stock, the shotgun coming up as he stared at Eewald's clothes. "Italian," he whispered. "I have located the weapon, as you see. I have searched and I have found it. Fornicator Italian."

"Daddy! He's not the one!"

"Wait," Mike said. "Prioleau's a dago?"

"Daddy. This isn't Corporal Rita."

"She always lies down," Melchior said.

The shotgun came up to Melchior's shoulder. He held his chin away from the stock and closed his eyes. "What?" Eewald said. "Who in hell *is* this?" Melchior, pointing the gun at the U.S.-issue fatigue jacket, squeezing his eyes shut, making small noises, pulled the trigger.

The unloaded gun clicked, a little bright sound. Melchior pulled again, jerking the barrel, and the gun clicked. In the hallway of his former home, in the middle of the century and center of the nation, blindly aiming at a soldier's coat, surrounded by the high exhausted throat sounds of his tall daughter, Melchior pulled the trigger again and again, and the shotgun made small clicks.

1963

It was bright night. Ellen had left Prioleau inside, chucking wood into the fireplace against a cold June, and had gone to the beach, which was shaggy with timber and staves and trees tossed up by storms. She climbed over and around black boulders, slid on rounded stones which rolled beneath her feet. At the water's edge, where the tide slapped kelp, she looked off to the right, around the palisades of the cove, toward the Navy's towers, from which signals, they'd been told, were sent to submarines. The towers were hundreds of feet high; there were twenty-six of them, girderwork and invisible guy wires, and they were covered with red lights to warn off planes. The lights blinked in a pattern that looked only random: a monstrous heap of firebombed wreckage, glowing.

To reach their house it was necessary to drive the coastal road, U.S. 1, into and out of Machias, Maine, to drive across the Machias River and then to cut uphill and into the back country, where a few white cottages offered gardens to the salt air which stunted them. Fog pooled in these hills, and marshes below rose and fell with the tides of the bay in which, half a mile from shore, seals sometimes fished. Inland, though, as the cracked two-lane road twisted across the stubby peninsula, all there was after a mile or two of driving were miles of green emptiness, the strong smell of the invisible sea, and every now and then a small shack with a lawn littered by children who watched the occasional car pass.

Eight miles from home, there was a mesh fence and a guardhouse, a sign which warned that the Navy's communication towers stood within. Five miles from home, there was a small graveyard and a T-junction; and then, off the left-hand road, in another mile, there was more sand blowing onto the road, and the low roar of the ocean, and then the shallow hillside on the high parts of which some fishermen's houses stood and below which the wide mouth of the Potter harbor lifted and sank. A dirt track began outside Potter, curving uphill and beyond the harbor, running parallel to the shoreline of dense fir forest. Ellen LaRue Spencer Eewald and Anthony Prioleau lived there in the house they had built.

Ellen looked out to sea, past the foaming rock and the buoys of lobster traps, toward Grand Manan Island, Canada. Prioleau came from the huge spruce at the meadow's edge —even now, in the coming fog, it dripped moisture though there wasn't rain—and he climbed over and around the great stones to reach her. She turned as rocks clattered, lifted her chin to him, then crossed her arms on her chest and looked out again.

In a while, he said, "What?"

"Valentina," she said, pointing out and up.

"Sorry," he said. "What?"

"Valentina Ter—I can't say it. She's an astronaut. A Russian. A woman, she flies rockets. They sent her up today, she's orbiting the earth, and I thought if I stood out here for a while I might see her."

"Fog's coming in."

"She's *over* the fog."

Prioleau, behind her, put his hands on her shoulders. A high plane, its winking lights just visible, went ahead of its engine sounds. "No," she said. "Just a bomber off the SAC base."

"I wish they'd stop that," he said.

"I wonder if they're flying to Birmingham to bomb Negroes or Cuba to bomb the leftover Russians. The fog's too thick now. She's up there, though. I figure she weighs about two hundred pounds and stands five foot tall and probably shaves twice a week. But she's up there. In a rocket. Imagine that. Hello, Valentina." She turned, balancing herself on the rocks, and leaned into him. She bumped her head against his chest, and he hugged her. Then she said, "Tomorrow's your birthday, did you remember? You were hoping I'd forget."

"Fifty-one," he said. "Except all the tourist girls, when I take the truck into Machias, they look at me and whistle, they figure I'm barely forty and a terribly attractive rural phenomenon. Don't you think?"

"You're okay for an older person," she said. "Happy birthday."

"Tell me that when *you* turn fifty-one."

"Oh, I expect I will. Let's give up, there's too much fog. Good night, Valentina." They balanced by holding each other's hand as they climbed from a wide rock slab and then over boulders to the spruce and the narrow trail that went to the house. Ellen said, "For your birthday, I intend to dynamite all the towers, by the way."

"No," he said, "we can leave that for Gus to do."

"Don't even joke that way, Tony."

"All right. We won't even talk about him tonight."

"Tell me that when we get through the rest of the night and don't talk about him."

They got through the rest of the night, they talked about Gus for much of it, and in the morning Prioleau drove past two- and three-room cabins, unpainted, roof-shot, heated with dangerous slender pipes poking through walls not much thicker than the tar paper which, between gaps in the warped clapboard, looked like filthy underwear seen through rents in ragged clothes. Useless refrigerators stood in dooryards, and dead engines, retained against their possible use or kept just because they had been there a while. Garbage spilled around the motors that didn't run and the lumber never used for repairs once it was scavenged. Withered dogs and wormy children stared. Sometimes a woman sat at a stepless front sill and watched the children watch. Sometimes a man with a beer belly swung a wood-splitting maul by the side of his shack.

At Sandys Point, it was rumored at night in fishermen's bars, smugglers brought drugs from the ocean in yachts to short Italian men who drove them in long cars to Boston, posing as tourists. This was an idea thrilling, once, to Gus, who even had camped at the point in hopes of seeing gangsters; he'd come home with a rash from poison oak. Prioleau wondered what he might come home with this time. Then Machias, with its A&P, its gift shops for the growing tourist trade, and, on a back street that was still mostly meadow, the unemployment office where Prioleau, using his wartime service and college degree as credentials, worked as a supervisor of those who oversaw the dilemmas of those who couldn't, and didn't, have jobs. When Ellen filled in at the library of the two-year community college across the river, she went with him in the truck. When she didn't, she stayed at the house and thought about Gus; and Prioleau waded through the day's boredom and early fatigue, supplying statistics in answer to questions forgotten in Augusta and Washington, and he thought about Ellen.

That morning was a normal one. Mackenzie nipped off to the bathroom in the little office rented by the government; he came out, hourly, a little more cheerful and red of cheek; by early afternoon, he would fall asleep at his desk or slide drunkenly along the green linoleum floor. Lilah Minton, married to a fisherman, interviewed and gave out incomprehensible forms and yellow cardboard folders filled with instructions on being jobless: *Keep this book even if you get a job. You may need it again.* Fluorescent lights buzzed and flared. Phone calls came. They went to lunch in shifts. They watched the large clock on the pastel-yellow wall. Three desks in a large room filled with gray filing cabinets and index-card drawers: the place where Prioleau made mistakes which were different from the ones he made at home. In the little bathroom, Mackenzie whistled a medley of tunes which Vic Damone had sung on the Ed Sullivan show. Prioleau thought of Ellen in the yard or at the beach, looking up: Hello, Valentina.

For his birthday dinner that night, they cooked on the beach at the rock slab, making a fireplace from stones, laying a grate across it, burning driftwood for the coals over which to grill the mackerel. They sat on rocks and drank martinis from a thermos, while Prioleau smoked too much and Ellen raised her brows at his cough. After the second drink, Ellen took his gift from the white canvas bag they'd carried down.

It was a cheap porcelain plate, chipped at twelve o'clock and two o'clock, and painted blue. The picture was of the old capitol building in Springfield, Illinois and it said UP TO DATE IN '39. Sitting opposite him, wearing a short yellow slicker against the wind and the blackflies, she raised her glass. "It was the closest I could come to 1944. Took me half a year to find it. The old man who runs the junk shop in Calais dug it up for me. Happy birthday, Tony."

"I love you."

"Sweetheart, I told you that a long time ago."

"Naturally you were right. Now, marry me."

"Once again: I have a husband who must hate me, and I don't want to file for divorce because I don't want him to know where I am. And it wouldn't be good for Gus. And you know all that."

"What would be good for Gus? This?"

"This is good enough for us, and it isn't the worst thing for him, and that'll do it, Tony."

"That'll do it."

"Cook the fish."

"Make love to me."

"Not on rocks in a cloud of flies with you waving that dish around. I'm forty-five years old. I'm too old for this. Cook the fish."

They left slender white skeletons for raccoons from the forest to carry off. They boiled coffee over what was left of the fire, and Prioleau smoked and watched the bony gleam of a lobster boat, late from its round of traps, curve in a wide arc that would carry it around Sandys Point toward Roque Bluffs. "You know what we need in our lives," he suddenly said to Ellen. "What we need is subject matter."

She looked at him as he had always imagined her looking at the high-school students she had taught in Pennsylvania

and Wyoming. He could not ever rid himself of the feeling
that she was older than he.

"Something outside us," Prioleau said. "Like war, or current events, or something."

"How about peace?" she said. "Might as well worry
about that, too. Let's see—they've done penicillin and they've
cured polio. You want to do life on other planets, Tony?"

They made the faces they made at each other when he
was to be foolish and she patronizing, but he went on. "I'm
talking about something outside of us. What we do is, we
worry about me and you and Gus. Then we worry about
Gus and you and me. Oh, and the garden. And money.
Whether your car might not start. But we never get out*side*.
You made me think of it, looking up there for the astronaut.
You think they call her an astronette?"

"Not on my time, they don't."

"Do you see what I mean?"

"I guess maybe it's all here, is why we do it. Maybe that's
all there is."

"Do you care?" Then he said, "I mean, do you mind?"

"Sweetheart, why should I *mind?*"

He hunched over his cigarette and mumbled, "I'm saying
I hope you don't get bored with it or anything."

She shifted over rocks to sit beside him with one small
arm over his shoulders, and she kissed him on the cheek,
put her other arm on his belly, kissed him again, and said,
"Please continue to beg. But you don't really need to."

Prioleau stood up and went down to the sea to fill the
martini thermos with water, which he sprinkled on the
coals. They scattered them, kicked the fireplace over, and
carried the canvas bag back up the track to the house, where
Ellen read the Boston papers he'd brought home and Prioleau read how Nero Wolfe and Archie Goodwin foiled

the archcriminal Zeck. In the middle of a paragraph describing how the 286-pound Wolfe had dieted himself into a disguise, Prioleau looked up to cite phony statutes of limitation, and the emotional needs of the middle-aged, and the undeniable fact of his birthday, and he asked Ellen to marry him at last—in a church or a synagogue, in a city office hallway, on the deck of a cod trawler in Force 5 winds.

She had finished the *Globe* and was back to the local papers. She said "No" again, with no new information, explanation, or excuse. Prioleau said nothing more and stomped upstairs to bed, finally falling asleep in the sound of the bell buoy off the point and the fog horn at Grand Manan. Of course, he woke. He came downstairs at 2:30 a.m. to confess his sudden wakefulness and usual confusion. And he found her on the sofa in front of the fireplace, looking peaceful and young under rough blankets, smiling, pale, and ready to defeat him again by saying, with all servitude, "Oh, Tony, it's terribly early. Go back to bed. I'll wake you for work."

So he did, and he drove to Machias with gummy eyes, having waked himself to sneak out early, without coffee or the smell of her skin, while she softly snored on the sofa. Everything lived to assault and injure him—a plague of motorcyclists with long, shiny hair and silver-studded black jackets who massed on the road between the towers and Machias; too many tourists on the street too early; clam diggers in trucks who scowled at him; unemployed artisans at the office who would not make sense of the reporting regulations; crippled fishermen whose pride made them deaf to instruction and incapable of talking straight; red-faced Mackenzie, who insisted on whistling one thousand permutations of "High Noon"; Lilah's slow patience.

He came home yawning and blinking, ready to resume the argument for marriage, ready to resume almost any argument at all, since he expected Ellen to be cozy on the sofa, rosy with rest, pleased, as usual, with his pursuit of what she claimed he already possessed. The house smelled of wood smoke from the night before: a low pressure front was settling over coastal Maine, and old men's bones—no doubt his own, Prioleau thought—would ache for days. The low squatted on them, driving the smell of creosote down the chimney, but Ellen wasn't there to complain about it. Ellen hadn't left a note, as sometimes she might, and she hadn't called, as she always did, when she was bent on an errand.

What Prioleau found was the lamp lighted on the table near the living-room window where they ate, and another lit at the far end of the room, beside the old deacon's bench Ellen often sat at, looking through the bay window down the meadow track through trees to the sea. What he had seen as welcoming light was only useless illumination of what he had cringed before secretly since the evening she had blundered, all sly chatter and tough eyes, into his shack in Illinois: the fear that she might decide on taking the rest of the journey she'd seemed so much to love. His sinuses squeezed his head with the rise-and-sink of tides, with the drumming of a long-dead generator. It had to be Gus, he told himself as he walked through the house to see whether she had taken something important, the absence of which would tell him that she'd grown bored with his silences, or was wounded by his inability to help her son. Their son. It had to be Gus.

And of course—pawing through underwear and long socks, unfolding dungarees, flapping sweaters, prodding a

cheap scarab bracelet—there were *two* boys, as Ellen liked
to point out. One was eighteen, one had just turned fifty-
one, and neither seemed to believe that the world was
steady, much less safe. Hello, Valentina. The old suitcases
were there, on the shelf at the top of the closet he had built
of tongue and groove but never had stained. And on the
bookcase in their bedroom lay the envelopes of photographs
she had taken from Philadelphia. Downstairs, in the desk
near her deacon's bench, were their birth certificates, all
three of them. He found a file folder labeled APPLIANCES;
inside was a small guarantee for an alarm clock they'd
thrown away years ago, nothing more. He lit another
cigarette, coughed another cough, and waited to get angry
enough to do something. But he got winded and scared, so
he paced the small living room, lit another cigarette, and
went into the room on the first floor in which Gus had slept
and sulked and hidden away for seven years. It was the
room into which they had gone, last thing at night, to
cover him and watch him sleep. It was the room into which,
at least once a year, Ellen had lugged a big metal garbage
pail and, pointing at the explosion of old toys, new records,
half-read paperbacks, and pictures of singers who seemed
to come in sets of four—all of them with carefully camou-
flaged pimples, Prioleau used to swear—and say, "Fill it up,
buster." It was the room into which he'd walk, years earlier,
coming home from work, to find her sitting on the bed,
her legs crossed as they'd been on the bed in Illinois, talking
low, or listening to Gus's voice going from high to low in
the squeak of his constant discomfort. It was the room in
which—they'd never found them, and they'd forsworn
looking too hard, though Prioleau had kept his eyes open
—Gus had possibly lain on the bed to write his unmailed
letters to Mike. It was also the room in which, as a boy, he

would play, singing—"Happy," Prioleau insisted to its darkness before he backed out. "Also, dammit, happy."

They had agreed not to look for him. He was seventeen. He would come home. He would be in touch. He had been raised decently, with the customary training against rape, pillage, and looting. He enjoyed food and cold milk. He would *not* drive with low people to Portsmouth or Boston and linger in barrooms or bad hotels. "Probably he's on unemployment somewhere," Prioleau had said after the first week. Neither of them had laughed. It had been just a month now, and what could happen in a month?

Possibly everything. Prioleau read the living room again, squinting like a detective in a mystery. It could say that Ellen had finally decided Gus was in sorest trouble. It could mean that she'd finally *heard* he was in trouble. It could mean that looking for Gus—like searching for her father, or traveling on toward Mike—was more exciting than living with a man to whom benevolent dourness was something like a way of life.

"Well, you're no spring chicken, either," Prioleau said. "You're not that much younger than me, even if you look it." He rubbed at his sinuses as the low gripped them. He sniffed and coughed. He walked out to the garage which sat twenty feet from the house and found what he had been certain from the start he would find, and what he'd wanted to forestall discovering: nothing. Her car, the valve-clattering, oil-burning convertible Corvair, was gone. So at least Ellen wasn't hitchhiking on the Machias road. How fine to know. She was gone, but driving herself: the pilgrim still on her voyages. He found himself at the door of his truck, one hand on the handle, and he couldn't remember walking up the drive to get there. Some women would be delighted to know that their husbands, whom they won't marry, still panic when they go; he practiced saying that, because he wanted to tell her. Where should he travel to tell her that?

Go inside and read a detective story, he instructed himself. I'm *in* one, damn it: The Missing Wife. The Case of the Missing Common-Law Wife. The Case of the Missing Son. Don't panic. No. How about I just walk around in circles and get cold and smoke? Don't panic.

No clothes missing, at least not her one good suit, the single pair of high-heeled shoes, the good leather pocketbook. Birth certificate still here, so she's not taking out a passport to skip the country with. Maybe she was kidnapped by a roving band of Hell's Angels down from Boston? No blood on the walls, and they wouldn't have wanted the car. A vigilante squad of the grouchy unemployed? Maybe she and Gus decided to run away together. Or, how about a nice long drive back to Wyoming? Maybe it's Mike's turn again. Unworthy Prioleau: you're a sore loser and a sore winner, and you're sore in-between. *Your* problem is, you never believed your luck—not in Illinois, and never here. You were always waiting for the bad part.

He was back in the house, kicking at the cold coals in the fireplace. He turned the television set on and ran through the stations. He turned the set off and, standing at the refrigerator, in its bright light and stale odors, ate from a hunk of cheddar, a slice of raw onion, a pickle, took a gulp of milk from the bottle. He hurled the door shut, and the refrigerator rocked. He put his palms against it in the dark kitchen; then he leaned his head against the freezer door at the top.

Maybe it's Gus, in trouble.

He slammed his palms against the door. "What about me," he said. Then, slamming again, and louder: *"Me."*

He went to the bedroom and put on rough trousers, a flannel shirt, work shoes. From the bureau he took the pocketknife Gus had given him years before on another birthday, and the first-aid kit, a cigar box filled with old unguents and tattered Band-Aids and half-empty aspirin bottles, dusty tape. He found his nylon rain jacket and went outside and up the hill to the truck. He came back down for the can of gasoline he kept in the garage for the lawn mower, and that went into the back of the pickup. Then he started the motor and turned on his lights. Now it was his turn to drive alone in a moonless night, falling ahead into his headlights, leaving behind him nothing but the dark.

He drove automatically, looking at nothing, he realized, because he expected to see nothing that might be of use to him. And though he was on his way to Machias, he didn't know what he would achieve by arriving there. But it was important to go. The radio, which gargled static as he passed the entrance to the base and its towers, told him that cherries in cans were a fair deal at the A&P. It told him that the killer of Medgar Evers was still at large, and that Valentina Tereshkova, after forty-eight orbits, had fallen down to everyone else. It announced that the Sunrise County Fair would feature death-defying aerialists, and a demolition derby, music by the Everly Brothers, and a song and prayer session with the Reverend Billy Horsefall and his American Youth Choir. Prioleau wondered what would happen if she weren't there to plant her late and always-futile garden patch with its fog-withered pole beans, or if their house weren't lighted along its foundation by the bright weeds she forced him to roam the roads for. He hit the steering wheel with his fist and shook his head. If someone told the story of Ellen LaRue Spencer Eewald almost

Prioleau and the man she had picked to live with, he thought, if someone at a party on a boat in Potter harbor told it over whiskey sours, people would smile. This was killing the story, and he didn't want it to die, or change too much. He turned the radio off because the song was harmonica and whistling, and he was reminded of Mackenzie doing his own interpretations of "It's All Right with Me." He struck the steering wheel again and then leaned on the horn as if it could say something for him, but the noise was nothing more or less than he could think to call in the dark cab of a dirty truck on a narrow lightless road.

It took him half an hour to walk from the American Legion post around the corner to the nameless room of a functionless hotel which was the other bar in Machias. He asked no questions, only looked—he saw young tourists in dirty clothes and whiskers, girls with severe faces—and he listened to talk that offered no useful information. Then he was in the truck and heading back out of Machias toward Woody's, the converted Esso garage where fishermen drank and sometimes, when they were drunk enough, beat each other up. It was square tables and low smoke, Eddie Fisher on the jukebox, and wiry men in fish-smelling clothes crouched to drink. He sipped beer which tasted flat and about which he would never dare to complain—Woody, round and strong and always angry, listened only to men who wore knives on their belts and whose days were passed in boats—and he tried to tune to separate conversations as though each were a staticky radio band, or one of the Canadian TV stations he sometimes received late at night. He heard of a sudden dearth of halibut, of Russian trawlers off Campobello Island, of a fire in a church in East Machias, about summer people buying Hovey's farm and of beatniks living like lice on the land. He smoked and sipped and listened. A short man with bulbous cheekbones and scars on the backs of his thick-wristed hands snarled, "One of 'em took a dinghy off of the landing near the gawdamned pound. Robbie Dunham's. Had a good gawdamned little outboard, too. They *ah* bastahds." Woody nodded curtly. The man with the cheekbones said, "Probably wanted to have a sex pahty with the ones already filthyin' Cross Island. You know about 'em." Woody knew. He watched Prioleau, who slopped beer when he put his glass down, who knocked his cigarettes from the bar and left without collecting his change, because he had to get to the truck and drive to ring Lilah Minton's doorbell and stammer at her husband and borrow a boat or, even better, pay for a late and dangerous ride by motor—Minton would sting him hard for a fee—and make his way to Cross Island, a trip no wise fisherman would make now, out into the Atlantic past Old Man Island, edged by shoals, which Prioleau, if he went alone, trying to read the charts by flashlight, probably couldn't avoid. But he had no place to go except there, where young people were gathering and maybe Gus with them, maybe, therefore, Ellen too. There was no place else to go.

The fog, or cold air, something—perhaps the deep stink of rotted bait for lobster traps—made him sneeze, sometimes in single convulsions, sometimes rapid-fire, exhaustingly, until the squeal of his sinuses sang in his head. The motor stank too, leaking fuel into the boat through a cracked rubber feed line from the gas can to the heavy outboard. Sweet exhaust came up into his face, and sometimes when he gulped to sneeze he drew the carbon monoxide in. He spat out poisoned saliva, he sneezed out poisoned mucus, he held the folded chart and steered clumsily with the little midships wheel of the Boston whaler under his free hand, while in the armpit of his left he clamped the flashlight so it shone on the mysterious chart.

The whaler was eighteen feet long, and Prioleau was certain that Gus would disapprove of its 35-horsepower engine, small compared to what powered other whalers in the area. It was quiet, though, and since he was sneaking, he was grateful. He ran the throttle low as he headed from the town landings, across the broad to where the tidal river necked down. Once he had passed the outside lights of the dairy on the bank above him, he opened the throttle and ran loud for a mile until he saw the red and green light at the Machiasport Bridge. Another quarter of a mile and he hooked with the river to the right, past Indian Point, and then, half a mile farther, Pot Head on his left. He had come this way as a passenger, by daylight, and nothing looked correct, although he could recognize the light on the steeple of the Congregational Church uphill behind the sardine cannery. Over the sound of water and his engine, he heard conveyor belts and large machines: fish were being gutted and packaged in oil. The tide ran hard, and the prow of the whaler lifted and smacked on it, making explosions of phosphorescence on the black water. His nose sealed up, and he didn't smell the sea after a while, or the rotten bait. He did feel the wind which now, in the blackness of the mouth of Salmon Cove, was picking up. He hoped it came from the east and that east was the right way to go, because that's where he was headed and that's where he'd been going—eight years of heading east as far as he could get.

The musette bag he'd borrowed from Minton, salt-stained navy blue, lay soaking at the front thwarts. He saw himself with his Swiss army knife open and clamped in his teeth, dragging his middle-aged body up the beach of Cross Island, dreadful commando on a midnight rescue operation, slashing what the local men called beatniks, snapping orders to Ellen, as Gus, mouth agape with admiration, cried, "Daddy!" When he laughed then, the flashlight drifted from the chart, the boat drifted from its course, and he remembered *You're really not good at this, are you?*

And Gus need hardly be available for clumsy rescue on an island sixteen miles from home. And why should Ellen be there? What made him think she'd steal a dinghy—she, who didn't swim and whose love of the ocean had nothing to do with her setting herself on its surface? Because. Because Prioleau had no place else to go. That's when you find places, he told himself: when there's no place else to go. That's how you found Patoka Plains. That's how you found Potter, Maine. And that's how come you're being steered by a smelly engine on lightless water to an island that's been abandoned since the Coast Guard closed their station there after the war. It's where you've been heading since your father got you to a college you could hardly limp through. It's where you've been aimed since you straddled the roof of a house and told yourself, Go ahead and laugh, it's all right. He sneezed.

The great combines in Illinois had slowly roared across the wheat or soybean fields, and he'd never had the wit to think of them as anything but ships. Grackles and blackbirds flew up around them, like the gulls in coastal France around what he remembered best, of all the decent memories from that short time: a man who might have been old, who surely was curved and knobby and small, strapped behind a horse and guiding a plow made of wood with an iron wheel, the man in dull colors, and the horse a dull brown, and the little field he worked a bright yellow-green. In the center of his field was a square of sandbags, and in the center of the square was a 20-mm. antiaircraft cannon with its round drum of shells. The German strapped into the shoulder harness of the gun had stepped up a little metal ladder to depress the elevation of the gun, and as the farmer leaned back in his straps, so had the gunner leaned in his, following the plow in its careful geometric trimming with the high round guns—right, then straight along, right, then straight along, right, then straight along, right again. Prioleau, sitting with his back to a stone wall up a slight rise from the field, had heard the gunner, growing bored, cry, "Ow! Ow! Ow!" His loader had roared laughter, and the farmer, looking up for the first time, hearing the make-believe fire and, seeing the cannon aimed down at him, had slowly placed his hand on his heart in a mockery of wound. The loader had stood to attention and had clapped his applause. The farmer had removed his brimless straw hat and, in his traces, had bowed. *You're no bloody fucking good to us at all.*

Prioleau remembered having thought that the small farmer in the small field, followed in his progress by wheeling seagulls, looked like some kind of boat. The combines in Illinois had seemed like battleships careering through high waves, and, often, on a call in the countryside, he'd stopped the van on small roads to watch the reaping over enormous fields, the machines disappearing and taking most of the sound with them, then appearing again a quarter of a mile off to bring the noise back. In the later years, he remembered, he'd eaten his lunch at the side of a country road, tasting no meat or bread or bottled beer, smoking cigarettes before he knew he'd lit them, and telling himself that he and Louisa were adults, were sufficiently adept, each of them, at taking care of themselves, and that if someone was being used, they were using wisely and well—the use was fruitful, you weren't alone when you needed not to be, and you didn't think you were vanishing since there was a person there, in the other chair or on the other side of the bed, and when you whined in your sleep or grumbled in your waking, you were heard and even listened to, and there was more than that.

If it wasn't love, it was comfort. And each had made the other feel wise, once in a while, and even necessary. Sniffing and squinting at the dark water, he thought that one day Gus, if Gus stayed alive, might demand that he explain about her. He knew that he would say, "We were friends. We were grateful to each other," and that he would feel cheap.

Thinking of her, and then of her father, he wondered if Gus thought of him as crazy, too. He was a buried man to the boy who had grown up with Mike, who seemed a founding member of the large club of boyish men to whom it is necessary that they celebrate their lives because they breathe. And he remembered the afternoon when Gus was sixteen and had phoned him at work. They'd argued, all of them, snapping at one another, during breakfast; it had been about Gus's wanting to skip school for reasons not much weaker than Prioleau's arguments for insisting he attend. Gus phoned him later, and they stumbled and muttered and paused before each other, listening to the crackle of emptiness over the wire. And Prioleau, watching Lilah do the most useful work in the office, listening to Mackenzie whistle "The Teddy Bears' Picnic" in a funereal rhythm, and wanting with great desperation to say something comforting and intimate to Gus, had shouted into the telephone, "You know, we have to sit down, one of these nights, and put a quart of beer on the table, hon, and really *talk*."

What was worst about it was not his foolishness and evasion, for he expected them of himself. It was Gus's assumption of exactly his tone and key, his willingness to escape his father the way his father dodged him: "Damn right, Tony. You bet. Hey, I'll talk to you tonight, okay?"

It was Ellen they relied on, he knew—not as buffer or referee, for they didn't only fail at understanding each other; he and Gus knew, sometimes, or at least they once had known, how to hug and, once, hold hands, and of course protect each other from what each suspected was a tendency of the world to devour fathers and children, using the fathers and children as teeth. It was Ellen they relied on as continuum, the medium in which they lived. If they couldn't talk now, or kiss each other good night or goodbye, her presence seemed to say, they might do better another time. And what was wonderful, Prioleau told himself, hoping that Gus knew it too, was that such utility was accident: Ellen lived her life, like a creature in a field, because that was what she did. Her service to them was very likely unintentional; they were other creatures in the same field. And, knowing not much more to think about her absence or possible destination, he sat in the borrowed boat and prayed that he steered toward her, and mourned in case he didn't.

He had struck out for Birch Point, and had run between Salt Island and Larrabee Cove, and the harsh coldness of the ocean was incontestable, and he shook. The light ran like water as he let the wheel go and tried to take a compass reading of 165 between the south end of Salt Island and the tip of Bear Island, shapes in the blackness. And now he was coming up on groundswells near the Avery Point light, which looked like a match in the fog. He heard the Avery Point horn and he saw, dreams of a burning city, the Potter towers, three miles down. Using the shrouded tower lights for a bearing, he went into black Machias Bay.

He heard the slap and suck and break of water on the

Old Man, and he grew frightened enough to turn the motor off and listen. The sounds jumped at him harder, and he thought, *Ocean!* and felt suddenly, in the scoot and churn of the little boat on hard tide, how vast the sea was. He dropped the flashlight and chart and turned the starter, and when the motor caught, he licked his lips. He retrieved the light and played it ahead, to his left. Seeing the white foam of water running through rocks which ringed the Old Man —two tiny islands with a narrow channel between them, joined at the top by a bridge of stone—he headed right, moving the light so he could see the humped shapes of the cormorants which flew from the single bald pine, stunted, which stood atop the leftmost island, the orange-yellow lichen spattered with guano and a luminescent moss, white water running at the base. Alone in blackness, with only the dead island in sight, he could have been off the Scandinavian coast. He might as well have been. This wasn't anyplace to do with what he'd called home, where he'd been born to circulate in hot counties with a lonely schoolmaster who often was mother, father, architect, and carpenter for them. This was another country from the one of make-believe planes and soldered circuits and wandering women in cars. This was as far as he could go. This, after fifty-one years, was where he'd been traveling to.

And *from*. From Mike, among other origins of flight. It had been a year ago that Ellen had called from home to the office, reporting a conversation with Gus about which Prioleau had not wanted to hear, and which she forced him to listen to, as he sat in the music of Mackenzie's whistling and Lilah's soft voice instructing the softer-voiced, shy, enormously muscled fishermen and craftsmen who wanted the money she could provide but who hated asking a woman for help.

"It was like he was ten and I was pretty," Ellen said on the phone. "I was changing after some garden work, and there I was, all breasts and underwear, and in comes our huge sixteen-year-old with his acne and dirty jeans, just *staring*. I put on a bathrobe and I waited, because he didn't look good. You know that look his lips get?"

Prioleau grunted, sympathy and apprehension at once, and he waited.

"He said, 'Do you hear from Mike?' And I said, 'You know I don't, honey. Do you miss him again?' And he said, 'He was only my father for a while, why should I miss him?' It was ugly, Tony. You know how he is when he gets the reins in his teeth that way, he doesn't let go. It was like *Perry Mason*, with this big beautiful kid coming at me from six different directions, cross-examining me. Did I get letters, did I hear from his family out there, didn't I ever write to tell him how Gus was doing? You know?"

Prioleau said, "What I know is what I hear in your voice you told him. You pulled both triggers at once."

"Not right away. I was very reasonable and very courteous. I just told him that it was better this way, because what had happened was so extreme there was no way to be rationally in touch with a man you run away from without much warning."

"You talked like a teacher," Prioleau said. "And of course he hated that."

"Hate is not quite strong enough to use in this case."

"It's the worst I know," Prioleau said.

"Listen. He walked around the room, touching things. He touched a pillow. And something about the way he did that—he was thinking about sex."

"He's always thinking about sex."

"About us and sex."

"Probably that, too."

She said, "So then he stops, he's standing next to the bed, and all of a sudden he grabs the pillow and throws it at me! His face was like a dog's—it was *rage*, Tony, a dog at a throat. Brr."

Prioleau breathed out over the phone, and the static of her sigh in response lay between them. He cut through it to bring her back: "I'm sorry I wasn't there to get some of that for you."

"No, I'm *glad* you weren't. He'd have hit you. You'd have hit him back. It was very terrible. Something would have happened."

An old woman with strong arms showing through a tight boy's shirt was weeping at Mackenzie's desk, and Mackenzie was doing her no good, and Prioleau watched them with sorrow, wondering whether he should fire Mackenzie, or simply fire himself.

Ellen was saying, "Tony?"

"Yes," he said. "Then what? He's going off on a cross-country hitchhike to find his original substitute father?"

"Don't make fun of it. Anything could happen. Anything. He's at a dangerous age."

Prioleau said, "I'm not making fun. I don't mean to be. I'm being worried."

"I am, too. Because—listen to this. He started ranting at me. *Vicious.* And he sounded like both of us, Tony. That was awful. I could hear our voices inside his. He was shouting. 'Sure. You can bite it off and go halfway across the country with your boyfriend. I mean, your lover, excuse me. But what about me? You fucked him and had me, but what about me? What about Mike? What does *he* get? *He's* the one who took care of us!' Something like that. Something ugly."

Prioleau heard his breath on the phone again. He said, very gently, "You didn't bother to tell him how you earned as much money as Mike to support you all? Or that people get a choice in their lives? That loving somebody makes a difference in what you do with your life, with or without a boy's opinion or approval, or whatever the hell I'm trying to say?"

"I said I loved you and I didn't love Mike. I said I lied to Mike when I met up with him in San Diego, and I lied to you when I left and stayed away, and I didn't want to live that way anymore and it was my life."

"Let me—thank you, Ellen. Thank you."

"Oh, shut up."

"Let me guess what he said next—about how it didn't seem to matter what he thought and what Mike felt, and he bit at his nails and slammed out."

"Pretty close. He managed to say 'fuck' three or four more times."

"Naturally. But: thank you."

"Don't you act like this, please."

"I'm sorry."

"Tony, dammit, for *what*?"

"Just sorry."

He thought of hot toast with so much butter fingers fell through it, and coffee ground with chicory served up with cream that rimmed the cup. He thought of Ellen's hair, and how for years she'd tried sounding Southern when she spoke so that the Yankees of Potter would know—so that Prioleau would know—that she was part of this man's language and life. He thought of Gus, and the smell of his armpits, and how Ellen had rhapsodized on the boy's sweet odor turned to the yeasty odor of growing up. He looked behind him at the twin-bridged stone clumps beaten by the Atlantic as the boat bucked for Cross Island and Northwest Harbor, which he'd been to once and would try once more to find—the wide sandy beach, the freshwater stream where mussels clung, the wrecked Coast Guard station, and perhaps the people, he would try to say, in any language he knew, who were his.

Art Boots was doing several ritual acts of dope smoking at the wide pool of Cross Island's Northwest Harbor spring, in the forest, away from the beach. Since he used big kitchen matches to light his corncob pipe containing opium and hashish, and since he wasn't content when he lit up unless the pipe sent gouts of light flaring before his face, he was glowing in the dark. He was also, since he toked with affection and since he was stoned, moaning a good deal, crooning to the plastic stem he sucked on. And since he was a leader, he was loud in calling the attention of those he led to the process of which he was a part. "Hey, somebody, hey: *get* some."

Wanda wore a black silk warm-up jacket with Air Force insignia on the left breast. On the back, in yellow thread, a dragon breathed fire. Over its head, in an arc, was KOREA. She wore combat boots, had gray sweat pants tucked into them, and graying brown hair tucked up into her black-watch cap. She smoked Camels, drank brandy from a U.S. issue canteen, and sat with her back against a tree, watching Art Boots.

Downstream, on the beach, not too far from the line of kelp which showed how high the tide came up, Gus was feeding driftwood to the fire while he listened to the radio he'd helped to carry from the 14-foot catboat tied to a lobsterman's anchor buoy. It was what Art called their listening radio. Gus had also helped them row, in the plexiglass pod beached nearby, what Art called their delivery radio, square, khaki-colored, very heavy, and understood only by Wanda, whose job it was to send the message they would send. On the smaller shortwave radio, voices from Canadian waters told of routine offshore patrols and the arrest of two teenagers who were drunk in a power boat.

Wanda came down, chunky and handsome, flicking a butt in a boy's dream of offhandedness. "He's getting amorous," she told Gus. "He always does when he gets full of dope."

"And he always is full of dope," Gus said.

"Fucking Indians," she said, squatting like a soldier at the fire. "Can't handle booze and they can't handle dope. Tonto and his friends, they can't manage stimulants." She shook her head. "So how are you, little brother?"

He shrugged.

"Don't be nervous," she said. "Or, go ahead and then don't worry about it. You never got arrested before?"

He shook his head.

"It's how you tell them. It's a message. It gets in the papers and somebody reads the truth, for a change. Anyway, they might not even get us. We jam them a while, they go a little crazy, we get on the boat and sail away. Dump the radio, go home, call *The Village Voice* and tell them about it. REBELS SEND ATOMIC SUBS IN CIRCLES, you know? I really dig the idea of all those submarines ending up under the ice or someplace."

"You can really do that?"

"*We* can, brother. Yes. I know everything in the world about radios you want to know. Art told you."

The voice came from the edge of the woods: *"Wanda!"*

She stood and sighed and pushed at the watch cap. "I'm going back there and mess with the horny Indian," she said.

"Kind of take his edge off so he stays quiet." She looked down at him. "Want to participate a little?"

"Uh, no, thanks, Wanda. Thank you."

"Yeah, you're still young, aren't you? Okay. See you later."

Gus stood as she left. He looked out to sea and saw darkness and the rolling water. He looked along the curved beach and saw, at the far end of the small cove, great rocks on which the tide broke. At the farthest rocky point, he saw motion, something bright, then only the stone and the haze which seemed to seal the sea away from moon and stars. The radio was silent, and he bent to turn the tuner. A deep voice in another language growled directions. He turned the radio off and heard sounds from Art Boots, angry Indian come home to lodge a protest on behalf of his victimized people, and reclaim his native land by canceling the Potter towers' transmission.

Gus walked away from that thought, not only because it didn't bear too much standing next to, but also, and mostly, because he could hear Art Boots snuffling and saying *ooh*, splashing with Wanda at the margin of the woods. He clapped his hands, as if the noise might soothe his gut or drive his thinking up and out, and he belched and walked farther along, toward the high rocks where he'd seen something—images of Coast Guard sailors carrying guns—just possibly flicker and go away.

He walked over flats that would yield sweet clams at low tide, and through marsh grass from which deerflies flew up. He climbed a steep ramp of stone, then had to use his hands to pull himself over a spur in which a million years of wind had eaten dish shapes and holes. When he stood, his hands in his dungaree pockets as the sweat dried and steady wind blew fog and salt and the vegetable smell of the flats into his face, he looked out to see the Potter towers, glowing, winking, so numerous and tall that he knew no one, not even a woman tough as Wanda, might silence or confuse whatever lay beneath and behind them. He thought again of the Coast Guard, or of the patrols which the Navy must mount, and he remembered how much he had loved Mike's long stories of combat in the Pacific, and books about dying under fire, and the kick of a rifle when Mike showed him how to shoot when he was small, and how he'd fought with Tony about that big quiet man's disdain for the Boy Scout uniform Gus had coveted and which his mother had finally bought for him at Sears.

Gus lifted his chin and posed, looking into the foggy Atlantic: Portrait of Romantic Youth in Conflict, he told himself, working hard to keep his grin. War babies have it tough. Yeah. Tell it to the Indians. If you're not careful, I'm giving you back to the Indians, his mother used to say, smiling. And they were all supposed to smile together at that, because Tony had some Indian blood. Unwise parental joke. According to Tony, every joke was serious if you looked behind it hard enough. Hey, Tony: *look*.

E llen walked around and around the abandoned Grassy Point Coast Guard post, which lay at the far end of the forest, on the other side of Cross Island from the radio and the fire and her son, whom she had spotted, she was sure it was he, when she'd climbed the rock outcrop and peered down at the cove. She closed her yellow slicker and walked, very purposefully, in the same circle. High grass lay behind her in a trail which also lay before her. The station, once a two-story house, had no windows left, and only one of its two doors. Most of the floorboards downstairs were gone, and all of the upstairs flooring and the steps—plundered by fishermen for outbuildings, probably, or for extra rooms on a saltbox house. Swallows lived there. In daylight, they'd explode around her when she walked in.

The problem was, she wasn't crazy. And only crazy mothers were supposed to hunt for their kids, and steal someone's precious dinghy and motor to get to them, after guessing that the tall straight back and curly head she'd seen a quarter of a mile out to sea in a catboat, heading east, was her son, making for his favorite boyhood place. Despite the binoculars, and the clear view down to the cove from their window, there was no way to be certain, yet she'd moved without thinking, without leaving word for Tony—whom, she suspected, had by now decided that she'd left him: the abandonment he'd waited so long for her to perform.

Mike had told her, when he was only a little drunk and only, then, bemused—the fury had come later—when they'd been fighting and she'd been speculating on where Tony was, that it was *storybook* stuff, lovers and fathers and children separated by so many miles and so much time. Storybook romance, to think of bringing all that separateness together in the middle of a perfectly satisfactory existence: she'd felt childish for hours, thinking of his big hands as they shaped wood and made real objects of use to grownups in their lives. Yes. And here she was, being a fool, frightening everyone, including herself, fresh from a stolen boat and a reconnoiter, spying on her grown son, pacing circles around a haunted house.

But it *was* Gus. And he was with some scruffy characters who looked like part of a motorcycle gang. And he was standing, all alone, like a lonely boy, beside a fire on a beach in the dark. And she was forty-five years old. She ought to know better.

"Better than what?" she said to the high grass and the

broken house, the forest of dark trees. Twenty years later, and she still was in transit, collecting men at the edge of the sea.

When she was little, and her parents were planning their party, they'd left her alone while they went shopping, and that was when she discovered the maraschino cherries. Uncle LaRue was still at the lot he owned and at which her father worked, but rarely after five o'clock, and not on the day before his New Year's Eve bash, when relatives she heard of all year but hardly saw would be coming to drink all night, until her father passed out or her mother picked a fight with one of the pretty aunts for what her mother would call unforgivable.

The old three-story house under very old maples next to the Pike was silent. Snow slowly fell in big floating flakes, and in the pantry, wide floorboards under her feet, she roamed in search of after-school snacks. Ellen stood on a dining-room chair to forage. It was a big jar, almost too big for her small hands, but she managed it. She ate sweet, sticky cherries with her fingers, and she drank juice over the rim of the jar. She wasn't ten and smart for nothing. She carried the jar into the kitchen and filled the empty space with water, turning the contents a rusty red-brown. Then she washed up and climbed the stairs to her room, where she lay on her bed, clutching her stomach. When she heard her parents, she dragged out *The Wonderful Adventures of Nils*, in order to be found in guiltlessness.

The room was blue, because once, when her mother asked her favorite color, she had said the first one that came to mind—dark blue. So the two windowsills of the corner room were enamel blue, and the bedspread was Prussian blue, and the linoleum was a white-streaked navy, and the wallpaper was a textured bamboo pattern in blue and dark green, and there were Prussian-blue curtains to match the spread, and a desk chair with a shiny blue cushion. *Nils* lay on the bed, and Ellen lay at the other end, curled onto herself and gasping. Her mother found her, diagnosed a burst appendix a few minutes later as she held her head in the black-and-white-tiled bathroom, and it was only when her father was starting the car and her mother was calling the doctor to ask that he meet them at the emergency ward that Ellen confessed.

So at seven o'clock that night, Ellen sat on the rocker in the living room, leaning back and forth, back and forth, working on her knowledge of injustice and the fact that kids have it hard, rocking her anger, sustaining it, as her father came in with her coat and boots and scarf. He sat on the sofa—it was dark brown and covered with a kind of wool that pricked her bare skin when she lay on it—and he said, "Pumpkin, do you know what consequences are?"

"I don't care."

"It's what happens because—if one thing happens, something else happens because of it. That's a consequence. You make one thing happen by doing the first thing. You ate the cherries. Do you know what a Manhattan is?"

"Daddy, this isn't *school*, you know." She could feel the pressure high in her nose, and she knew that her face was red and that she'd cry soon.

"But you know. It's the drink I make sometimes at parties."

"And everybody gets drunk. Sure."

"I wanted to serve some Manhattans tonight. I wanted to put some cherries in them."

"I said I was sorry! I didn't eat them *all*, you know."

"Just most of them. And you ruined the rest with water."

"There's enough left, Daddy."

"So the consequence is that you get dressed up warm, and you walk exactly three blocks, and you turn to the left at the streetlight near the mailbox, and you see if Mr. Matuski's store is still open, which I think it might be, and you spend your own money on a jar of cherries for us, and you come right home. I'll wait near the door. I'll expect you. Understand? That's the consequence."

She courteously informed her father that Mr. Abraham Lincoln had already freed the slaves, in case he hadn't heard the news, and then she dressed—he checked her coat pocket to see that her money was inside—and she left. She didn't say goodbye, and she knew that he was smiling, and she marched. Instead of walking toward Matuski's, she turned the first corner and went back, down the street behind theirs, moving away from the Pike and downhill. She passed a closed gas station that was shaped like the Shell insignia, and when a dog inside the garage began to bark, she ran. There were fewer houses, larger lots, and then fields. She recognized the diner they sometimes stopped at for Cokes and the big low building where the United Parcel Service trucks came from, and then there was an endless field with baseball diamonds. She walked it in the dark, kicking the feathery snow, and turning, once, to look at her footprints in the bright moonlight. But the field was too large and she was too small, so she ran for a while, until her pride arrested her, and she walked again, urging the time to pass, sensing that *now* he'd expect her to be halfway home, and *now* on their corner, and *now* on the squat brick stoop.

She stopped to look toward the road, expecting a slow-cruising Buick with her father's big hands on the wheel. A wood-paneled station wagon went by, and she walked deeper into the park. There was ice on the iron barbecues and on the benches, ice on the seats of the swings. She climbed onto one anyway, and she didn't swing, but rocked, though not in anger now so much as fright. The park felt gigantic, and dark all around her. She didn't turn to see how bright the moon might be; she rocked slowly back and forth on the swing, feeling the night, assuming that the only light in suburban Philadelphia lay on the little assembly of swings and seesaws before her.

She listened for the sound of a car's horn or her father's anxious voice. From the forest on the other side of the monkey bars something called a low complaint. "Owl," she said loudly, to prove to whatever witness that she wasn't scared. As further proof, she hopped from the swing, walked to the monkey bars—her neck was so stiff from being held erect and fearless that she reached to rub it, then stopped lest she give herself away. She climbed the icy pipes and insisted that she balance herself on the next-to-highest tier of bars, leaning her knees against the topmost. She put her hand over her eyes and stared into the dark forest. "Owl," she said. "I keep telling you, it's just a dumb bird."

Then she heard the snarl, and then the roar, and she cried a high wail and slipped on the bars and fell. She lay on the snow and cried, tried to throw up but couldn't, found that she could breathe after all, and then remembered the beast sound from behind her. She was on her hands and knees when the light struck her. It was a big car, skidding and slipping on the field, bucking toward her in low gear. She closed her eyes and the lights grew brighter, the growl of engine louder, and when she was opening her mouth to wail, the shape bulked high in the lights like shadows in her room after nightmare, and it swooped upon her, then stopped, glaring.

It was Uncle LaRue, of course, violating everyone's idea

of punishment. It was her father's father, long called Uncle by her mother, soon enough to adopt the name himself. He was as tall as her father, and broader, and softer of chin and voice; he smelled of Prince Albert pipe tobacco and the Lava soap he used at the garage. He hugged her, he kissed her nose, he said, "You're all right, yes?" and he led her by a hand to the car.

She sat in the front with him and looked down the lights at the little circle of swings and seesaws, the island she had sought in a sea of snow and early evening. Uncle LaRue relit his pipe with a big kitchen match struck against the dashboard. She watched it flare before him, and the sudden brightness in the dark car made her cozy and safe and adventuresome-feeling.

"So," he said, turning the lights of the car off in case there were police, he explained, and driving in the blue moonlight toward the road.

"I didn't get the cherries."

He tapped a bottle beside him. "Matuski's was open," he said.

"Were they scared?"

"Yes."

"Were you?"

"A little. I thought you'd take care of yourself all right. But I was worried, sure. Were you?"

"Nope."

"Not a little?"

"Nope."

"Ah."

They bumped off the curb and into the dimly lit road. He turned the lights on. The tires hissed in the melting snow. Uncle LaRue's pipe steamed good smells. The streets weren't familiar. They passed small houses close together, and then a stretch of wide road with stores on either side where trolley rails gleamed. Uncle LaRue drove toward what seemed to be a wall of shops, and she pressed her feet together, then relaxed them when she saw that they were in an alley and then near a door over which a light shone. He said nothing, so she did too. She followed him through the door and there was a tiny corridor of stools at a marble-topped counter. A fat man in a white uniform was combing a huge mustache. When he saw Uncle LaRue, he smiled a very tired smile and drew a cup of coffee, then raised his eyebrows and pointed with his thumb at Ellen. Uncle LaRue said, "Milk and pie, Herbie," then went to a telephone on a shelf above the Coke cooler.

Ellen closed her eyes when Herbie put the pie down, for fear that it was cherry, but it was apple, a wide slab, and she said her thanks and bent to it. She heard Uncle LaRue telling his son the news, but she didn't concern herself with his words or what her father's reply might be. She ate the second piece that Herbie set before her, and looked down the counter toward the small window at the front of the diner, where on a strange street the cars of strangers went to places she was certain she never had seen. The pie was gluey on the roof of her mouth, and the best food she'd eaten in her life. Uncle LaRue sat beside her, smoothing his gray hair back, blowing his big nose into a paper napkin, saying things to Herbie that were too low for her to hear, though she was next to them. She felt his stringy strong arms through his coat when he carried her from the diner, and she lay against him on the drive home, listening to his pipe against his teeth, smelling the Prince Albert and the oil that always clung to his clothes, feeling his arm as he shifted gears, and wondering then—or was it only now that she wondered, so many years later, him alone in his attic room with his match-sticks, with everyone else dead except Mike—whether she was meant to be rescued this way by large men, or whether she had learned to command such tender help.

He had seemed to understand. It was after the funeral, and after she had served canapés and hamburger Stroganoff made with cream of mushroom soup, and a good deal of Rolling Rock beer and two kinds of whiskey to relatives she'd called by going through her dead mother's battered telephone book alphabetically. It was eleven o'clock at night in her twenty-second year in the season before Christmas, when the relatives were gone and she hadn't reached her father because you can't place a call to every house in New Mexico asking for the man you mostly called Daddy and spent too many months of your life chasing from boarding-house to salesmen's hotel. She and Uncle LaRue sat in his little room upstairs, he with the wakefulness of old age or madness or both—his white eyebrows were still, his large red nose dry, his eyes too, the constant sense of preoccupation like a mask imposing calm upon his flesh—and she, now in a nightgown and slippers, offering the jar of cherries before her so that he could reach with the fork she'd brought. He took none, but he held the fork in sympathy, as if at any second he might use it, and she dipped and chewed, drip-ping syrup and crushing heavy sweetness around her tongue, really sensing nothing but the wet weight of syrup, and eating rapidly, head bent to the jar, until she had to place it carefully on the floor and let her head droop, and start to cry.

Uncle LaRue dropped his fork and walked, on his bare clean feet, in dark serge trousers and his brown horn-buttoned sweater, to kneel before her where she sat, and to hug her as if she were tiny. She smelled the tobacco, and the Lava he still used because she bought it for him. She smelled the camphor that lingered in his sweater, and the whiskey she had carried upstairs for his mourning's nightcap. She started to rock, and he held her while she cried for more than her mother. "I know you been scared," he said in his rough low voice. "It's hard when you're little and they send you out on your own at night. Your daddy's been scared for you too, you know."

She nodded her thanks and rubbed her face in his sweater. When he asked her if she wanted milk and pie at a special place he knew, she kissed his bristly white whiskers and carried the cherries downstairs. She sat on the living-room rocker and was quite still for a while. She began to rock back and forth, but stopped herself, got up to wash the dishes and get some sleep before rising early to drive to school and teach, come home to climb the stairs to Uncle LaRue, who would be at his window and counting, having counted her too as she turned off the Pike to their house.

"You'd think I'd have learned better," she said. They were probably, even then, erecting tents and rolling the raceway flat. Men were building bandstands for the Sunrise County Fair, and other men with grease in their knuckles were tuning engines for the Demo Derby. Mothers would hold their children's hands as cars crashed and the boys howled their pleasure at the impact. That lardy, rich-voiced preacher would be sleeping on his wallet, waiting to deliver a service crying danger to the nation's soul. It would be a day in the summer sun for Down East families, and you'd think she'd have learned better.

And then she asked herself again, following her own trail in the dark, around the house, through wet grass: "Better than what?"

Art Boots woke because he rarely slept for long. Sometimes, he'd explained to Gus, when they were all getting friendly in Manhattan down among the Puerto Ricans on Avenue B, young braves went crazy with anger, but not enough to kill. They'd prowl outside towns too small for military detachments, and they'd find a drunk farmer or cowboy or even male child, and they'd slit his eyelids so he couldn't ever sleep again. "That's a lot of staring, you know?" he told Gus he had told Wanda. She'd been in her oil-on-canvas phase, and she'd painted a lean white face with enormous eyes, unlidded. Hung on the wall opposite Art Boots's mattress on the cockroach- and butt-littered floor, the face had watched Art and Wanda make love.

That was when Wanda worked for the technicians at Bell Telephone and Art was dropping out of Indiana, where he'd been a teaching assistant in the American Studies program. In New York, he worked for the Department of Health as a venereal disease detective. A clinic would pass him the name of a voluntary patient who had listed his or her "contacts," as they liked to call the people who had smeared their emissions on one another. Art told Gus his routine would be to visit each contact and counsel a trip to the clinic, while trying to extract the names of other contacts. His conclusions, after a month on the job, were, first: "There ain't no one in the city of New York don't fuck everyone else," and, second: the work was highly dangerous and underpaid. Fifth in a chain of contacts had been a contender for the lightweight championship of the world, and fourth had been a heavily muscled Mohawk Indian who did high girder work on a new building in the financial district near Trinity Church. After Art had visited each, the boxer visited Art, while he ate hot dogs at the stand just off the Staten Island Ferry entrance. Bloody and cut, but mostly bruised beneath and over the ribs, Art had left the public-health field and had taken up market research, which paid by the week and which confined itself to processing questionnaires about dishwashing liquid. The pay was better and the hazards were merely psychic—a kind of danger, he'd explained, with which he'd always lived. Often, he would describe for Gus how he thought the Hispanic and the Indian had performed their sex: he always portrayed the Indian as recipient of the boxer's love, and this image had become for him a useful emblem of what he warred with. "We have taken it in the ass for two hundred years," he'd say he said to Wanda, who by now was working with clay at night, using a kiln at Pratt to which a friend had access. She made Indian bowls, Indian-*looking* bowls, and they stored hash and grass in them, and roaches for emergencies, and the money they made by working during the day at market-research jobs, on one of which they had met the curly-headed boy who drank too much beer during his lunch break and who was too nervous to sustain a conversation for more than minutes.

The three of them practiced shoplifting together, though Gus refused to participate in the minor breaking-and-entering jobs Art occasionally sallied forth on of an evening. Gus lived with them for a week before Wanda grew bored with clay, with Pratt, and with New York, and especially with her certainty that her first husband would find her, by chance, on a street corner and try to force her home. So: by stolen car to Massachusetts, where they purchased equipment, and by second stolen car to the shores of New Hampshire, where Wanda's parents kept a summer house and a small boat. Then: by stolen catboat up the coast to Maine, along which they did some pickup seamanship and thievery, taking Gus home toward the towers which Art had never seen, since he'd left New England before they were erected.

So the story went. And here they were, the kid off walking the beach and pretending to stand watch, Wanda adjusting her clothes and zipping her jacket to the neck, Art Boots reminding Wanda, "Just because I sometimes talk like an asshole and do these drug numbers, I want you to remember I am not a patsy."

"No," she said, in the bug-ridden darkness, "you're not a patsy. You're a crazy fool."

"I am on the *war*path."

"You are impotent."

The match flared, the pipe burbled, and Art Boots sighed. "You want some?" His voice was weak because he was holding the smoke in. When he had let it out, and had sighed again, he said, "Sex is a distraction."

"Sex is sometimes difficult for you, is what you mean," she said. "Okay. Listen, I'm not complaining, except I am so bored with this."

"You tell the kid to watch those subs come up like dolphins asking for directions tomorrow, then you tell me about bored, queenie."

"Queenie? What's that, I'm a dyke because you can't get it up more than soft-boiled? Is that it? You're such a goddamned—listen, I can live without your cock, Art. I'm talking about running around like this."

"We're not running around," he said along the stem of the pipe. "We're lying around." He giggled.

"That's what I mean," Wanda said.

"You know, I really cannot get myself to give a shit *what* you mean. Except, pay attention now, we are not doing sociology on Bleecker Street with coffee and existentialists from NYU. You could get yourself shot in the tit for this. And maybe not just by Uncle Sammy and the machine-gun types. I'm talking *me*."

"Oh," she said, in a voice from *My Friend Irma,* "you're so *man*ly."

Prioleau, the motor off, was drifting, wind in his face and his fingers stiff with cold. He couldn't use the light now, in case there were people watching, so he couldn't use the chart to match the shape of the beachless little cove into which the boat bobbed. He thought, though, that this was not the place he'd been to before, and as the breakers showed their strength, he became certain. There was a seven- or eight-foot rock face here, beyond the round stones on which the waves rumbled, and he knew that he might lose the boat. From the musette bag, working by touch, he took a roll of gauze bandage, a roll of tape, and the antiseptic cream, and he zipped them into his jacket pockets. He felt for the knife in his trousers. He was equipped—for a picnic, family picnic, nothing more. He was as much of a Boy Scout as Gus had wanted, once, to be. There was a single oar in the boat, and he hefted it, reversed it, prodded into the rocky bottom. It was shallow enough for him to walk, though too fast for him to keep his feet, he thought. And how do you get out of a boat in water like this?

Holding the flashlight, he told himself: You fall. So, with a hip at the edge, he fell, one hand on the boat's painter. He went to his knees, was knocked down face-first by waves, pulled himself up with the rope, losing the flashlight, and thudded his forehead into the ring to which the rope was attached. As deft as ever. The ebb tide sucked at his feet, so he balanced by holding the gunwale, pushing when the tide broke in, planting his feet when it receded. He got, finally, close enough to the small cliff to see that he might wedge the boat among rocks and tie it to a rotting weir post and hope, mostly for Minton's sake, that it would settle and stay. He did what he could, and then, with eyesight adjusting, he started to climb.

The ocean wouldn't let him go, and it was no less than ten minutes before he could catch breath enough, and feign strength enough, to convince his muscles that he could haul himself by his hands to the point where he might find a foothold and then climb. He did that, and then he slid down, climbed back up, fell back into the sea, then started again, and then, at last, rolled over the edge of the little palisade to lie on his back, panting, starting to go cold.

He caught his breath and turned over to hand-and-knee his way up the incline toward level ground. The rock burned his knees, and he began to feel his bruises and the slices made by rock, which were stung now by salt. He saw nothing. Then he saw ferns and brambles, sandy soil, the forest, a more solid blackness in the night. Fog, thready and gathering before, was now massing to settle. Go get some combat. Or some little failure, why not? Go *ahead*. So he did, hearing, *You're no bloody fucking good to us at all.*

He walked into trees, fell over roots, was slapped and slit by branches. When he sneezed, he held his nose, and his ears almost exploded. Insects came up, clouds of gnats, buzzings of deerflies; they hung at his eyes and went up his nose, and

he slapped himself and sneezed into his sleeve in an effort
to be silent. He slapped again, and his wedding ring—Ellen
wore none—bruised his eye. He sneezed into his sleeve,
crushing mucus from the last sneeze over his upper lip, and
he walked ahead, fell ahead, on spongy forest floor, graceless
as ever on peat and moss, and not pausing to consider how
little he knew where he went.

A panic went around the island. Ellen heard the
sounds and simply, without looking for their source or
nature, followed her thigh-deep track in the grass to the
doorless front of the old house, then stepped inside, allowing
herself one quick circuit of the narrow room and finding, by
feel, what she sought: the remains of a fire someone had
made, no doubt on a family picnic or summer vandalism
trip, and a three-foot piece of driftwood which, crouching
now alongside the door, inside, she hefted like a baseball bat,
waiting. A cloud of swallows flew above her, diving near.
She thought of real bats and she shuddered.

The sounds grew louder, then disappeared, and so did
the waxing and waning of insects, the low shriek of distant
owls. Then there was the soughing of high grass, and then
a footfall outside the door.

The large shape—she saw at once that it was too bulky for
Gus—came farther, and then in, and the foot scuffed on the
rotted sill, the shape said, "Oof" as it staggered, and she was
already whipping the wood around, even as the timbre and
tone of the voice registered, so that she was unable to stop
hitting Prioleau very hard on the shoulder blade and was
incapable of crying his name as he made a vicious sound in
his throat and flailed his arms in a mockery of fistfight.

She went to her knees against the wall, covering her face as the open hands slapped and then became fists and a foot came up. She finally said, "Tony!"

And it stopped him in mid-swing, so that he stumbled. "Pardon?" he said, so politely that she laughed.

The shape backed up, came forward, and when she felt his fingers, she seized them. "Me," she said.

And of every question he might have found to put, he said, with delicacy, "Ellen? Is it okay I'm here?"

She pulled herself up along his hand and arm and felt for his face, then neck, and held on. He did too, though uncertainly, as if she were fragile. She knew at once what his question meant, and the tension of his wrists and forearms, but she said nothing in reply, wondering if she still needed the advantage which, even here, she felt herself insist upon.

The fire was out, or mostly out; a few coals lived beneath white ash, and the wind kept them secretly alive. Wanda had coaxed Art from the margin of the woods, and they slept at the dark fire in army surplus mummy bags, two green cocoons or corpses near a sloppy puddle of sandy gear. Gus, wearing a sweater, sat under a shawl of blanket on the rocks above the sea like a soldier in winter, like a *Saturday Evening Post* picture of Indians in a story about their perfidy and the white man's courage and loss. The fog collected and settled, and soon he couldn't see Art Boots or Wanda, or the clam flats, or even the ocean which broke not far beneath him. Soon, he knew, the dawn would start heating the day, and the fog would light from within, like a giant globe, and then it would blow off—march off, rather, stalking slowly in front of the wind until they were caught in clarity and compelled to act.

His father had been a technician during the war, and had worked with radio waves and TV. This had been one of his attractions for Art, Gus knew, though he was certain that Wanda had understood how little he comprehended of their plan. Gus knew, or suspected anyway, that their radio would have no effect on the giant transmitters off Potter. And he suspected that Wanda knew it, too. She was here for Art. Art was here because he hated his life—or for a reason, Gus thought, he'd understand when he was much older, and maybe forgiven.

The question, of course, was whether he, or they, would become any older. What they were after was sabotage, treason, something like an act of war.

Forgiven by whom?

I didn't mean forgiven, he corrected himself.

Oh, yes, you did. He had been accepted by Bowdoin, and what he should be doing now was shopping for clothes in Portland at one of the preppy stores. What would a freshman buy? Let's see—30-06 bolt-action rifle and box of shells, a Korean War surplus field radio used for guiding scout planes, the machete of course, and the Very pistol about which Art had lamented until Wanda had come up with extra cash for it. Art had seen a movie in which a man had blown a German vessel out of the water by firing the flare from a Very pistol down an engine hatch, and the idea of a *thunk*, a trail of feathery smoke, and then an explosion, had been captivating to him. What the well-equipped freshman needs for higher education.

I'm sullen, Gus thought, sitting with the blanket over his head and shoulders, holding it closed from inside with both hands. I'm sullen and spoiled and horny for Wanda, also

208 of 276 Frederick Busch

scared. I'm scared of Wanda, Art Boots, the radio, the gun, the machete, the Very pistol, the island, the morning, the Navy, the Coast Guard, and what my parents are doing. Because they're *not* writing me off. She never would, and he never could. Because of her. And I'm essentially a teenage jerk. Which is an insignificant person to be on the morning of the smallest revolution in the history of Indian warfare.

He moved his head suddenly and sniffed, looked around. Then he understood the source of his worry: fog sirens were silent; he heard one, miles away, at Machias, and then none; it was starting. He watched the fog mass itself and start to glow, very faintly. It was starting.

Art growled. His mummy bag wiggled, its foot end came up, and the bag thrashed, a giant larva. Wanda was already partway out of hers and struggling with Art's zipper, which was stuck, and he was swearing, complaining, softly howling. Wanda lay on him to keep him still, and she tugged at the outside lanyard of his zipper until she'd opened enough for him to creep out. She took off the jacket she'd slept in, opened her woolen shirt, took a bar of laundry soap and a toothbrush from a knapsack, and walked toward the stream. When she turned, where the stream splayed out like arteries, near a tide pool, her heavy breasts swung, and Gus held his breath. Then she took off the shirt and scooped water onto herself as she leaned over the pool. She winced and cried out in a high voice—just like any girl someplace, Gus thought. She scooped and lathered and rubbed, her breasts hanging. Gus wanted to be in a cool dim gas station, hearing the men exchange opinions about brake pads while he pretended to listen, but looked instead at a wall behind a shelf of wrenches where there was a calendar photo of a girl with heavy breasts who didn't care if you looked at them.

Art and Wanda spoke while she dried herself with her

shirt—Gus watched as she stretched to reach under her arms —and then dressed in the shirt and jacket and looked tough again. Gus didn't hear what they said because the wind was blowing past him down the cove to where they stood. But he could hear occasional fragments when the wind eddied; Art spoke Gus's name and Wanda shrugged. They wouldn't wait for him because he had nothing to tell, never had known anything about radios or the schedule of offshore patrols. Art was urinating near the cache of equipment as Wanda wrestled the radio and reached behind it to make an adjustment.

I am— "Hey," he called down the beach. "I'm sorry."

Art, bending over their gear, looked up, then stood. The machete in its sheath was on his belt. He was unzipping the canvas rifle case.

Gus stood on the rocks of the point, holding his blanket around him. "I'm too young," he said, too softly for them to hear.

Art smiled at Gus and cupped his scrotum, wriggled his hips. Wanda was blowing the coals into flame and was setting sticks across the fire. The smoke blew into Art's face and he sidestepped, hand still over his balls. Gus sat down again, with his back to Art and Wanda, and watched the fog roll away. He heard the far-off chug of a boat and squinted to see whether it might not be a launch filled with sailors and guns. Though he could see nothing but the hard metallic glint of sun on sea, he heard the boat stop: lobstermen, pausing at traps.

When he turned, he could see Wanda at the radio again, rigging a long line to a nearby tree. Art was in the tree, hauling on the wire. The coffee would boil, and they would sit and drink some. Art would take a hit or two of his mixture, and then he would remove from his knapsack the greasy, often-folded papers he'd prepared. And then, while Wanda kneeled at the radio, thinking thoughts Gus knew he'd be unable to understand even if she wrote them on a blackboard for him—freshman orientation—Art would hold the microphone close to his mouth and start to read what he'd been preparing for weeks.

And the question, now, was surely not of getting off the island. There was one boat offshore, and that belonged to Wanda, courtesy of robbed parents, and he could never reach it; reaching it, he probably couldn't sail it alone. And Art would be standing in the water, legs braced against the tide, pumping 30–06 rounds at him as he swam—a rehearsal for his war, or maybe all the war that Art would need. The only other boat he could leave in would be the one in which they surely all would be forced to, hands locked behind them, under arrest. So the question was simply of getting away. Away from the radio, and Wanda's old eyes, and Art's hash pipe, and the declaration Gus did not want to hear as it went out over the dawn air to collide against the Navy's transmission and slide down into the sea, like water sprayed at a wall.

So the answer—his muscles formed it, and he responded before he thought, *Again*—the answer was to run. He stood. Art, perhaps alarmed by the way he did it, stood too, and Wanda looked over her shoulder as she poured coffee. He stood. He released the blanket. Art pointed, and Wanda stood. Gus was moving, going around the point farthest from them on the beach, where he had thought during the night a movement of bright yellow might have shown. He took off, chuffing and panting, sliding on wet rock out of sight of the beach, then striking for the forest above and away. The ocean boomed here, there were small caverns, and he couldn't hear whether Art Boots was shooting a rifle at him, and he couldn't think about it either, because all he was was fugitive, animal flight. *Again* was all he heard in the surf and caves.

He had reached the far end of the rock bed on which waves broke, and now he had to climb up, sliding on slippery stones and crumbling sandy soil, pulling plants out by the root as he sought for handholds, tearing at the island like a man in despair who tears at his scalp. He got up, hearing nothing but the general roar, and on his knees and elbows wriggled toward the edge of the woods. Then he stood, with his hands clenched at his chest, to look behind him to see whether Art Boots and his technology had risen in pursuit. He was alone. He ran into the forest. He was in his eighteenth year, and in pursuit of what had brought him there.

What they didn't do was exchange information on how Ellen had known of the people on Cross Island and why she had assumed that one of them was hers. They did not go into boat theft or navigation by amateurs even in calm weather. Nor did Ellen ask how Prioleau, too, had learned what she'd discovered. And no one raised the question of Ellen's wordless flight from the house and Prioleau's response to its emptiness. She didn't forbid anything, she thought; but she understood that she had relied on the probability of what they each had done, and on the eventual conjunction of their separateness. And she didn't tell him. She sat with her back against the wall, near the door, close to where she'd slugged him with driftwood, in the ruins of a Coast Guard outpost, and he sat beside her, under diving birds.

"I saw Gus," she said.

"At Northwest Harbor?"

"Did you see him, too?"

"No," he said. "I couldn't get the boat to go that way, I didn't really know how to find it. I just figured he'd be there. Is he all right?"

"He looks healthy enough. I peeked. I didn't see him too well."

"Who's he with? Some guy at Woody's said something about a sex party."

"Some guy at Woody's would. He'd wish. I can't figure it out. There's a big, strong-looking girl there who's dressed like a man. And somebody else I didn't see. Gus's alone. I mean, he stays off, away from the others."

"Doesn't he always," Prioleau said.

"I wonder where he learned to do that?"

"Bad genes, huh?"

Ellen rustled in the yellow slicker, looping her hands to hold her knees bent before her. She leaned against Prioleau, then leaned away. "You're supposed to do your best when you raise a child, so when he's on his own he makes the right decisions. It said that in the Boston *Globe* on Sunday."

"And the Portland papers on Saturday," he said, "and the Manchester papers on Tuesday, and Brazil, probably, two weeks ago. People are having a tough time with their kids."

"So I was wondering, Tony: do we do that, or do we storm the beach and kidnap him?"

He leaned and kissed her on the cheek.

She said, "And?"

"Remember I told you I stormed a beach? In the war. Sneaked onto it anyway, off a fishing boat? Radio, pistol, forged papers, fear, dread, a real civilian commando."

"And you don't approve, in principle, of storming beaches because of that time?"

"I'd love it if he'd let us help him. But it sounds like he's mixed up with a bunch of bums. Beatniks. Some kind of crazy skulduggery. I don't know—" He heard the whistle of cloth and draw of grass before she did, because she'd been listening to what he said, while he, she knew, was making noise more than sense in order to delay a decision he wanted to be hers. She watched him sit straighter. "Did you leave a trail of bread in the forest?" he said.

She pushed off on his shoulder to stand. He reached for the driftwood she'd struck him with, then he stood too. "I hope he doesn't hate us for letting him grow up and then we come here to take it all back."

He whispered, "We're not doing that."

"Well, we are," she whispered back.

"Tell me what you want me to do, Ellen."

"All I knew was to get here. You're going to have—"

He hushed her. They waited. They heard panting, the bursting of insects against something on the move, the crushing of weeds and the rasp of small branches on clothes. A bird screeched a long melody of warning and then went silent. Shadows moved on the sill. Then Tony jumped out of the door and wailed a wordless alarm. She went after him.

And there they were: a bulky middle-aged man with a Cro-Magnon club, crouched in front of a tall boy with a dirty face, its lower half faintly irritated with acne, and the small woman with her braided red hair reaching arms out toward them both. Prioleau stood from his crouch. Gus put his hands behind him. Ellen folded her arms across her chest. They stood in front of the ruined house, between the ocean and the woods, and stared at each other.

Ellen said, "Ask it."

Gus and Prioleau said, "What?"

"If you mind if we're here," she said.

"Who?" Prioleau said.

Gus said, "I beg your pardon?" Then: "You heard it was about Indians, didn't you, Tony?" He clapped his hands before him and nodded once, hard.

Ellen's head dropped almost to her right shoulder as she stared at her son. "Did you arrange this one, Gus?"

Prioleau said, "I'm lost. Who'll tell me about it?"

"Oh—you *child*," Ellen said, still staring.

"Who?" Prioleau said.

She sat where she was: let her legs drop from under her and sat as if she'd been tripped. With her legs before her and her hands on the ground, supporting her torso's sudden weight, she looked up at Prioleau and Gus and said, "Sit down and tell it, Gus. Tony, sit down. If you don't tell it, Gus, I think I can. I will. But you start."

Prioleau said to Gus, "She's ahead of us again."

"No, I got here first," Gus said. But he moved a step closer and sat.

"Are you all right?" Prioleau said.

Gus looked up at him and shrugged.

Ellen saw how young he looked, and she made fists in the dirt, held the sandy earth in her hands so that she wouldn't rise to hold her son. "Sit down," she told Prioleau. "Listen."

Fuck him," Art Boots told Wanda. "We don't need him. You know that."

"You think it's safe to let him, like, *roam?*"

"It's an island, am I right? What's he gonna do on an island? Put a message in a bottle for the Treasury Department? Do the radio."

"At least you don't have to make a goddamned speech."

"I wrote a very lovely and dignified talk, just in case I had to use it."

She said, "I heard enough speeches from you."

"Listen, babe, I heard enough shit from you, too."

"Hey, Art, how about we do business and then get the hell away from each other for a year or two?"

He struck a match and cuddled the pipe.

"Old Gus'll be disappointed if we split," she said. "He's a very romantic kid."

"Yeah. You loved it, didn't you? I mean, you told him so many details, man, I couldn't even remember the story of my life after a while. Alleged story."

"Alleged life," she said.

"Here it comes," Art said. A white boat with two white sails was making for the cove. "You won't even need to use the radio."

She said, "I wouldn't know how, probably, if I did."

"Well, we're on the air, anyway. Contact my broker, would you?"

So Gus talked and Ellen listened, and Prioleau shook his head when he thought they weren't watching him. They weren't. They were looking at each other, and he looked at both of them and tried to understand what Ellen wanted him to know to be true. New York, and journeywork as a clerk, and scratchy nights at the YMCA, and then Art Boots, the Indian revolutionary, and Wanda, who was an artist or a long-line technician for Bell, and the recital of theft and evasion. Prioleau thought of the mysteries he read, and of how many scenes came down to this: the detective—he looked at Ellen, who frowned as she decoded what her child said—with an audience of the guilty and the innocent, who permitted idle talk and an exchange of information useful to the reader until he—*she*—saw fit to shake the kaleidoscope and force events to make sense.

Before he knew he'd say it, Prioleau butted in with, "Stop the towers with *what?* You know what kind of transmitters you're talking about, Gus?"

Ellen said, "Never mind the technical verities, Tony. It doesn't make any difference."

He said, "It's just the only information I happen to possess."

"It doesn't matter," she said. "They weren't doing that."

"What?" Gus said. His face grew younger and younger. Soon, Prioleau thought, Gus would have to turn his shaving brush in for a washcloth, if they sat there much longer, swatting at bugs and listening to Gus confess—which was what he seemed to want to do. Behind them, the window frames and buckled clapboard made faces on the wall of the house. The swallows seethed. Gus said, "What?"

"When you talked with them," Ellen said, "what was the most interesting thing you told them about? What got them the most excited?"

"The towers," Gus said. "Art went crazy. He wanted—the first thing he wanted to do was blow them up."

You're really not good at this, are you?

"You're sure," she said.

Gus sat very still, his legs folded beneath him, his hands folded in his lap. He looked like a disciple, Prioleau thought. "No," Gus said. "No. It was the island. I told them about Cross Island, how the towers screwed up a nice view from the point, and from Potter, and from this place on the island I used to come to a lot when I was a kid."

Prioleau made himself silent, didn't permit himself to comment on the template Gus used for determining when he was and wasn't a kid.

Ellen was nodding, saying, "Sure. I knew it. It's the island, Gus. You see it, Tony?"

Prioleau said, "No." He tried to light a cigarette, but it was too wet. He sat with it in his mouth and looked at the book of wet matches.

"Stop that," Ellen said, and he obeyed. "Gus," she said, "I'd bet you something that this Art Boots person never came from here. I'll bet you. That's why they took you along, sweetheart. So you could show them Cross Island."

"They couldn't afford maps?" Prioleau said, crumbling the damp cigarette in his hands.

"They probably figured that a native son, a good old Down Easter like Gus, he could show them everything they needed. He spent his summers on boats, Tony."

"Yes, ma'am," Gus said. Tony thought of rubber ducks and bubble bath.

"So the radio and all of that—the Indian stuff, that was just to fool you, Gus. It gave them a reason to give you. Oh, he sounds like he's angry, and he's probably part-Indian. But so what? So's Tony. Oh, my. Oh, dear. Gus."

"I don't want to talk about this," Gus said.

"That's all that all of this is good for," she said. "You have to."

"I don't want to talk about it any more, Mom."

"You talked to them about Tony, didn't you? And how he was part-Indian too?"

Prioleau stood and walked back toward the house, because he didn't know where to carry what he finally understood— that Gus had let himself be used, he'd thought, by Indians, so-called, so that his father, Tony, this slow, stupid, faraway father, would join the little revolution, or anyway know, somehow, that Gus loved his daddy and had staged an assault on all the Navy's submarines to send for him. He didn't want Gus to have to see his face. He didn't want to see Gus's. He looked into the empty house, trying to find some place they could leave what Ellen was drawing up.

Somebody croaked in his chest, "A sixty-fourth Indian, maybe. I don't know. Maybe a little more, a little less. Not a lot, pal. I mean, I hardly knew her. She might have been half Negro for all I know. I never did care." He wondered if they heard him.

"So they let you come with them to start an Indian uprising at the Potter towers. You thought Tony would hear about it, and get angry about Indians, and he'd come and fetch you," Ellen said. She turned as if from a telephone, and her voice was low: "It's for you, Tony."

Still looking into the cold darkness of the house, Prioleau said, "I'd have come to get you. I'd have come anyway, Gus."

"So you came up here to start a war with that ridiculous speech-on-the-radio business and bring the armed forces of America to a dead stop. And they let you come so they could follow you to this island, which would be perfect for something *else* they had in mind. Gus? Honey? You think that's it?"

"I would," Prioleau said. "What else, though?" He turned, but they weren't listening to him. They weren't looking in his direction. They sat opposite one another, on the ground, and they spoke to each other about him, who stood at the hollowed-out house.

Gus said, "Ma."

"Baby," she said. "Sweetheart, I hope—"

Prioleau saw it, high and arcing, trailing pink smoke. He pointed as it disappeared on the other side of the forest.

Gus said, "What?"

"Some kind of flare, I think."

"The Very gun. He said it was armament," Gus told Prioleau.

"He's signaling a boat, I bet," Ellen said. She stood up and walked toward Prioleau, then stopped. He waited for her to return to Gus, but she stayed where she was. "It has to be coming in from Canada, right? The delivery."

Prioleau remembered Gus's boyhood all-night watches in a wet pup tent near Sandys Point, and the fishermen's talk about cars taking contraband from the point to Boston. The boyhood watches do go on. And loose talk comes true. He looked past Ellen to their son, and he wondered if in Gus's mind something insisted on hearing Art Boots on an adolescent warpath, telling his radio audience that the white man had gone too much farther than far at last, and that nationhood stolen by white imperialist lackeys must finally be made good. He wondered whether Gus had imagined his father coming by boat or helicopter, and for what reason—to join with them? to rescue his son before the Coast Guard came to lock them up? to hold their hands and be dragged with them from the beach and into jail? "Gus," he said. His voice made the name snap: "Gus." His son looked up.

"Probably drugs," Ellen was saying. "I don't know. Is it worth that much to smuggle cigarettes, or do they ship them by truck from down South? Unlicensed liquor? Does Canadian whiskey turn a profit?"

Prioleau said, "Gus."

She said, "No, it's probably drugs. He signaled the boat, and they'll drop the—dope? Whatever it is. They'll drop it off. It's probably *heroin*. And Wanda and what's his name will sail back home. I bet you that boat belongs to whoever's paying them for it. I bet you it wasn't stolen."

Prioleau said, "Gus?"

Gus was gray-white, his tan had disappeared. He sat on the ground, the fingers of his right hand in his mouth. He nibbled. Prioleau remembered the hand: it brought the bus stop back, a small town in Illinois on a spring morning, and a stiff-backed boy with a frightened face who ate his fingers and said, "I heard you were my father."

Ellen, reading his mind as usual, said it loudly so that he would stop lamenting, Prioleau knew. He knew that he depended on her for it. "He'd have come, honey. He *did*." She said it again: "Gus, he did show up."

Prioleau saw her stepping from the next bus to walk across the highway toward the son she'd sent to find him.

But Gus didn't own that history, Prioleau remembered; Gus was owned, was set in motion by it, moving yet. He said, "What should we do?"

"They don't want you," Ellen said to Gus, while looking at Prioleau. "They don't need you anymore."

Prioleau said, "Wish them all the best in their business venture. If they get away, you get away." He was looking at Ellen. He knew Gus watched them both. "Wish them a fruitful life and high profits."

Boy Scout hatchets and condoms carried so long they wore a ring in the leather wall of a wallet, Prioleau thought, and medicine for pimples and a hot hand in the bedroom in the dark. He walked over to where Gus sat and he clumsily went to his knees. He closed his eyes and reached, struck Gus's shoulders, seized his neck at the back, and pulled him in. Gus rocked forward, didn't hug back, but received what Prioleau gave—gesture, his own discomfort, safety in his bulk, his body's heat. As they kneeled opposite each other, touching but pulled by their muscle and bone in different directions, Prioleau thought to say—but he didn't speak—

that they'd have to see if Minton's boat had stayed in place and he must ask Ellen where she had beached the dinghy she'd stolen. He thought that they were safe as long as they hugged, but would be shamed as soon as they leaned back. But of course it was Ellen again who solved it all. He imagined how she had run to launch herself, arms spread like a child in a rough game, flapping slicker and red hair, for she landed on them both at once and they lay in a heap —"*Mo*-om," Gus complained hoarsely—all arms and legs and breath and sealed-away sight.

Ellen said, "Relax. It'll pass."

The hardest times were when they had you in their sights, friends of course, and also foes; but when they were your lover and your child, and you stood before their eyes as finally pathetic as you knew you would be, those were the times they saw you stark. Whether trying to tell her you had stalked her skin all day, thinking of her breasts flattened out as she lay with her arms above her head in the wind that whipped the curtains and made her shoulder, when you kissed it, smell like the sea. Or watching your son turn fourteen and grow arms and legs like a spider, and balls like a horse, seeing in the worried dark sockets of his eyes, fugitive as game birds, the woundedness of being young. Or moving to touch his face because you must. Those were the times when they had you naked, and you must let them. It was like that, on Cross Island, standing up and back from Gus and looking into his pallor and possibly hatred—of himself, and of his parents for baring the undeniable fact: he still was small. But Prioleau stood, breathless, conscious then of the stink of his sweat and the itch of his bites, the pain of his bruises and open cuts, the slight distance he had moved from Ellen and Gus on the splayed heels of his work shoes, the blush going over his cheeks and neck and probably chest. Looking at Gus, he wanted to turn away, or to weep, or to hold him again. He stood to see, and be seen—he could give that—and as he did, he felt the strongest lust for Ellen. Wanting her, he wanted Gus away, safe but away, so that he and Ellen might slam at the earth with each other until something yielded.

He turned away on exhausted feet—he thought that every small bone in each foot was broken—and he shuffled through grass back down toward the rock ledge. As he kneeled to let himself down to the sea, his struck shoulder blade throbbed, and the muscles of his neck grew so weak that he was sure his head lolled. He descended clumsily, carelessly, hurting himself. His knees grated, he wondered why he didn't hear the bone and cartilage groan like wood in an old abandoned house. He slid the last few feet, turning his head away from the rock because the crystals, glinting in the sun, hurt his eyes, and because he was certain that if he kept looking in, he would see a fossil, fixed there forever.

He didn't see the boat. He waded in, sliding in the surf, tripping and going down, numbing his elbow as he fell. The cove bent to the right, and tall boulders in the tide made a tentative sort of shelter, so he went to the right, where fir trees grew almost horizontally, needles yellow from salt and cold. He ducked under the firs and followed the slimy shoreline into sudden chill and deeper darkness, and an A-shaped cavern where the small explosions of ocean on rock sounded suddenly grand. The boat, trailing its painter, came back on the ebb and butted him, as he waded, in the chest. He seized the stern, slicing his lip on the propeller but holding on, and then he blindly pulled the boat as he backed into sunlight, the pressure of which on his face told him he'd been closing his eyes in the dark.

He stood, soon, in the surf where they slid down the steep rock face, feeling like a buoy and glad to be of real service at last. He pointed the boat in, and Gus held the prow while Prioleau tried three times to pull himself up and in, and finally made it. Then Gus helped Ellen in, stepped in and around her to sit in the stern while she stayed forward, and Prioleau opened the pet cock for fuel, opened the throttle, turned the starter, and slumped.

"It's just a loose clamp, Tony," Gus said.

Prioleau nodded, turned again, got nothing. The tide rocked them, and they sat on it, looking at the dead engine. Ellen leaned to find the oar and passed it to Prioleau, who pushed them off with it and then, holding it halfway down the shaft, paddled against the tide to get them out. The water was ankle-deep, and Gus and Ellen bailed with their hands.

Gus said, "You might have loosened a clamp, Tony."

So Prioleau crawled over Gus and found the 12-volt car battery and resettled the alligator clamps which went to the starter. He came back on sore knees and tried the engine again, and it caught.

Ellen said, "Smart person, Gus."

He shook his head.

Prioleau raised his eyebrows, and Gus read them well enough to know that he should tell how to steer away from Northwest Harbor and its commerce. Gus pointed, Prioleau ran the engine low, and they made for the sea.

They were silent. A funnel of wind danced over the water ahead of them, making a matte cat's-paw on the shiny surface of the waves. The footprint of the wind came toward them, and when it reached them the whaler bucked and then went steadier as the cat's-paw rippled away. Near Wauchula, once, in a half-built house in southwest Florida, they were alone at night on a sandy rise that, in the darkness, looked over nothing. His father was drunk on warm beer and was pacing the bareness of softwood floorboard they had laid within a frame of two-by-fours. The boy sat near a kerosene lantern and looked at *Goode's World Atlas,* waiting for his father to return them to the old hotel in which, because lumber was dear and they were poor, they would share a bed, then rise early so they both could start another new school. Looking up from an annual rainfall map of South America, squinting into and through the hard white light, he saw emptiness beyond the bones of the house without walls. Bugs went at his eyes and nose, and he brushed them away, still peering. There was nothing outside.

And inside, coming close and then treading away in a careful half shuffle of high-topped shoes, his father, in one of his white shirts worn under farmer's overalls, sniffed—as if the boy were giving off an odor of which the father didn't approve. His big white face wrinkled, his clear eyes stared, and then he drank from his bottle of beer and paced toward the other side of the house.

He went back to the atlas, this time following with his finger the outlines of the ice ages in western Europe. From the other side of their house, nearly invisible because it was the boy who occupied the light, the father said, "What a life."

"Scuse me?"

"What a life, I said. Kind of a conversation opener. You feel like talking to me?"

"Yes, sir." He closed the book and looked in his father's direction. "Sure. You tired tonight?"

"I *am* tired tonight, that's right."

"You sucking up some beer might make you tireder, I guess."

"*That's* true. If I had some branch I could mildly tincture with some corn, I'd have my energy up in no time. Beer will slow a man down."

"You unhappy tonight?"

"Oh, my. Well, are you?"

"No, sir."

"Are you happy, then? Are you half hysterical with joy?"

"I'm all right."

"*That's* true. You are all right. You're a good man for a boy. You're fine. Only I think you might be something like too old for a kid."

"Scuse me?"

"Only if you excuse me first and for longer." The bottle rolled on the floor, empty, and he heard his father uncap another with the church key he wore on a brass chain. "I've been running you around, haven't I? All these rinky-dink little towns and cities with their rinky-dink little schools."

"You like to travel."

"You?"

"Me? I'm eleven years old."

"What does *that* explain?"

"Scuse me?"

"*That's* all right. I was baiting you"—he drank, and then the boy heard him slump against a stud and slide to sit on the floor, grunting—"I was being touchy on account of it occurred to me tonight, again, how much I should apologize for how we've been living."

"That's all right, Daddy."

"I like it when you say Daddy."

"Yes, sir."

"No mother for most of your life. Father who drifts as hard as any nigger picking at crops. Good women who don't stay, hard drinkers and good-time girls who stay too long. Cold food, and—what's the name of that hotel?"

"The Yale Hotel?"

"That's right. That's the one. It's as close as either you or me will ever get to Yale University, Tony."

"Yes, sir."

"Not that we need to be there. You'll do all right. We got a background in education going for us when you need to be in college. There's a Prioleau, did I tell you? There's one of us, never mind how distant, teaches agriculture all the way over in Tulane. We'll be all right when it comes to that. What I worry over—you live kind of secondhand, if you were to ask. You wouldn't. Well, you might, when you hit the teen ages and get rebellious. But you're a good young man. You remember I told you that, hear? And don't say, 'Yes, sir,' if you please."

"Uh—"

"This has been Hamlet's soliloquy, ladies and gentlemen, brought to you through the miracle of unwired radio. Let's put the beer in the truck and go to the Yale Hotel. Wouldn't that be restful?"

So they drove, slowly because of the beer and the rutted roads, through sand and palmetto and saw grass which, in the darkness, with the windows open, was more heard than seen—the hissing of leaves and snaky weed on the windshield and door, and then the occasional wet slap of a leaf against his face, from which he flinched each time. His father reached out a long arm and squeezed his neck, then pulled him. Tony slid over to ride the way his father wanted him to, which was up close to the shift lever, their shoulders touching—the way his father's women rode beside him as Tony crouched on the flatbed and looked in through the small rear window at the single silhouetted shape.

The smells in the cab were of beer gone stale in the mouth, and of sweat caked up salty from the day's hot work, and

gasoline fumes leaking from the corroded muffler. He tried
to place himself at a school named Yale, or someplace in
Texas, or anyplace without his father and the motion—new
classrooms, the faces looking up as he walked in to one more
first day; orange lumber, bought cheap because undried,
warping in the sun as they worked; roofs on which they
rode in spite of his hourly mistakes; his father's dimpled
flanks as they showered from a rain barrel after building a
porch; his confidence, each time, despite his father's growing
reservations, that this was what his life was supposed to be—
and he couldn't see, in the hot cab and its cloud of smells,
driving through indistinguishable dark shapes, how he
might come one day to live another way. That frightful
blankness, blank as the dark his father carried him through
in the pitching truck, must be the bright future his father
sometimes mentioned—the life that was different from this.

And he, the little boy, had been right, Prioleau thought
as they came up on the Old Man, which looked in early sun
and shadow like a single shape, its dividing alley of sea wash
hidden. There always was something ahead that was blanker.
He couldn't imagine why he missed his puzzled wandering
father now, fleeing with a family from rescues and crimes.
But he missed him, as if loss were sudden and new. No
matter what that man had done and been, he had been the
man who straddled the roof and laughed. He had been the
one who carried them through the nights and strange
landscapes, and who had made them, finally, homes. It had
been that man's hand at the back of the boy's thin neck, in
whatever nameless countryside.

Shiny black cormorants ranted and pointed their long
beaks at the sun; they jumped into the air from Old Man
Island and dove. Gus called over the engine, "I guess I need
a job or something, don't I? And a place to live?"

Ellen shook in the cold. She hugged herself and bent low in the prow as if to duck the wind. She looked past Prioleau to Gus, who looked at the shimmer of sun on bare sea. Prioleau was thinking of jokes he could make about his working in the unemployment office and helping men find jobs. He said nothing.

Ellen shouted, "Maybe Lilah Minton knows about some summer work, Gus."

Gus, behind him, called, sullenly, "How do you know it's just for the summer? And a place to *live*, I said."

Prioleau was listening for sirens, or the grind of helicopter engines bearing law enforcement and television reporters to the scene of a crime entertaining to viewers in towns like Potter and Machias. He heard nothing except sea wind and the slap of water, the ugly buzz of the borrowed motor, which drove them at the coast.

"I think we're all right," he said.

"Tony," Gus said over the sound of the engine. He made his complaint, in two syllables: "Da–ad."

Prioleau couldn't keep the expression from his face. He didn't know what it looked like, but he could see that Ellen was red, that she rubbed her eyes with her fists. He said, "Yeah?"

"You're not listening again," Gus said.

Prioleau turned his face, seeking someplace to look, but there was no place except the ocean around them, Gus behind him, Ellen ahead. In their sights, he hung his face before them. Ellen, whom he saw looking over his shoulder at Gus, seemed for an instant out of focus, and then she came back.

1980

The clock-radio woke him at 4 a.m., when New York was as dark as it got, and while he sat on the side of the bed and rubbed his face, and while below, on West Eighty-sixth Street, the usual sirens nagged and whooped, the neutral radio voice told him, "Good morning. Billy Horsefall, the self-proclaimed Reverend of the Airwaves, and a staunch advocate of conservative causes, is dead at seventy, felled by an assassin's bullet. Reverend Horsefall, walking with an unidentified companion from her car to his motel in Rock Hill, South Carolina, was shot twice in the lower back and side by the assailant, who was not identified. The British Foreign Secretary has unofficially stated that the President's handling of the crisis in Afghanistan has placed the European allies in, and I quote, an untenable position vis-à-vis Moscow. And France's aerospace program suffered a setback yesterday, when Philippe Bu, head of the Chatelaine missile project, drowned in a boating accident off Lorient,

France. Back in a moment with news of the presidential race."

Gus was in the kitchen, boiling water for instant coffee, snapping the waistband of his undershorts, looking from the streaked dusty window down to the street. When the powder foamed in the mug, he shoved the window up and carried his coffee onto the fire escape. Even before dawn, in the black air where the breezes lived, the mugginess brought a sheen of August sweat to his chest. The hot coffee made him hotter, but he drank, splaying his toes against the emptiness under the metal slats, leaning at the waist-high railing, looking over the gritty mist, which seemed to be cooking at an even 98.6.

WQXR played Elgar, which he heard when he stepped out of the shower, but even melody was too much weight by then, so he turned the radio off and dried himself and dressed in the silence of the small apartment, fear of the trip maintaining the coffee's heat below his chest as if it were solid. Dressed, and sweating again, he went through his rooms, unplugging everything, kicking laundry and shoes out of his way, checking for wallet and keys, lifting the canvas suitcase, leaving, locking himself out.

At the garage, he overtipped the man who brought his car. At traffic lights, he was so cautious that taxis honked him into haste. And, getting onto the Connecticut Turnpike, hearing the news again—the death of Billy Horsefall and the President's stern blundering—he thanked the man who handed him his toll ticket, thanked him twice, despising himself, as he accelerated the untuned MGB, for cowering before everything he met.

After a while, riding through Massachusetts and then New Hampshire, he drove with the radio off, tried to think clearly of work, of a brief he'd brought to read, and then the road took over, the heat and dazzle and cramp of the long drive, and he aimed himself toward Potter and home, to which he'd been summoned.

It was a long drive, handsome enough for a while but finally nothing more than gray cement with lawn on either side, and too many cars, and too much light in the eyes. To relieve his boredom, he inferred design on the part of trucks which overtook him and the fast cars he chose to pass. He clenched his jaw, and read the mirrors nervously, and swiveled his head unnecessarily, saw danger in each driver's careless drift, and soon he was in the passing lane permanently, his headlights on the bright beam, pushing at cars, blinking at tractor-trailers, refusing to slacken his speed, making of an August morning an emergency—as if by getting more quickly to Maine he might prevent something from being what it was: deadweight immovable fact. His jaw grew sore, and his tongue, which had been pressing, he realized, at his teeth. All right, he whispered in the low car, driving rudely and dangerously, all right: say it. Go on. But there was nothing he had to say which needed suppressing. Surely he would have to speak once he was there, but those words would have to be forced up and out, and there was time—and he slowed suddenly, raising a cry of air horns from behind him, and he swung into the slower right-hand lane without looking to see whom he'd endangered, because suddenly it was important to get there later, later than that, to nearly not be there at all.

So he alternated between rabbit bursts and hog waddles, menacing unnumbered dozens of recreational vehicles and family cars, trying to get home, and trying not to.

"Gus, can you come home?"

"What do you mean, Mom?"

"Can you?"

"What? Tell me what."

She'd made the noise of someone cold, or someone breath-less after running, and then she banged the receiver on something and rang off.

And instead of calling her back to ask, he'd arranged for vacation time and postponement of a trial, choosing to pack underwear and socks and cancel the newspaper delivery rather than learn what he was sure he'd wish not to know. He'd thought to telephone home the day after his mother's call, from the office, where he'd divided his day between arranging for time away and sitting in the firm's law library with what amounted to, in numerous volumes, the historical compendium of speaking cruelty of others. In this matter of his client's son having written, but not having formally published, a book his client saw as defaming his wife, now dead, it was difficult to know whether he should bring the suit for libel or for slander. If you tell a falsehood that injures the reputation of someone else, the charge is slander. If you publish the falsehood, the charge becomes libel. And the libel lies not in writing the words but, accord-ing to the law, in "showing" them through publication. Did his client's son, in "showing" publishers his manuscript, actually publish? Or was the submission of the manuscript a "telling"? Defense for each might vary, Gus's senior part-ners thought, and first he must know the nature of the charge.

He had stayed in the library, growing hopeless, framing two lines of attack in his clumsy childish hand, its loops too round and corrected to speak of confidence. And he hadn't called. There was nothing to ask for but the truth, so he hadn't called.

It was dusk when he reached Portland, and he turned off to find a motel. He suddenly steered to the right, hit the brakes hard at the start of the exit ramp, waited for traffic to thin, then backed, on the gravel margin, until he was heading east again. A huge orange sun filled his driving mirrors as he fled toward the darkness of the coast. I'm thirty-five, and it is time.

There were moccasin wholesalers still open, on Route 1 beyond Freeport, and a few souvenir shops, but then the roadside grew darker, and the chill of the coastal air increased, and sand blew from the roadside onto his car. Patent infringements and matters of divorce he handled as favors to friends, the probate of murky wills, a case of libel or slander, and the impossibility of finding legal secretaries who would take a smaller salary than his own: though he drove at a reasonable speed now, his practice of the law pumped up and down inside his body as though he were speeding. Because he knew that he was coming close to home and that being a child involved laws he found cruel and unbreakable.

And then the drive through potato fields—WELCOME TO WASHINGTON COUNTY, THE "SUNRISE" COUNTY—where of every place in America, the sun was said to rise first. And then blueberry barrens, and weeds in sand, the cracked road narrowing, a very few cars on the road now, his own lights showing him only scrub and tattered houses. And then the swoop down the hill—a new supermarket and drugstore in a giant macadam parking lot—and then the bridge over the Machias River to ride past a new service station and the A&P, now open at night. And then the bridge outside town, and uphill again, above the marshes that rose and fell with tides which prodded the inlets of the bay. Small craft lay on their sides, tethered like dead livestock to poles protruding from cracked mud. And then the long run out, the rise above clam flats, from which he saw the blinking, burning

Potter towers, and the descent to the final straightaway, past the entrance to the Navy base, and the dark road oppressed by forest, and the graveyard, and black Potter itself, only the harbor sparsely lit, a few big craft bobbing at anchor, and then the same road, with a few more trailers, one new split-level home, but essentially the same: unpaved, unlighted, uneasy.

He parked above the house, keeping the car at the very front of their drive, as if in readiness for a getaway. He left his bag in the car and walked down the gravel of the drive, stepping carefully, as if at the last he might change his mind and escape, never having been seen. There was no fog tonight, and he could see foam at the lip of the cove and down to the right where, as a boy, he had stood fifty feet up on the cliff to dare his own worry about heights, and what broke below. It was the view his mother often sought, her journey away while caught in the house, sitting at the bay window, staring down. He tried to steal it, but it stayed foreign and familiar: a photograph of some place he'd visited often and to which he might never return.

The light over the side door was on. His mother, standing beneath it: erect, almost stiff, wearing blue jeans and a bulky dark sweater, her hair almost brown now, with a good deal of gray, which had appeared in the last six months. Her throat was taut and veinous. Crow's-feet at her eyes, frown marks at her mouth, a lean hand barely touching her lower lip—she looked handsome to him, and her small bare feet made her charming, but he was frightened as he stepped up onto the side porch to get hugged home.

She didn't hug. She waited until he stood before her, leaning over her. She looked straight ahead, at a button, perhaps, on his shirt. She reached out, as if someone were dreaming them both and the nightmare slowed them terrifically, and she seized handfuls of shirt. She pinched, and squeezed, and wrung the cloth, pulling him closer, in that slowness. She twisted, and dropped her head, laying her brow against the front of his shirt, pushing her head at his chest. He heard the stickiness of her mouth as her lips parted —through the insects and surf and the Grand Manan hooter, he heard that. She said nothing, or not words at least. Her voice made sounds: "Dooh. Oh. Dad."

So he knew at least its name, or a name they could use for summoning something of or about it. It was he who did the hugging and the pulling in. And it was he, as well, who did the crying, reserving the right, as if she were a witness he must plumb for facts at another time, to question in a redirect. *Why didn't you call me?* he would ask her. And *why didn't he ask you to?* And *why have I been cheated of my obligations?* And *how?*

Because, as Tony had told him, she was several parts witch, or anyway smarter than both of them, she knew his mind. Her head moved against him. She opened her mouth again, but this time for breath. She said, "No. No. He's alive. I'm sorry. I should have told you right. He's alive."

He pulled her hands from his shirt and snapped her arms down. She winced. He stepped back and in a snarl he'd heard through his boyhood from Tony's throat—when Gus had come home drunk and had wakened his mother to announce that he was man enough to puke in cars and over rugs; when he had called from college to ask for money because he loved a girl too rich not to be bored by the diversions he could afford to offer her—and in his father's voice, he said, "What're you trying to do? You tell me. Tell me!"

And this woman who would punch a man as large as his father for risking their lives through bad driving, and who had once frightened off a crazy student in the Machias library by raging through his amphetamine high and driving him with slaps to the face out onto the campus lawn—this woman stood before him in the posture of a chastened child, head still down, and listened to the dummy play ventriloquist.

"Mom?"

She only nodded.

"Tony's all right?"

She raised her face up and looked ugly and old. "Sick," she whispered.

"How fucking *sick?*"

She swallowed, and Gus began to cry again. She touched his shoulder and dropped the hand back down. "He's been dying for a while," she said, and her calmness was in the slow pronunciation; the despair and fatigue threatened her voice, like a storm outside a window.

Counselor may question on redirect, with the understanding that this is not a hostile witness. "And you couldn't call me up on the telephone?" Counselor is reminded that the witness is his own, and *not* hostile. "Mom?"

"It would've been bad for his dignity, Gus."

"Oh. His dignity. What, he thinks something like this is only his?" Counselor will be warned. "I don't understand this."

"No," she said. "It's very hard for me, too."

Counselor will comport himself as an officer of the court and will *not* wipe his nose on his fingers and wail. "Okay, okay. I'm sorry."

"Gus, he's crippled and all broken and—I don't even know if he's still breathing. Your grief does not come first."

And at thirty-five, and still her child, he retraced, by moving forward, the step he'd taken back. He stood close

enough for her to hold again. He offered what he had to
give. But she was in the other part of her life again, and the
loss felt suddenly heavier to him, and he was lonelier than
he'd been all day.

"Mom," he said. "What should I do?"

She said, with some gentleness, "Be quiet a lot. Come with
me. Remember who he is."

In the downstairs bedroom, which he thought of, still, as
his, Tony lay under covers in weak light, grinning at him.
The remnants of raven hair looked fake now, like a barfly's
Saturday-evening wig. The face had fallen in to the bones
beneath, which looked crude, the pale skin polished and
pierceable. The teeth seemed gigantic in the thin lips' smile,
and they were yellow, wet-seeming. The dark open eye was
puzzled, and then recognizing, then familiar and glad. His
father's mouth moved, and Gus heard the same voice,
though no sound had yet come up. Then: "Gus," as if a
favor long sought were offered and received with gratitude.

Gus held his breath and leaned to kiss his father on the
mouth. Tony's hands remained beneath the covers. On the
rock 'n' roll posters around them, thin boys leered and
smirked under greasy pompadours. Marilyn Monroe pouted.
Mickey Mantle and Willie Mays leaped for fly balls in
centerfield. His father lay in a permanent wink on the bed
Gus had poured his boyhood into, and from his father's
mouth, as Gus hung over him supported by his forearms, as
if his father were a woman and he, pausing, made love,
there came—he breathed it in, he wanted to want it—the
gases of corruption. He inhaled again, leaning there, and this
time he found what was true: the smell of sour vinegar, a
deeper animal stink, but only what might come from a man
who dwelled alone in the process of his life. Gus bent lower
and kissed him again, this time on his cheek, where the

unshaved stubble of whisker scratched his face as it had on no-shaving Saturdays since he'd been small.

Like a speech he had prepared: "Daddy, let's all go to sleep and then I'll come in and drink some coffee with you and we'll talk. All right?"

The head whispered, "Mornings. Better. Mother says. Baby about pain." The teeth showed, then went away. The open eye did too, and Gus looked up to his mother, who was not weeping, and who stood in the doorway, watching them.

"I gave him his Demerol," she said. "I think he—it's only sleep. He's asleep."

Gus stood up, his legs still pressed against the bed. "I always wondered what I'd do," he said, almost crowing. He spread his arms and folded them across his chest, an athlete who had just performed.

And she knew, of course. Because she said, "You always wondered what you'd do about everything."

Which was enough to lead him silently from the bed, looking back—it was a head above sheets, an exaggerated sculpture of Anthony Prioleau—and into the living room, where they sat on the deacon's bench, the ocean behind them down the slope, while his mother poured brandy into blue Mexican glasses and they drank and sat without speaking. They drank more, and then she said, "Cancer of the lung."

"Oh, my Jesus."

"At the least," she said. "And not calling you was his idea."

"But he was glad to see me."

"Being glad has nothing to do with it. I'd expect you to know that by now, Gus."

"Yes, I do."

"You mean you wish you did."

"Or that. All right. Listen, I'm sorry for before. That was an outburst you didn't need. This has been insane for you."

She shrugged. The tears were suddenly there, and with no loud snuffling, or shakings of the head. She wiped at them, and they were gone. They seemed to have left tracks on her face. "Well, you know we expected something. He's sixty-eight years old. He had the pain, and Dr. Bettye in Machias gave him pills for everything from bladder problems to angina. We went to Ellsworth, finally, and they kept him there and did something—it's called sputum cytology. They didn't even operate. They wanted to give him radiation, but he said no and they didn't argue, and he said no chemotherapy either, so that was that. They let him come home and become a drug addict." She laughed. "You remember those creatures you got mixed up with when you were a kid, on Cross Island? It was during your smuggling and revolutionary phase. I kept thinking, Maybe Gus knows where we can get some marijuana. It's supposed to help, isn't it?"

"I was a true asshole, wasn't I?"

"Well, you were true, I'll tell you that. It's hard to look at him, isn't it?"

"What's wrong with his eye?"

"The cancer got up into the neck. It's going after his brain. There's a nerve it got already, and he can't move his eyelid. I close it at night, or he does. He can sleep that way. He has to keep moving it up and down when he's awake. So it doesn't dry out and get sore. His belly's filling up. His bones—that's what the Demerol does, Bettye told me, it works on the pain in the bone marrow. Aside from that, though, he's in excellent health."

"*Can't* they operate? Can't they give him medicine? Why doesn't he let them? He's not committing suicide."

"What makes you so sure?"

"I can see him not talking about how it hurts. I can probably understand why he didn't want me to see him. No, I can't. I can guess. But I do *not* understand why he doesn't *fight* it."

"He knows he can't win. He knows he can't even start. He knows he has to die." Her face worked, and she looked down at the brandy, which moved in the glass, a level that showed which way her world was tilting.

"And he had to keep that in, too. Everything. What is that? Why? I remember, I was throwing a ball once and he jumped for it—a beautiful leap, he looked like Willie Mays when he went up. You remember? He came down funny and said he thought he should take a break, and we found out a week later he was bleeding inside from a torn muscle? And not one word. Nothing."

"He's pretty strong."

"You think of that as strong?"

"Not *right*. Not correct, you know: not easy on the rest of us. But, yes, strong."

"I wasn't criticizing him."

"No, you shouldn't do that."

"And you know what? I always felt as if I didn't know who he was."

"Your father who loved you. He let you know that."

"Yes, he did. But I wanted—"

She shook her head, looked at the blue glass. "I think the rest was for me. Was available to me. Sometimes. And for him, of course. He lived alone a lot."

"You too."

She smiled. "You too."

"We were always in orbit, you know?"

"Sweetheart, it beats collision, every time. Why are we talking like this?"

"Because your son is an idiot and he doesn't know what to do about a father who's dying."

"Oh, that." She barked a small laugh, and he did, too. He poured the brandy again. "Are you trying to get us drunk, Gus?"

"It's a thought," he said.

"I couldn't get drunk if I swallowed the entire bottle. I tried, once or twice. It's like not being able to sleep. You are simply stuck with seeing the night go past. Do you sleep all right in New York, with all that noise?"

"What noise?"

"Big-shot New Yorker."

"That's me. The big-deal bachelor attorney, you know: I flit from fee to fee, from girl to girl."

"You do? Girls?"

"Oh, it's okay, Mom. I have some friends."

"Now, you know what I mean. Do you love anyone?"

"You met some—"

"Yes, and they were charming. Do you *love* someone?"

"I'm waiting for the goddesses to arrive."

"You can't do that for long, can you?"

He shrugged.

"I hope you can, if that's what you want. I wish you wouldn't," she said. "Can you practice law in Maine?"

"I can tell you things. But I can't file papers or process them. But I can sure as hell help. You mean—"

"I'll need you when he dies, if that's all right with you. I thought about that."

"Oh, of course. Of course."

"And I'd like you as a witness tomorrow. That's why—
that's one of the reasons I was so pleased you came tonight."

"You haven't got *wills?*"

"We do have wills. Of course. No. It's—oh, my. Gus,
we're being married tomorrow. It's the one thing I never
did that your father wanted so much. It really doesn't matter
now, but we're going to get married tomorrow afternoon.
We're going to do that. Isn't it corny?" He didn't answer.
She moved on the bench to put an arm along his shoulders,
and then she curved the arm around his neck, and put the
other out to touch his hands, and then she held him and they
sat together on the hard bench.

And later, down at the beach, looking up the slope to
see her bedroom light go out, then go on again as she failed
to sleep, he walked over boulders to climb the slab of rock
on which they had eaten their picnic dinners and stood to
look across to Canada, or up, as he did now, in the mild
winds and the sound of the ocean ebbing back from the
rounded black rocks with a leeching hiss. August was the
time for shooting stars, and he looked above the winking
towers at the unreasonable depth little planets might fall
through, burning, because the closer you came to the earth,
the greater your endangerment. But he saw no shooting
stars, only the ones that were fixed, and so much not a part
of anyone, not useful for wishing upon, or praying to, or
crying at, or for listening to the little peep of a story you
might think you have to tell. And he smelled no wood
smoke from their old picnics. He heard nothing of his
father's deep reluctant laughter, or his deeper silences, or
the high silver sound of his mother's conversation. It was
a small rock beach on a very large ocean underneath a sky
too wide to really see. And he was younger than he wished

to be, and aging faster than he wanted to, and there was nothing, now, to hold him at the margin of the sea, or maybe anywhere else.

The sky ran down to him, the ocean banged on the coast in his direction, the trail from the house came to stop where he stood, and the family died or was dying or would die in its own good time at his feet. It was he, he was the missing part he'd been trying to find, poking at a black jigsaw puzzle in the dark with his eyes closed. It would not be a long, bitter joke, merely a cruel story, only if he—in a distant city, or driving on a heat-shimmered road, or groaning in a woman's bed—knew what it meant, this history of simple rise and fall.

Walking up the trail in the darkness, he thought that now, at least, he knew what it was he didn't know. He wondered if that was enough to emerge with from the fabulous design of their lives. He went up to the house to lie in the extra room on the second floor if his mother was sleeping, or to sit with her if she was still awake, and smile his healthy teeth: his white man's minstrel show.

She gave him the time with himself. Though he heard her bed creak, and he thought several times, waking, that he heard her go downstairs to check on Tony, and though he waited, each time, or thought he did, for her to slowly come back up, signaling that what life was left continued, he did sleep. Fatigue and simple fear gathered momentum as the night progressed, so that each time he wakened and fell back, it was into a deeper unconsciousness, and morning was like feet of water through which he had to swim before he could rise and dress and walk downstairs and out to his car for clean clothes and shaving tackle, holding his tiredness around him like a film of the water he'd surfaced from, until he finally came from the bathroom to acknowledge that his father lay in his own boyhood room, his mother was in the kitchen making coffee, and his dreams were lost.

He drank his first cup of coffee with his mother, watching crows in the meadow and gulls above the point. She didn't talk about the night, or the day now on its way. He told her about an arbitration at which he had argued the side of a paper manufacturer from Nova Scotia and how, by losing his temper and shouting at his adversary, he'd intimidated the arbitrator and won. She talked about medical bills, and he about the cost of renting office space in New York. She told him of divorces in Potter, and the falling price of lobster, and how halibut was too expensive for anyone to buy. He told her about a woman who worked in the district attorney's office who refused to date anyone but Jews and him, saying that his demeanor was of Jewish loss. "You should be proud of that," his mother said, "or bored to death with her. Let me guess which." He told her to take the savings book and checkbook into Machias and withdraw most of her money, explaining that when a man dies his assets are frozen until his will is probated. And then she told him that she'd done so a week before. He slowly shook his head. "I don't think you understand," she said. "I know what to do. I'm ready. My problem is, I can't stop hating it. You see, I don't want to give *in*. It's what has to happen, all right. I just hate it." When he nodded, she stuck a finger into her coffee mug and twirled it, whispering, "I really hate it, Gus."

His second cup of coffee was with his father. The room looked no different, even in its dimness, from the way it had looked the night before. His father was no different, either, and when Gus first sat beside the bed, his feelings were from his first entry—terrible alarm, dismay, enormous undifferentiated pity. Tony lay still, but the head had a tinge more of color, and one eye was more alert. The other, its dead lid slid back for the day, looked up and in. If he watched only the paralyzed eye, over which his father slid the lid from time to time, Gus felt that he was a penitent in audience with a saint's statue of arrested pain. He tried to see the eye that blinked. His father licked his lips and showed his yellow teeth. He said, in a voice with little air behind it, "How're the Yankees doing?"

"The baseball team?"

"Did Jackson start hitting yet?"

Gus said, "Oh, he always comes around late in the year. He's hitting the long ball, and his average is, I don't know, I think in the .280s. He was in a bad slump for a while. But he's coming back."

The head nodded a little. Tony said, "They love the Red Sox around here so much—I always thought it was so they could hate the Yankees more. You know, everybody likes to hate New York."

"Jackson's really terrific. I don't know, I think it's something like ninety runs batted in. He hit his four hundreth home run, you know."

"He's tough," Tony said.

Gus said, "You feel okay this morning, huh?"

"It doesn't hurt as much, dear. Thank you."

"Dad. I was wondering."

The teeth were bared again, and his father's voice sounded stronger, as if all his throat muscles were working. "I keep wondering, too." He meant it as a joke, and Gus made a snickering noise for him. "Ah," Tony said, as if something had made for comfort. "How's the law, counselor?" Gus made his hand move. Its chewed finger pushed his father's dead lid up and down on the eye that felt like a hard-boiled egg.

"*My* law? The job? I love it. I honestly love what I do."

"You needed it."

"Really? Why? I mean, I'm sure you're right. But how do you mean that?"

"Evenness," Tony said. "No—regularity. *Law*, I guess. You know, A plus B equals C. I didn't get that right."

"No, I know what you mean."

"A code, hon. That's what you want. Something that says what to do. Plus a good fight once in a while?"

Gus said, "I like that part of it. I like advocacy. I like the little wars. And whoever fights smartest, that becomes a part of what happens the next time, because it's in the books, it's some more of the law."

"You liked history in college."

"That's right. That's what the law is."

"My father taught history. He taught everything, I suppose. I think you get your temper from him. He could go on a tear—of course, he was very gentle with us, mostly."

"You too, Dad." Gus blinked his father's eye.

"I was always too embarrassed to, to shout too much, I guess."

"I loved growing up with you. I don't mean it that way. I loved being your kid. I still do."

"You're a nice boy, Gus."

"You too."

"Yeah. Ah." His father breathed shallowly, as if trying to catch his breath without confessing breathlessness. "Read some, Gus?"

"Okay, Dad, don't you talk for a while, that's right. You rest a little, is that what you mean? And I'll hang around and read you—here's a paper, and I'll, no, here's this book you were looking at, all right, you lie around a little, and I'll—" He chattered on, made every noise he could, from rattling the newspapers to thumping the paperbound book on his leg, putting all the sounds he could summon into the air around the bed, as if they might cover his father's sudden pallor and the new lines beneath the flesh of his face, and he opened a page and started to chant, as if the language were new to him, and its rests and pauses and accents translated on the spot into words approximating what lay beneath him on the page, distorted by a magnifying glass which didn't hold still. Someone in Spain had murdered a politician and a detective inspector who drank too much was driving someplace with his very articulate wife and a sergeant of police who fancied the wife as much as her husband did. He closed his father's eye, and the other one closed on its own. There were Basque guerrillas who said some Marxist words, and a woman who had gone to America to teach, and a corpse in a hedgerow, and then it turned out to be the woman herself. She was revealed as a NATO intelligence agent. Everyone was puzzled. A monument blew up. The inspector had a double Fundador, and his wife got hold of his gun and fended off a neo-Nazi who had loved the woman before she became a spy and came home to reveal a Fascist cell. His father was sleeping. Gus put a hand above his father's mouth and felt the push of little breaths. He laid the book on the bedside table and watched his father sleep. And again, he thought of Mike, his father too, dying alone, long ago. That made it easier, somehow, for him to bite his finger and let more tears come. He did his crying in silence. His family was good at that.

His mother went to Potter for the mail, and they each pretended appetite and nagged one another into lunchtime, and she gave the Demerol to his father, and went upstairs to put a skirt and blouse and loafers on for the Reverend Van Eyck, who was due, his mother said, "to humor us in all this senility."

The Reverend Van Eyck arrived in a jeep which had no top. He was tall, pudgy, with blond hair which fell in front of his eyes when he waggled his head, and which he swept aside as if it were earthly clutter for which he had little patience. Dressed in khaki trousers and a navy blazer, with a fine white cotton sweater over a blue broadcloth shirt, with hands just a little dirty from doing actual work, he adjusted his gold-rimmed circular glasses, offered Gus a manly hard handshake, accepted coffee as if it were a real achievement for Ellen to have brewed some, and stood on the side lawn with them—"We don't want to disturb Mr. Prioleau, I think"—and offered them, in a rumbling voice punctuated with brays and long vowel sounds, his best advice.

"I always enjoy the counseling part of my ministry, and at no other time do I enjoy it so much as before a wedding." Here he lowered his voice and paused. Then: "Of course, this is a singular occasion. We have, first, the heartbreaking fact of Mr. Prioleau's sad illness. And then, second, there is —well, I honestly don't know how to describe it. The redundancy, in one way, of performing a service to create wedlock when in truth you have hallowed your lives to-gether with love and mutual respect over such a long pass-age of years." He drank coffee, smacked his lips to tell Ellen that she had done herself proud in the making of coffee. A long, clean finger with a wide dirty nail erected itself before them. "Still, it does no harm, it never can do harm, it would be *well*, were this marvelous marriage to be hallowed in the language of the Lord's book and in His eyes and the eyes of the community. Matrimony is, after all, called by many of us *holy* matrimony."

His mother said, "Gus? Could you get me a drink? Some of that cognac we drank last night?"

The Reverend Van Eyck paused, as if to let himself be seen to notice and then dismiss as mere fleshliness the equivalent of a long fart. His eyes widened, then subsided. Gus left to carry a grin into the house, and to fill two blue glasses with an inch of brandy, take them back out into the sun and cool breeze bearing salt up the meadow. As the Reverend Van Eyck spoke, he handed a drink to his mother and they raised their glasses, clinked them, nodded and drank. Gus sipped. His mother drank the cognac off, and as if they had arranged it, he took her empty glass, gave her his own, and watched her drink it off.

"Because while we, while the church, has never wished to disapprove of love faithful and long in its service, and the obvious devotion attendant, it *is*, finally, the intention and usefulness of sacrament to, as it were, stamp with heaven's imprimatur what man on earth has done. And woman, naturally. It is 1980, and we are neither fundamentalist nor primitive in our views of sexual behavior."

"That's how we got Gus," his mother said, holding her empty glass.

"Pardon?" the Reverend Van Eyck said.

"I said, that's how this person came to be. Sexual behavior. Tony and I produced him. It took us two nights and three days of pretty much nonstop sexual behavior. Of course, we were having fun. That's how Gus got here. That's why he is so nice. A little sexual behavior in the heartland is what it was. I am *so* sorry to make you drive out here, Mr. Van Eyck. It's a lovely day for it, but I think I don't want to get married anymore."

"That man is dying." The finger woke, stuck up, then shifted to the horizontal, pointing at the house.

"Yes."

"In the eyes of the Lord, we are judged whether or not we wish to be, and by His standards, not our own. I would only advise—I seek nothing more than to be of use—"

"Yes. Yes, this is my fault. I'm sorry. I truly do apologize for wasting your time and making you look ridiculous."

"Ridiculous?"

"Now, you never mind that. Please. Accept my apologies, and thank you, thank you very much. I don't want to be married right now. Really. Thanks."

"I hope that this decision is the right one for you. And I suppose you wouldn't care to hear—"

"Oh, no."

"No. Then, good day. I thank you for this *excellent* coffee. I commend you for having tried to change your life."

"Reverend, my life doesn't need me or you trying anything for it to change."

"I see. Then, good day."

"Maybe so, Reverend."

"Yes. Then—"

"Bye."

He walked with dignity around the house to his jeep, and he backed around the MGB with care. He drove slowly, and they watched the dust of the road gather and drop before they turned, Gus to look at his mother and grin, Ellen to face away from Gus and look at the gray enamel paint on the clapboard of the house, at which she threw her brandy glass and on which it shattered with a disappointing soft splash. He watched her walk on stiff legs into the house, and then he ferreted in grass and pebbles along the foundation to collect the bright-blue shards and throw them away.

Talking calmly about it inside, and not, as he'd expected, weeping, his mother sat with her slender legs crossed and her penny loafers kicked off. She spoke about gestures, and not making any more of them if she could help it, and how the last gesture had been made by Tony—a good one too, she thought—in letting Gus live without Tony's illness in his life as long as possible. "It made it tough, mostly on me, but on him, too. But it was a gift for you, and you take it, and look back and tell yourself you enjoyed some of that time away from this."

"I did," he told her right away. "Thank you, I did."

He understood what they were doing, now. They were evading nothing, and hiding nothing, and living with the dead, but making no more of it than they'd made before, when the dead had seemed—at least to him—further off.

"Wasn't I unfair to poor Reverend Van Eyck? I suppose I saved him from unpleasantness, though, and surely a lot of theater. I mean, can you see that profoundly pompous man standing there while he weds a sixty-two-year-old harlot to a man in his grave? And pretending, because it's his Christian duty to pretend, that it's a normal living-room wedding? Even the room would have been wrong. He'd have had to sing the sanctimonies in a *bed*room. With rock 'n' roll posters all around."

He spent a good deal of the afternoon wondering just how far off the dead are—how distant they stay. If he had spoken of it to her, he would have asked at what time in your life, according to her experience, you're free of the people whose lives you come shouting from, bone yard after bone yard, into what you promised yourself will be life. But he didn't, because she was getting ready now, and he simply followed and performed.

She went in to check on Tony more frequently now, between chores. Gus didn't; he hid within the busyness. During the next days, they got ready. They vacuum-cleaned the floors and the upholstered furniture. They swept off the porch. They polished mirrors and cleaned the living-room windows, wiped at smudges on the refrigerator door, and swabbed the top of the stove. They talked some in the mornings. The ashes were shoveled from the fireplace, the toilet was washed and the bathroom floor mopped, and, when he couldn't find more work in the house, Gus, using the manual mower because the gasoline engine would be too noisy, stayed outside and cut the grass. It began to rain, a soft rain of thick consistency, cold drops on warm air, and slow fog gradually sealed away the view down the meadow and up along the road to Potter, so that the house and lawn, and a part of the neighboring meadow, were isolated by weather and walled by the echoes of the wheeze-and-clatter the mower made. He sweated against the rain, and the wet grass kept clogging the blades of the old machine, but he stayed with the work. He felt safe. It grew darker, though not very, the air was a deep mustard color falling onto the grass and high weed. Without pausing, lest he be summoned, he rolled the mower back to the garage, and then he walked back to the margin between the meadow and the lawn with an old, blunt, long-handled scythe. He took his shirt off and threw it on the lawn. And with hurting muscles, for he hadn't done this work since he'd come home from law school for summers, years before, he cut high brush.

Slowly, because he liked the work, and because he didn't want his refuge invaded, and because it seemed important to do the job correctly, they were getting ready after all, he spread his legs, swung from the hips, letting his arms and upper back follow the thighs' swivel, biceps loose and forearms taut, and he cut. Then he shuffled and stepped, planted his legs wide again, and he swung. He marched like that, in slow motion, in the rain, down the division between meadow and lawn, until he reached the start of the hedgerow that went, on the right-hand side, down to the blackrock beach. And he didn't want to stop. He didn't dare. He walked into the fog and away from the house, along the track, bordered on the left by birch growth and on the right by tangles of hedge he couldn't cut. But the trail was overgrown, and it would do. Facing downhill, he cut to trim the trail. His motion threw him forward, so he reversed himself, his back to the sea, his face toward the house softened in outline by hanging fog. He worked backward then, swinging the scythe, stepping back, tensing himself to swing again, going away from the house, and from his mother who arranged things, and from his father who, like a god, disposed the day and its emotions within which each of them worked.

Sometimes the long, gently curved metal blade clanged on a rock in the trail; then the scythe would skip upward and sail to his left, pulling him from the grace with which his movement had begun, and making him trip. Sometimes he swung with too much effort, his teeth clenched, his mouth so tight that his lips burned, and he would miss everything and spin in a clumsy circle, to stand again facing the beach, which by now he couldn't see. Then he would turn himself to stand correctly, and take a larger breath, and flail on, with as much control as he could find.

It was a long track, and he was too scrupulous for such rough work, even if the work might be argued as necessary, and so he was washed with sweat and rain by the time he reached the spruce at which the trail ended and the jumble of rock and detritus began. He panted and blew, looked into the fog, dropped the scythe. Ocean cold came up to him, and he folded his arms for warmth, but didn't go back up to find any. He went deeper onto the beach, walking with effort over the slippery smaller stones and climbing the large ones, until he was at the picnic rock again. He could smell the fog, and the salt behind it, the flung seaweed and rotting jellyfish and small crabs marooned in tide pools. He heard the fog sirens going down the coast, near the Potter harbor and across, at Grand Manan, at Machias and Roque Bluffs, at Sandys Point. The Potter towers were obscured, and so was even the mouth of their own small cove. He went on, moving away from the trail, descending a slope of small stones, then climbing the palisade he'd made, as a boy, into a Tripoli fortress. The stone point ahead of him was invisible, and so was the sea below, but he knew where to go, though he crawled the final feet on his hands and knees. It was where the cliff seemed to end. in the fog, and where it seemed he would fall to the ocean. But he knew, feeling his way, to go ahead—his hands read the rock before he recognized formations—and he dropped, making a little peep of fright, three or four feet down, below the edge, to a protrusion of rock that slanted upward and on which a boy could lie to look down at the tidal foam on the base of the fifty-foot cliff. He scraped his chest and arms on the rock, but remained on his stomach, lifting his legs so there would be room, and he stuck his head out and stared. He heard the sea, though he couldn't make it out for the fog, and he breathed its smell in deep, and he knew that he had come as far as he could. He shook in the cold, he closed his eyes, lying on his belly in his boyhood's secret place.

He wanted to say something about Tony and his dying, some kind of prayer, or anyway a summary—the last drama he'd allow himself during what was surely coming very soon. There was absolutely nothing. He thought of Tony, but there was too much of him in Gus's life for one event or face or word to summon, or be of sufficient service. He thought, without knowing why, of Mike, who had lived so long without him. He thought of his mother, and then of his mother and Mike, the three of them camping near Yellowstone Lake, and of his bus ride into Illinois, and Tony receiving him on that long, wide, silent street in the early morning, and of the meal which Tony had served him on the sticky wooden table in the dark store, his silence as he watched the scrawny kid inhale mushy pie and cold milk. He saw his mother, off the bus and in the road, looking at them the next morning, as if they were a picture she had painted, and then he imagined her walking through the fog—he started to laugh into his arms—and finding the scythe, and knowing where he was, and carrying it up the slope of the beach to this rock, making a dry joke about Father Time getting younger every day, or commenting on his sense of humor in selecting implements to wield—he was trying to laugh harder now—and he made himself stand, surrounded by thickening fog, alone in it, and he climbed out, though his spine tingled with fear of the height. He crawled back toward the safer width of the palisade, savoring the solitude, but lonely too for the living house and the dying within and those who were stranded between. He went back.

In the house, he shivered with cold. He remained in his wet clothes, however, because his mother was making preparations, and she strode past him, walking heavily, as if he weren't there, or as if she were angry at him, or as if something so terribly much larger than he were suddenly

the issue and she wanted—she said this with her footsteps
—wanted him to know that there was no discussion of what
was about to occur.

She turned each light off: the kitchen light, the side-
porch light, the light on the table in the living room, the
toll lamp near her deacon's bench, the night light near the
phone, the hallway light. And then, in the darkness of the
blackened house, she wept as if no noise she made could
waken his father. She wailed, first low, then high, in ugly
noises, alien to her usual control and alien even to this long
emergency she had lived in with his father. She said no
syllables: the sounds were only for her to hear in the dark
hallway of the house she had lived in first and last and all
the time with Anthony Prioleau; the sounds were for her
sake alone; she was giving herself the only measure of comfort there was—the pure and undeniable fact of her pain.

He did not move to comfort her. In the darkness too, he
stood around a corner, shivering in a body that did not
understand what hers, or his father's, now knew. On the
other side of the wall he waited, and his mother wailed.
And soon enough, mercifully enough, for he was crying
with his head in his palms and his nose crushed against his
fingers so he'd make no sound, he heard her sigh. It was a
long, an infinite, expulsion; it went on, it went on, it went
on. And then she walked, a brisker walk than before. And
on his toes, in his wet socks, he sneaked behind his mother.
Like an evil child, but in fact only a decent and a dumb one,
he peered around another corner—into his father's room,
which once had been his and never would be again—to see
the only light in the house, and to see a fugitive good-night
kiss.

His mother stood, her arms at her sides, her hands as
loose-looking at the wrist and fingers as if she had been

carrying enormous weight and only recently had released
it; she seemed exhausted, unable to move. She shuffled
closer to the bed. His father, beaten by the day and frozen
for a while by Demerol, slept. One hand was under the
pillow, as a child's might be—as Gus's must have been, once
upon a time, and in the same bed. His father's mouth was
open. The yellow teeth showed. His breathing was deep,
judging from the rise and fall of the sheets, but there was
no snoring noise, no sound of lungs that worked. His mother
stooped, very stiffly, to kiss his father good night. She had
kissed Gus good night that way, he knew. Now she kissed
Tony good night. The wail began, and she jammed her
flattened left hand between her teeth and bit. He could see
the jaws work and see her rise almost to her toes because
of the pain. Her jaws worked and she was biting harder, up
now on her toes. And she remained that way—at first un-
changing, it seemed. And then he bent forward, clutching
his gut as if he would vomit, for he saw the blood she drew
from her left hand, while her right, now clenched, remained
at her side. The blood ran down the back of her hand and
onto the back of her wrist. Something of a marriage was hap-
pening; he knew it, and he knew that he should leave them
alone in it. He could not, and he kneeled on the edge of their
lives, and he spied.

How she moved, in that ceremony of pain, he could not
imagine. She did, though. Stooped above her husband,
giving herself all the pain her jaws enabled her to, she
reached for the syringe on his bedside tray. As she did, her
right hand opened above the tray, and the vial—he knew it
must be Demerol—fell onto the white paper towel which
lined the little cocktail tray. She moved her bleeding hand
from her mouth, it shook, and the blood ran onto her chin.
But she made the hand work, and she filled the hypodermic

in a slow and endless pulling back of the plunger—back it went, and back, back, back further, all the way, she was at the limit, and Gus felt profound relief, and at the same instant his father felt gone to him and he wanted to make her stop, give him a minute more with Anthony Prioleau, but he held his stomach like a sick little boy and watched his mother lean once more to kiss the weary sleeping face; he watched her tie the rubber tourniquet on his arm—his father stirred but slept—and saw the dutiful vein rise to the surface.

She snorted. She did it again. She was panting, but through her nose, like someone who was passing out. He heard her make the sound; then she edged the syringe onto his arm and pressed. It pierced the pale and unresilient skin. A tiny bubble of blood rose. She stopped. She shook her head. She snorted again, she bent to kiss his cheek, she pushed the syringe further, more blood came, she leaned, she kissed him good night, goodbye, she pushed, more blood, another push, another kiss, she leaned forward, she leaned back, she shoved it with her chewed hand and leaned to kiss him, missed his face, leaned and collapsed across his chest with her hand on the pillow above his head, and she heaved like someone struck or dying, and with the fingers of her healthy hand she reached under herself and over his face and neck and pushed the plunger, crying aloud in almost a man's baritone voice, and flushed what Gus knew was an overdose of Demerol into his father's vein and up and into his heart. As he watched, his father stopped. His father slept deeper, while his mother lay upon him, her face in his pillow. He slept deeper and deeper. Gus watched his face to see if it would change. But all it did was stop. Gus was on his knees in the hallway, only as tall as a big boy watching around a corner to see his parents in bed might be. Gus was a big boy, and he was watching his parents at their wedding, on their honeymoon, and before he wept for his father, and before he wept for his mother, and before he wept for himself all alone, he crawled down the halls with his shame so that if she sought him later or in the morning his mother would not know that her son had trespassed so profoundly as to watch her finally, at long last, marry Anthony Prioleau in what the Reverend Van Eyck would surely acknowledge as a private ceremony.

On some mornings, the red-tide algae, which turned
the shellfish poisonous, lay so solid and dark against the
shore, lobstermen said, you could roller-skate to the traps.
Oil scum from a slick laid down by two tankers off Hatteras
still, in early sun, made rainbows on the surface of the
tidal pools. The paper companies' trucks shuttled inland,
carrying old trees beheaded for the sake of memo pads, and
the forests thinned like the head of a sickened man, the
trees replaced by chemically treated seeds which possibly
poisoned the water table, as surely the airborne blueberry
sprays did, making children sick a dozen miles from the
bogs and killing others in the womb. While statesmen in
Augusta fought to build a great refinery off Machias, and
the legislature begged for inland dams, and while the land
and water slowly, but not so slowly as before, went away
while they watched, the price of gasoline had risen that
summer, the influx of tourists had diminished in response,

and the local economy had sunk. So what they were doing, in the Boston whaler they'd borrowed from Lilah Minton, tall, silent fisherman's widow, as they speechlessly motored from their cove in the direction of Canada, was preparing to add to the general pollution and local decline.

They had managed it formally and well, with little conversation. They wore clothing suitable and silly at once. Sitting forward in leather pumps and stockings and a tan twill suit, a cream-colored blouse she had ironed the night before, and white kid gloves, her feet planted flat on a greasy layer of rotted bait and gasoline and candy-bar wrappers, Ellen faced Gus as he steered the boat. He was wearing a suit of Tony's, too large for him in the shoulders and chest and waist, too short in the leg. Sporty dark figures showed on his socks under the narrow trousers, above his canoe moccasins. The shirt he wore, of bold blue stripes on white, was his own; the necktie, narrow and red and of cheap material, was Tony's. He kept the suit jacket buttoned as he steered. They headed out of the cove and toward deep water at dusk, the water choppy and stained orange over the dark dirty blue, winds picking up, and waves too, so the boat bucked and slapped.

Ellen held it with both hands against her stomach, her legs extended for balance. She didn't look down at it, but only at Gus, or the shore behind them, as their cove became just a part of the ragged stone coast. It was the sort of vessel you might imagine for sale in a stall in an Italian town—squat, dark, with a patina of gold on the two looped handles, something dignified and fake for the mantel of a tourist's fireplace, in which plastic birch logs glowed in the light of a hidden red bulb. Gus looked from the sea behind Ellen to the urn on her lap, then looked up again, and out.

The motor beat its simple cycle, and so did the sea beneath the boat.

What they didn't speak of were the ease with which wills are filed, the simplicity of motion with which a child can gather his father's bedclothes and drive them, hidden in a paper sack, to the smoldering dump past the shacks of the very poor, and throw them away with one swing of the arm, the emptiness of the bed thereafter, the Reverend Van Eyck, who actually stammered on the telephone to offer his service and services, the noises made in the house by those left behind. Nor did they speculate on whether the story now ended. They had huddled together, then had avoided one another, and now they were separate, though working the same boat, not speaking because their language was as beside the point as Tony so often, with his silences, had said it to be.

Ellen lifted a hand to her hair and with the antique buttoned white glove smoothed what had been coppery red and dazzling in sun but which now was a soft brown-gray. Gus watched her, she was ready, and he turned the engine off. The sound was of wind around them, sometimes hard enough to whistle, and the hard cuffing of water on the hull. He cleared his throat as if he ought to speak, but he didn't. Ellen's eyes were running but her lips were tight, and the strong wind drove her pallor away and blew color into her face. Her chest rose and fell as she breathed in late-August air, like an athlete making ready. She worked the top of the urn loose, and the pottery disk fell from her fingers and spun on the bottom of the boat, then stopped. The boat rocked, she gripped the side and leaned over, holding the urn by a looped handle, and she poured. Prioleau rode on the air.

Gus, watching, had neglected to use an oar to steady them, or to turn her side of the boat to the lee, so the winds from Canada swept the ashes toward Gus, into his mouth and nose and eyes. He turned his face away from the wind and Ellen finished pouring. There was a little plopping sound as she threw the urn overboard. And then, as he wiped at his eyes, and as he sneezed and pretended to cough, rubbing at his tongue, he started to cry. But his mother was laughing at the face he'd made, and when he turned to her, she mimicked him, her tongue hanging out, her gloved fingers brushing it, her eyes wide with his horror. Gus reached over the side with both hands, rocking the boat, to scoop seawater up and gargle, spit. She raised her hands and shrugged, held the gesture, then let her arms fall. He wiped his mouth with the sleeve of the borrowed— inherited—suit. The urn had sunk. The powdery film had been turned into sea. The Potter towers burned. They sat in their silence in the noise of water and wind. Then he started the motor, and the boat's white wake tore a long imperfect circle that would close against the rocks below the house.